To Rose

THE ANDROS CONNECTION

BY

THOMAS HUDGIN

A Novel of Adventure and Intrigue on the High Seas

Thomas S Hudgin

27 October 2012

Shadow Line Press
www.shadowlinepress.com

ISBN 13: 978-0-9712875-5-6

Printed in the United States of America

Published by Shadow Line Press
www.shadowlinepress.com

The Andros Connection is a work of fiction. Names, characters, and incidents are products of the author's imagination or are used fictitiously. Any resemblance to actual events or locales or to persons living or dead is entirely coincidental.

May the gentle winds fill your sails,
And the warm, tropical sun brighten your spirit.

This book is dedicated to my wife, Barbara, and my son, Chris, who sailed with me for many years and gave me the strength to make this book possible.

TABLE OF CONTENTS

PREFACE

Born with a love of the sea, I've always dreamed of sailing the oceans and exploring tropical islands. Ever since I could remember, I would sit on the beach along the coast of the Carolinas searching the southern horizon for that illusive tropical paradise of white sandy beaches, coconut palms, and crystal-clear coves.

When I completed my college education with degrees in chemistry and mathematics, I received an officer's commission in the US Navy and sailed the Pacific Ocean on tankers and repair ships. Little did I know that the valuable experience gained in deep-water navigation and seamanship skills would be put to use again years later.

Continuing to pursue that spirit of adventure following my tour of active duty, I earned my wings as an instrument-rated, private pilot and bought my first airplane. Every opportunity I had, I'd fly to the tropical islands of the Bahamas and charter a sailboat to explore the northern and secluded central islands.

Following my retirement after working thirty years in the pharmaceutical industry, I purchased a thirty-foot sailboat, named it *Mystique,* and sailed to the islands of the Bahamas. Itching to do more challenging blue water sailing, I signed on with two others to sail a thirty-eight foot ketch from the islands of the Caribbean to Europe. Despite the fact that this voyage nearly ended in disaster, I still possess a keen fascination for exploring the clear waters of the tropics.

Although this novel and characters are fiction, the places mentioned and sailing experiences are real. I have a high degree of respect for the local folks of the Bahamas and Colombia where much of this adventure takes place. They are proud, honest people living in a paradise unequaled anywhere in the world. This story is not intended to poke fun at their lifestyle, but is simply a story that could occur anywhere at any time. Having been to and explored the many places mentioned in this novel as well as having done my homework, the Bahamas and Colombia seemed to be intriguing settings for this tale.

Chapter 1

River Debris

"Mayday! Mayday!" a voice cried over the short wave radio.

Sleeping in his cabin on board the *Southwind*, Jason suddenly opened his eyes and sat up in his bunk.

"What the . . . ?" he mumbled. He looked around the cabin trying to figure out what startled him, but there was just silence except for a faint hissing sound coming from the sailboat's radio. "Must be dreaming," he grumbled, scratched his head and plopped back down on the pillow.

"Help! This is an emergency!" the voice pleaded again.

Certain he'd heard the voice this time, Jason leaped out of bed, rushed to the chart table and turned up the volume on the radio. Again, there was silence. Then the plea for help returned, "Hello, anyone out there? This is Maisy . . . on Andros. Someone please help me!" she begged with a quivering voice.

Jason could visualize the tears streaming down her face as he frantically picked up the microphone and hollered, "Maisy, this is Jason Shannon on the sailing vessel, *Southwind*. Can you read me? Over."

"Yes, Mister Jason, read you weak but okay. My family is lost on a fishing boat in a terrible storm at sea. I need help finding them. Are you near Andros? Over."

"I'm in Wilmingtown, North Carolina, a long way from Andros, but perhaps I can find someone closer to help you find your family."

"Oh, thank you, thank you so much. My father, brother, and mother were on a fishing boat, and a terrible storm came. They have not come back. Over."

"Maisy, when did this happen?" Jason asked.

"Two days ago. Some friends looked for them yesterday and today . . . and . . . and . . . ." The radio went silent.

"Maisy, listen, I want to help you. I'll call the U.S. Coast Guard. They can arrange with the Bahamian authorities for a search. Tell me about the boat and where this happened?"

"I . . . I," Maisy started crying.

"Maisy, I understand. I can help. Try to tell me what happened. I know it is hard for you."

"It's a thirty-eight foot wooden fishing trawler. I heard they were ten miles offshore when the storm came."

"Offshore where?" Jason asked. "Andros is a large island."

"Mr. Jason, it's Moxey Settlement on Mangrove Cay where I live. Do you know Moxey Settlement?"

"Just a minute. I have charts of the Bahamas. Wait." After a few precious seconds, he said, "Maisy, I found it. Moxey is on the southeast side of Andros. Can't the local police help?"

"Moxey is a tiny village. No police here. My friends have tried, but nothing."

"What about Nassau?" Jason asked.

"Nassau is far away. I need help now!"

"Understand. I'll call the Coast Guard immediately. How can I reach you? Do you have a phone, an address? Can I call you back on the radio; say tomorrow at the same time?"

"Yes, thank you," Maisy's voice quivered. "My address is 17 Papaya Lane, Moxey Settlement, Andros. We live above our store."

"We'll find your family." Jason tried to sound convincing.

"Okay, Mr. Jason, thank you."

"All right. I'll call you on the radio same time tomorrow."

"Yes, same time tomorrow," she repeated. "Oh, I hope someone finds them quickly."

"Me too. Take care of yourself. Talk to you tomorrow," Jason said.

"Goodbye"

Jason looked up the number for the Coast Guard and called. They agreed to send out a search party and call him tomorrow with a status report. When Jason put down the phone, however, he felt helpless with the deep, sinking feeling of knowing that he could do so little almost a thousand miles away.

He tried to fall back asleep but knew he couldn't.

The following day, Jason waited impatiently for news from the Coast Guard, but by three p. m., there was still no word. Desperate, he called the local Coast Guard station and was told that they had indeed launched a search off the east coast of Andros but had found nothing. They promised to continue for another twenty-four hours. Finally, at the previously agreed upon time, Jason sat down at the short wave radio and picked up the microphone.

"Calling Miss Maisy. Are you on frequency?" Jason waited for several minutes. He repeated his call, and finally, the call came back.

"Mr. Jason. Are you there? This is Maisy. Over."

"Yes. I'm here. I have good news for you. The Coast Guard is searching for your family now and will continue until tomorrow."

"Yes. I know. I saw the planes fly over today. Oh, I hope they find them soon."

"Of course. So do I."

"Thank you, Mr. Jason." She was sobbing. "Thank you so much for your help."

"I wish I could do more. You are so far away. By the way, just call me Jason, Okay?"

"Yes, Jason."

"Uh, Maisy, listen. I, uh, want to call you tomorrow, same time."

"Yes, Mr. Jason, I mean Jason. I'll be here at the radio tomorrow. Take care."

"Okay. We'll work this out. Try to get some sleep." Jason felt helpless. "Bye."

Jason stared at the silent radio and tried to imagine what Maisy was like. A flash of fantasy danced in his head. Was she young? Pretty? Was she as sweet as her voice sounded? Swirling like surf flowing across a sandy beach, his thoughts vacillated between exciting adventures in the clear waters of the central Bahamas—a paradise teeming with colorful fish, white sandy beaches, and sprawling coconut palms—and the unfolding disaster Maisy was experiencing. Finally, in a tangled state of bewilderment, he made a decision.

He had to find Maisy. He had to see her in person, put his arms around her, and comfort her. But she was over nine hundred miles away.

In his late twenties and single, Jason was more fortunate than most. His inheritance from his father's estate set him up to an easygoing life style that gave him the opportunity to own outright the thirty-six foot sloop, *Southwind,* and a cottage on Wrightsville Beach, North Carolina. With an associate's degree from Cape Fear Community College in engine mechanics, he'd opened up a car repair shop in Wilmingtown six years ago and his business had grown to six employees. Being his own boss, he had the luxury of time and money to sail to the tropics on a whim.

Later that morning, Jason left the *Southwind* and returned to his cottage at Wrightsville Beach. He set his notepad down on the kitchen table, and immediately called Jeff, a sailing buddy who lived in Wilmingtown. A year younger than Jason, Jeff was just finishing his second year at the local university for his MBA degree and had a steady girl friend, Lori, whom he had been dating for several years.

"Hello?" Jeff answered.

"Jeff, listen, you won't believe this. I heard a distress call on the short wave radio this morning on my boat. It came from a girl on Andros Island in the Bahamas."

"Yeah? What happened?"

Jason told his story.

"Wow!" Do you think it's for real? It almost sounds like a prank, like some kid playing a joke."

"No, no, I don't think so," Jason said. "I think there is a Maisy, and she's really searching for her family involved in a freak storm accident."

"This sounds too dramatic, like something you would see in the movies."

"Well, I believe it's all true, and I want to find her," Jason said, more determined than ever.

"You wanna do what? You're crazy! Oh sure. Just race down there and stand in the middle of the jungle of the largest island in the Bahamas and sing with your arms stretched out 'There she is, Miss Maisy!' and she'll miraculously appear before your eyes, right?" Jeff attempted to hide his sarcasm. "I happen to know Andros is huge."

"It's not funny. This really did happen. Maisy has a broken heart. I want to find her."

"You really must be desperate. So, how you gonna do that, fly to Andros and sweep her off her feet? You certainly can't sail. It would take you a week to get there."

"I'll work it out. It's not impossible," Jason said.

"Well, whatever, Romeo. Keep me posted."

"Hey, changing the subject. How 'bout you and Lori joining me at the marina Saturday and spend the weekend on the *Southwind*," Jason suggested. "I want to do some cleaning and, well, we can go for a sail down the river in the afternoon."

"Sounds good to me. I'll check with Lori and call you back in about an hour."

"Okay, See ya," Jason said and hung up the phone.

But Jason could not get Maisy out of his mind. He looked at his charts and did some calculations. "Let's see, 925 nautical miles from the mouth of the Cape Fear River to Moxey Settlement," he muttered to himself. Studying the chart details, he noticed a solid line of hazardous reefs along the east coast of Andros from Moxey Settlement north to Coakley Town, a distance of thirty-five miles.

His Andros Island sailing guidebook warned that the passage through the channel to Moxey Settlement should be negotiated only in favorable light with the sun high and behind so that the shallow coral heads and rocks could be seen easily. That was disconcerting to Jason.

"Maybe I could meet her in Coakley Town. Coakley would be about a week's sail from Wilmingtown," he muttered again. Then he shouted, "Why not?" With a wide grin on his face, he stood up, walked to the front window, and gazed beyond the surf into the vast Atlantic. His mind flooded with illusions of Maisy, imagining a pretty island girl just waiting to be rescued over the horizon. "Yes, I have to do it," he howled and pounded his fist on the windowsill in a sudden burst of excitement.

A short while later Jeff called back. "How 'bout we meet you on board at nine a. m. Saturday," he suggested.

"Yep. See you then."

Late Friday night Jason called Jeff. "Hey. I have to take care of a little problem at the shop tomorrow morning, so it'll be around noon before I can meet you at the boat. I was gonna scrape the barnacles off the hull along the water line. Perhaps you and Lori could start on that project before I get there. You know where everything is. Then in the afternoon we'll take her out for a sail."

"Will do. We'll see you on the *Southwind* tomorrow," Jeff acknowledged.

The following morning, instead of driving to his shop, Jason drove directly to the marine supply store. He thumbed through the stack of navigational charts for the Bahamas and selected what he needed and placed them in his shopping cart. Then he grabbed a couple of recently updated guidebooks on sailing to the Bahamas, customs forms, and a yellow quarantine flag. Satisfied with his stash, he rushed back home, sat down at his kitchen table, and began an extensive checklist for his journey south.

At the boat dock, Jeff treaded water along the hull and attempted to remove the barnacles with a large sponge while Lori read a novel in the cockpit under the shade of the Bimini cover. Suddenly, something bumped against the rudder. Completely unaware of the jolt, Jeff continued scrubbing near the water line. Working his way forward toward the bow, he paused and hollered to Lori, "Hey, Sweetie, hand me the scraper. I can't get all of these stubborn barnacles off the hull with this floppy sponge."

"Where is it?" Lori grumbled and slammed the book down on the bench seat.

"It's in the toolbox, in the engine compartment. Where else would it be?"

Lori, a beautiful blue-eyed blond slightly younger than Jeff, ignored the tone and stomped below to fetch the scraper. Moments later, she emerged from the cabin, grabbed the helm with one hand to maintain her balance, and leaned over the side of the cockpit to hand him the scraper.

"Find it?" Jeff asked impatiently a second before he saw her head peak over the railing.

"What do you think this is?" She waved it in front of his face.

"Wow, you're in a nasty mood today."

"You started it," she snarled. "Okay, I'm sorry. It's just that I was at an exciting part in the story and you made me stop."

Jeff kicked his feet hard under water to propel himself upwards so he could reach the scraper. At that moment, something bumped the rudder again only with enough force this time to sharply spin the helm half a revolution. Lori let go of the wheel and fell onto the cockpit deck.

"Ouch! That hurt," she shouted.

"What are you talking about?"

"You kicked the rudder and made the wheel turn. You twisted my wrist."

"I didn't touch the rudder," Jeff insisted.

"Well, something did." Lori massaged her wrist to ease the pain.

"Oh, it was probably a log floating in the river." But when Jeff looked in the direction of the stern, he saw nothing there.

Determined to find out what had caused the helm to jerk, Lori leaned over the back of the boat and searched the water. A steady tropical breeze blowing up the Cape Fear River roughed up the river surface just enough to prevent her from seeing more than a couple of inches down. With her curiosity still burning, she climbed over the railing onto the swim ladder and stepped down until her feet were a foot underwater. Holding onto the ladder with one hand, she reached below the surface with her other hand to feel the rudder. She touched something weird.

"Oh, my God!" she screamed and scrambled up the ladder into the cockpit. "Jeff! Jeff! Somebody is under the boat! I felt a hand! Get out!"

"What? You're joking!"

"No. Quick, get out! It must be stuck between the rudder and the keel!"

Instinctively, Jeff swam toward the ladder to climb back into the boat.

"No, no! Swim the other way! Hurry! Up to the bow." Lori held her hands against her face and screamed. "A body is stuck next to the ladder. Get out! Oh God, please hurry!" She ran up to the bow and paced wildly back and forth. "Jeff, get out! Where's Jason? Why isn't he here?"

Jeff was preoccupied, trying to find the fastest way to climb aboard to respond to Lori's emotions. He rapidly swam to the bow and propelled himself onto the floating dock. Scrambling to his feet, he grabbed the rail near the bow and leaped over onto the deck. Lori rushed over to him and threw her arms around his dripping body. Her lips quivered and tears ran down her cheek.

"It's okay. We'll be all right," he whispered gently in her ear and continued to hold her tightly against his chest.

When she began to melt in his arms, he released her, and ran back to the cockpit to see what had frightened her. He searched the rippled water all around the stern, but found nothing. He turned the wheel until the rudder reached the stop, then turned it fully the opposite direction. It moved freely.

"Jeff, it was there, believe me, it was there!" Lori whimpered. "It was a person, a *dead* person. We need to call Jason."

"I believe you, I do, Honey. Jason said he would be here by noon. Let me think. There is a tidal current in the river and the tide is coming in . . . toward town. So, that means whatever it is could be drifting toward the bow and beyond, unless it's caught in a snag. I *have* to find it. I am going to get my snorkel and fins, and search for it. It has to be nearby."

"No, Jeff, don't! Let Jason do it. What if the body isn't dead? I mean, what if it grabbed you or something? I want you alive. Let's get off this boat, get out of here. I'm scared."

"That's crazy. Jason will be here soon. I can take care of this. No dead body is going to grab me. It'll haunt us if we don't find it now and tell the police. The body will drift too far away and be impossible to find. I *must* locate immediately so we can tell the authorities what we found."

Lori was too distraught to argue anymore and sat on the bench in the cockpit. Jeff scrambled into the cabin, put on his snorkel, mask and fins in record time, and leapt over the stern into the river.

"Hey, toss me a rope," he said. "In case I do find the body, I want to tie it to something on shore or the dock to keep it from drifting further."

Still quivering, Lori begged, "Please hurry, I need you."

"Don't worry, I'll be careful."

Lori quickly opened the storage compartment under one of the seats in the cockpit, pulled out a twenty-five foot rope, and tossed it over the side. With the rope held tightly in one hand, Jeff swam with the current away from the boat up river with his face under water. Two hundred feet away, Jeff stopped swimming, jerked his head up, turned around, and shouted to Lori, "I found it! You're right, it's a body. It's stuck in a tree snag on the bottom about three feet down. I'm going to loop the rope around its ankle and fasten the other end to that tree trunk on the bank." He pointed to a live oak tree with one of its limbs extending over the bank and hanging just a foot above the river. Jeff ducked beneath the surface with the rope trailing behind him.

Forty seconds ticked by with no sign of Jeff. Lori started screaming, "Jeff! Come back! Oh please, someone help! Jeff, please come back! Help! Please, something's wrong! Jason! Where are you? Help!"

A few seconds later, Jeff surfaced, jerked the snorkel out of his mouth, and took a deep breath. He was holding the other end of the rope. "I did it," he shouted back to Lori. "I just have to tie this to the tree and I'll be right there."

Lori held her hand over her mouth again in an attempt to control her shaking. "Please hurry, I want to go home."

"I know. I'm coming."

Jeff's feet sank in mud to the top of his ankles as he trudged toward the riverbank. He leaned forward, grabbed the tree limb, and pulled himself out of the muck onto dry land. After securing the rope to the tree, he realized that the only way he could return to the boat and avoid the blackberry briars, thick brush, and debris on the riverbank, was to swim. With a running leap, he dove into the river and swam rapidly back to Lori who stood on the bow of the boat.

Her hand was still covering her mouth by the time Jeff reached the ladder and climbed aboard. Immediately, he gave her another long, wet hug.

"It's all over," he assured her. "We'll call the police, and the rest will be in their hands."

Jeff disappeared into the cabin, dried off, put on shorts and a tee shirt, and rejoined Lori in the cockpit.

"Okay, now we can call the police," he said. He looked at his watch. It was 10:55. "Jason would do exactly what I am doing. We're on the right track."

Lori handed him the cell phone. He dialed the number for the Wilmingtown Police.

"Hello, Wilmingtown Police, Officer Jenkins speaking, can I help you?"

"Yes, my name is Jeff Chandler. I am on the sailing vessel *Southwind* at Harbor Marina, slip 34, on the Cape Fear River. Uh, well, we found a body floating in the river a little while ago . . . ."

"Wait," the officer interrupted. "You're going too fast. I need to get this straight so I can write it down. You said your name is Jeff Candling?"

"No, Jeff Chandler," Jeff repeated a little slower while catching his breath.

"Okay, Mr. Chandler. Now you say you found a dead body floating in the Cape Fear River near your boat at the Southwind Marina, slip 34? Where's the Southwind Marina?"

"No, no, no. I'm at Harbor Marina onboard the sailboat *Southwind*. Do you know where Harbor Marina is?" Jeff knew his impatience was showing.

"Uh, yes. Where is the body now?" Officer Jenkins asked.

"It's in the river. I tied a rope around one ankle and the other end to a tree a couple of hundred feet from the bow of my boat so the current wouldn't carry it away."

"Very well. I'll dispatch a patrol car there immediately. Stay there until we arrive. What's the telephone number where we can reach you?"

Jeff gave him his cell phone number.

"Thank you, Mr. Chandler. We'll be there shortly."

Jeff passed on the information to Lori who had settled down by now and was willing to wait for the police to arrive.

"Jeff, please call Jason now," Lori said.

"He'll be here soon. Like I said, he'll be proud of how we handled this."

In ten minutes, a police car with flashing lights screeched into the parking lot of the marina and two policemen got out and headed down the dock to slip thirty-four. When they arrived at the *Southwind*, Jeff eagerly greeted them and invited them to come aboard. The four sat in the cockpit under the shade of the Bimini cover while Jeff recounted the events that had led to the discovery and securing of the body to a tree. One of the officers, named Paulo, explained that he was a certified diver, and wanted to get into his wet suit to locate the body.

"Good. You can change in the cabin, if you wish," Jeff offered.

"Thanks," Paulo said. "I assume you're the owner of this boat."

"Oh, no, sir. Jason Shannon is. He'll be here shortly. We're close friends. He lets us use his boat sometimes."

"Roger that."

Officer Paulo climbed over the rail onto the dock and headed for his police cruiser to collect his gear.

"He'd better get that creepy body outta here fast," Lori said. "I'm still worried that something worse is gonna happen." She stood up and paced around the cockpit.

"Like what? I told you I tied it securely to the tree." Jeff desperately tried to calm her nerves. "And besides, it's dead. Nothing else can happen."

A few minutes later, Paulo returned to the *Southwind* with his diving tanks, suit, flippers, mask, and regulator. After changing in the cabin, he emerged ready to jump over the side.

"As I said earlier, the body is tied at the end of that rope just ahead of the bow." Jeff pointed toward the tree limb hanging over the water's edge.

"Thanks. I'll go take a look and get it out of the river so we can take it to the morgue for further investigation."

Paulo leaped over the railing and swam up river until he reached the rope hanging from the limb. He then dove beneath the surface for several minutes. When he poked his head out of the water, he signaled thumbs up to his partner standing on the bank where he found the body, and asked for help in towing it onto the bank. Officer Paulo dove down again to free the body from the snag.

While the policemen hauled the body ashore, a small paneled truck squealed into the parking lot. The side of the truck read "Wilmingtown News." Quickly two reporters with cameras rushed over to the bank where the body was being untied at the water's edge along the riverbank.

"Oh, no! Now we have to deal with the news media. I can't believe this," Lori complained to Jeff as she placed her hand over her mouth.

"Hey, don't worry. They aren't gonna bother us," Jeff said hopefully.

Officer Paulo dragged the body out of the water, placed it in a plastic body bag, and slid it along the grassy bank to the parking lot. The reporters continuously snapped pictures at the scene as the policemen lifted the body into the trunk of the cruiser and shut the lid. After a brief discussion with Paulo, the reporters headed toward the marina docks near slip thirty-four. The other police officers sat in their car and prepared the incident report.

"I don't wanna be in the news," Lori said. "Let's go down to the end of the dock and hide, pretend we're fishing or something. If they can't find us on the boat, maybe they'll go away."

Jeff shook his head knowing this scheme wouldn't work. "Reporters have noses like hound dogs. They'll find us."

In an attempt to appease Lori, however, Jeff hastily grabbed a fishing pole and tackle box off a shelf in the cabin. They raced to the end of the dock, plopped down on the edge with their backs to the reporters, and threw an empty line in the water. A few seconds later, the reporters rounded the corner on the dock and walked straight for their boat. Jeff watched them out of the corner of his eye. He heard one of them call his name and then knock on the cabin roof. When the reporters assumed no one was on board, they returned to the parking lot. Jeff sighed with relief.

"Hey, I gotta hand it to you. Your crazy idea worked," Jeff conceded.

Jeff continued to watch the reporters in the parking lot as they talked again with the police. Moments later the police and reporters returned to the dock and marched to the *Southwind*. As the investigation team rounded the corner of the dock, Jeff heard Officer Paulo shout, "There they are. At the end of the dock. I told you they were here." He pointed straight at Jeff and Lori.

"Damn! We've been caught," Jeff complained.

"Now what?" Lori asked. "I just wanna go home. Tell them I'm sick and can't deal with this right now."

"We're stuck. We'll have to see what they want and get it over with."

"Damn is right!" Lori snorted.

As the two reporters approached, one yelled, "Hey, you Mr. Chandler?"

"Maybe."

While one reporter reached for his notebook and pen, the other took pictures of them. "Yeah, you're Mr. Chandler all right. The police told us that you found this body floating by your boat this morning."

"Then talk to them about it."

"Is that your boat, the *Southwind*?"

"Yeah, sort of. Is that important?"

"What was your reaction when you first saw the body?" the reported asked.

"What do you think my reaction was? Do you think I jumped up and down with joy?" Jeff threw his arms in the air "What kind of reaction would any normal person have? You already know the answer to that stupid question."

"Hey, I'll ask the questions. You just give us the answers."

"Then don't ask me stupid questions."

"Stop it, guys," Lori said. She turned to the reporter. "Look, we are innocent people minding our own business. We had nothing to do with this crime, or whatever it is. If you promise to be kind to us, we'll help you with your story. Deal?"

"Okay, ma'am," the reporter said. "And your name, please?"

"Lori."

"Lori who? Lori Chandler?"

"No, just Lori."

The reporter frowned. "All right. I'll let that go. Now tell us what happened."

Jeff recounted the events to the reporter who took copious notes on a pad of paper while the photographer snapped numerous pictures. When Jeff finished with his tale, the reporter said, "Thanks, guys. The story will be in tomorrow morning's paper." With that, the reporter and photographer hurried down the dock to their car and spun the wheels out of the parking lot.

Suddenly, all was quiet again except for the gentle lapping of the waves against the hull. Lori wiped her forehead with her arm and looked into Jeff's eyes. Then she threw her arms around his neck, and with a tight hug whispered in his ear, "Let's go home, please."

Jeff looked at his watch. It was a few minutes before noon. "Jason should be here any moment now. We have to wait for him. Besides, he offered to take us sailing this afternoon. Don't you want to do that?"

"No. I'm too upset. I just wanna go home."

"Okay. As soon as we tell Jason what happened, we'll take a rain check on the sailing."

Just past noon, Jason pulled into the parking lot. Walking along the dock a few slips before the *Southwind*, he waved to Jeff and Lori and called out, "Hey guys, everything all right?"

"Yeah. Nothing happening here. All quiet," Jeff yelled back.

"That's a lie!" Lori shouted. "Everything's happened."

"Oh?" Jason climbed over the railing and jumped on board.

"Well, let's just say you'll read about it in the paper tomorrow morning," Jeff said.

"What? Paper? What are you guys mumbling about?"

Jeff shrugged. "Nothing big. Just the police and a dead body."

"Oh really?" Jason's eyes widened.

"Will you stop playing games, Jeff?" Lori interjected. "I'll tell you what happened. It has been the worst day of my life." Lori told Jason the story.

When she was finished, Jeff said, "Listen, Jason. Lori doesn't feel well after all of this. I think we'd better head for home instead of spending the weekend on your boat. I'm sorry, but thanks anyway for your offer."

"That's okay. I understand. Hopefully tomorrow, she'll feel better. I'll call you tomorrow."

"Thanks. See ya tomorrow." Jeff and Lori climbed over the railing and headed for the parking lot. Before they got into their car, they looked back and waved to Jason.

The following morning Jeff crawled out of bed, wove his way into the kitchen and turned on the stove to make some coffee. While the water was heating, he grabbed the newspaper off the front porch, sat down at the kitchen table, and read the headlines on the front page. His eyes quickly focused on a headline and picture at the bottom of the page: *"Sailors Find Body in Cape Fear River."*

Fully awake, he muttered to himself as he stared at the picture, "Oh my God, that's us. I can't believe they really did this."

Jeff grabbed the paper from the table and ran down the hall to the bedroom. "Lori, wake up. You gotta see this. They have us on the front page of the paper. The whole story is there, the body, the boat, us . . . everything!"

Lori rolled over and rubbed her eyes. "What story? Are you kidding?" she said as her mind quickly recovered from a sound sleep.

"The paper printed our story with a picture of me and the body. And they mentioned the name of the boat and your name, too."

"Turn on the light. Let me see that paper," she insisted, now fully awake.

Jeff reached for the light switch and handed her the paper.

"Good grief! So much for privacy," she groaned as she glared at the headline and picture. Half way through the article she said, "I see that the police found no identification on the body except for a belt buckle and shirt label in Spanish . . . and a bullet hole in the chest. One possibility, the article says, is that the man was an illegal immigrant and may have run afoul trying to escape from a ship in port. The police are checking reports of missing persons along the river. They also said you are the owner of *Southwind,* and that I'm your wife. I'm not your wife. I'm your girlfriend, right?" Lori asked uncertain what Jeff's response would be.

"Right, I'm not surprised," Jeff said. "They always get their stories screwed up."

She was obviously dismayed. "Crap. Now, everyone knows who we are."

"So what?"

"Well, I'm afraid people will harass us with questions or think we had something to do with the body."

"Don't be silly. We did the right thing," Jeff assured her. "No one is gonna bug us. We were just minding our own business working on the boat."

Later that morning, Jason called Lori. "Hey, Sweets, feeling better?"

"Hi Jason. Yes, I think we'll make it," Lori said.

"I guess you guys saw the paper this morning."

"Yes. But as usual they got a few things mixed up."

"I know. It's no big deal. Let the police deal with it now. Say, are you two up to having dinner on board the *Southwind* tonight?" Jason asked.

Lori checked with Jeff and then said, "Sure. What time?"

"How 'bout seven o'clock?"

"Yes, we'll be at the dock at seven," Lori agreed.

Early that evening Lori and Jeff arrived at the marina parking lot and walked along the wooden dock to the slip. The *Southwind* floated calmly on the river as if the events of yesterday had never happened.

"I feel creepy about going on this boat," Lori said. She stopped in her tracks next to the *Southwind* while Jeff leaped enthusiastically over the railing.

"Come on, it's over. We hafta move on," Jeff said.

"I know." She reluctantly climbed aboard and greeted Jason, who was in the cabin looking over charts of the Bahamas.

The sun hung low on the horizon while a light breeze blew in from the southwest, creating small, sun-drenched ripples on the river's surface.

"Ah, it is a perfect night for an evening on the river," Jason said trying to cheer everyone up.

"Well, maybe," Lori said, still bothered over the events the day before.

She walked to the back of the cockpit, leaned over the rail, and examined the water around the rudder to see if the body might have returned. Instead, she saw a piece of waterlogged paper stuck in the rudder hinge just below the water line. She reached over the rail into the water, retrieved it, and handed it to Jason, who read the faded scribbling:

Ramos a la porta 2 A.M. – BMW

Jason mulled over it for a few seconds and then tossed it into the trash. "Well, welcome aboard again, gang. I'll fire up the grill. Help yourself to some drinks in the galley. Are pork chops okay for you two?"

"Super," Lori said. She went into the cabin to prepare drinks while Jeff sat in the cockpit with Jason.

"Okay, friend, tell me more about this amazing Maisy you heard on the radio," Jeff said with heightened curiosity.

Before Jason could respond, Lori retrieved pork chops and three potatoes from the galley. She handed them to their host to put on the grill in the cockpit. Then Lori retreated to the galley and proceeded to prepare dinner.

"Maisy, yes, Miss Maisy," Jason said with a broad smile, "I'm going to find her. I'm sailing to Andros."

"I figured you would. When are you leaving?"

"In two weeks. I want you and Lori to come with me."

"You're kidding! In two weeks?"

"Why not? She needs help." Jason turned on the propane gas and threw three chops on the grill.

"By the time you get there, it'll be over," Jeff said. "She'll already know what happened to her family."

"Perhaps, but she is lonely. She still needs help."

"You mean, you're hoping she needs you," Jeff said, half-jokingly.

"Maybe." Jason turned his back to hide the smirk on his face and flipped the meat on the grill.

"Well, am I right?" Jeff probed.

"Okay, you're right," Jason admitted. "But I'm going, regardless, and I want you two to join me. I figured it would take us a week to get there, a week in Andros and a week to sail back to Wilmingtown. For planning purposes, however, I would count on a month. Are you in?"

"Wow, what an offer. Sounds intriguing. I'd better check with Lori."

A few minutes later Lori returned to the cockpit and announced, "Dinner will be ready in ten minutes. How are the chops coming along?"

"Perfect. They'll be ready just in time," Jason replied. He leaned closer to Jeff and whispered, "What are you waiting for? Ask her."

"Wine sure would taste good right now, Lori," Jeff hollered into the galley. "Check in the cabinet under the refrigerator. I bet Jason has a bottle or two just waiting for us to have a toast."

"Roger on that," she shouted back.

"I'll ask her after she has had a couple glasses of wine; let's get her loosened up before we pop the question."

"You sneak. You really know how to manipulate her," Jason chuckled.

"Oh, sometimes," Jeff snickered.

Lori filled three glasses, passed them around, and returned to the galley to finish dinner preparations. Before she returned, she managed to gulp the wine down and fill her glass again. Soon she handed the trays of food to Jason and Jeff and joined them for dinner under the Bimini cover.

Jason proposed a toast, "Cheers. Here's to three great friends on the *Southwind.*"

"Yeah, to the three of us," Lori and Jeff said in unison. They clinked the three glasses together and took a sip. "And here's to the three of us sailing on an exciting adventure to the Bahamas in two weeks," Jason toasted again.

"Yeah. To our exciting adventure to the Bahamas," she repeated and tapped her glass again with Jason and Jeff's glasses. She fell back against the seat and let out a giggle.

Jeff learned over to Jason and whispered, "She didn't get it. I'll try again."

"And here's to you and me sharing a great sailing adventure with Jason to Andros in two weeks on the *Southwind*," Jeff toasted to Lori.

"Uh, that's what I said . . . wait, you said what?" Lori questioned.

"You and me," Jeff repeated.

"You and me?" What do you mean 'you and me'?" Lori asked with a concerned look on her face followed by a silly grin.

"Oh, Jason asked us to sail with him to the Bahamas, and I said 'yes, we would love to go'," Jeff said excitedly as he put his arm around Lori's waist and pulled her closer to him. Lori gulped down the rest of the wine in her glass and waited for the alcohol to rush to her head.

"You didn't discuss it with me," Lori said drowsily.

"So, are you saying no?"

"I'm saying yes." At that moment, she fell into Jeff's lap, put her arms around his shoulders, and closed her eyes.

"See, I told you she would agree. Just a matter of wine and time," Jeff laughed. "Are you makin' fun of me?" Lori quizzed as her eyes opened again.

"Of course not," Jeff said and nudged Jason in the side.

The three finished dinner under a brilliant red sunset emanating from the western sky. Around 10 o'clock, Jason suggested they stay on board for the night. "You two can sleep in my cabin and I'll sleep in the guest cabin," Jason offered.

"How 'bout it Lori?" Jeff asked.

"Yeah," she responded, leaned back, and fell asleep on the cushion in the main cabin. By 11:00 o'clock, the lights were out. Lori had come full circle . . . she was ready for the adventure.

Shortly after midnight, a small boat snaked its way silently into the marina and crept slowly toward slip 34. Two unshaven, grimy men muscled the skiff forward with wooden oars being careful not to break the surface of the water. When they reached the *Southwind*, Jason heard one of the oars accidentally smack the wooden dock. He raised himself up, rubbed his eyes, and glanced at the clock, wondering if he'd been dreaming. Then he heard a splash. Now awake, he peeked out the small port window above his bunk to see what was out there. Suddenly a streak of light flashed across the deck and then focused on the *Southwind's* stern. Alarmed, Jason leaped out of bed and crawled quietly on his hands and knees into the cockpit to get a better view. He watched the two men as they turned the boat around and paddled slowly out of the marina, but not before he observed the damaged port bow on the skiff. Concerned, Jason returned to the bunk and lay awake for another hour trying to unravel the visit of the mystery callers.

Chapter 2

Coral Sun Ray

Later that morning, Officer Jerry Black, carrying a stack of investigation papers, walked into Captain Jenkins' office at the Wilmingtown Police Station.

"Captain, I've got the preliminary coroner's report on the body we found at the marina two days ago. The man was shot in the chest and then died from drowning. There was no identification on the person except a Spanish labeled shirt and a Spanish belt buckle. So, we suspect he might have been an illegal immigrant."

"Okay, check along the waterfront for any reports of missing persons or ship crew."

"Roger that, Captain. I'll get on it right away." Officer Black hustled out of the Captain's office, headed down the hall to his desk and picked up the phone.

"Hey, Paulo. Jerry here. We've got an urgent assignment to take care of," he said to his partner on the floor above him.

"Oh yeah? What's that, pal?"

"Just talked to the Captain. He wants us to check out the ships in port for possible missing crew. It's 'bout that body we found in the river. Since you're better at Spanish then I am, you've been drafted to go with me, okay?"

"Is that what the Captain said? 'Draft Officer Paulo into this mess'?"

"Well, not exactly. I'm telling you . . . I mean asking you to come along and help," Jerry hedged.

"Okay. Just wanna get things straight. I know you," Paulo laughed. "Gimme 'bout twenty minutes to wrap up a couple of things. I'll meet you in your office."

A short while later, the two headed down the highway in their police cruiser looking for ships along the Cape Fear River. By mid-afternoon, they'd visited several vessels tied to the piers at the State Ports and were exhausted.

"Paulo, it's already 3:30 and we're getting nowhere on this case."

"Yeah, I know. However, we've got time for one more ship, and then I suggest we call it quits for the day. All right?"

"Okay. I believe there is one more ship at a private pier just down the road," Officer Black said.

They pulled off the main highway onto a pot-holed dirt road that led to a wooden shack adjacent to a locked chain-linked gate. Wired to the center of the gate was a faded sign that read: *Yarrow Shipping – No Admittance*

On the porch, a scruffy old man sat in a broken, plastic lawn chair propped up against the side of the building. He appeared to be sleeping with his head down and his hat pulled over his eyes. Jerry stopped his cruiser in front of the gate just as Paulo rolled down his window to shout at the guard.

"Hey buddy, you work here?"

The old man sat motionless except to raise his hand slightly to tilt his cap to one side of his head just enough to see out of one eye. He stared at the cruiser but remained silent.

Man, this guy's a real fireball," Jerry whispered to Paulo. "Do ya think he's alive and breathin?" he snickered.

"Who knows?" Paulo said. "But I'm gonna find out." He leaned out the window again and hollered, "You're a lively one, aren't ya? Are you the guard for this place?"

"What do ya think? I ain't sittin' here for nothin'," the old man snapped.

"That's what I figured," Paulo retorted.

"What do ya want?" the old man asked.

"We want to talk to the Captain of that freighter tied up there," Paulo insisted and pointed straight ahead toward the end of the pier.

"Why?" the man grumbled.

"We're doing an investigation, a missing person's investigation," Paulo said.

"There ain't nobody missing," the old man insisted.

"Look, I told you we want to talk to the Captain about this matter. Now I am ordering you to open the gate . . . please," Paulo said in a threatening tone.

"The Captain's busy," the old man mumbled then got off his chair, turned his back, and walked into the shack.

"Would you believe this arrogant bum?" Paulo turned to Jerry. "This guy's definitely got an attitude. I'll fix his goose."

Paulo picked up his clipboard, got out of the cruiser, rested his hand on his gun in the holster, and walked into the shack. The guard had just picked up the phone to call someone, so Paulo waited for a moment to find out whom he was calling.

"Rafael, there are a couple of policemen here. They wanna talk to Capt'n," the guard mumbled. After a pause, the guard continued, "I know, I told them that." Another pause, then, "But they insisted they wanted to talk to him . . . something 'bout a missin' person." Still another pause. "Yep, I told them that, too. Okay." He hung up and turned to Paulo.

"Like I said, the Captain's busy and no one's missin.' Now git."

"Git nonsense! What is your name, Sir?" Paulo shouted in anger.

"I don't have to give you my name. I ain't done nothin' wrong. I told you the Capt'n' is busy, now go home," the guard repeated.

"I am ordering you to give me your name and let us through the gate! You're obstructing justice! We're here on official business and will get a search warrant, if necessary," Paulo screamed and kicked the guard's chair in a state of frustration.

"Okay, okay, I'll let you in. But I warn you. The crew will not let you onboard. Liability, safety issues, you know. You might get hurt."

"We'll see about that. I'll ask one more time. Your name?" Paulo warned

"Jago."

Paulo made some notes on his clipboard and proceeded out the door to the cruiser.

"Man, this guy's nasty. I mean really nasty. And he smells worse than nasty, too. I bet he hasn't had a bath in two years! We may be onto something this time," he remarked to Jerry after he got into the car.

When Paulo closed the car door, the guard came out of the shack, unlocked the chain, and opened the gate. Paulo signaled a thank you gesture out his window while Jerry drove the car through the opened gate. Jago raised his hand and responded with a gesture that could have been interpreted as something else as they continued down the narrow dirt road to the pier. From their vantage point, they could see no one milling around the dock or on the decks of the medium size cargo freighter. On the dockside of the ship, a large, opened cargo door with a ramp led to the pier. High on the mast a Bahamian flag flapped in the steady southwest breeze. Jerry parked the cruiser on the dock next to the ship, and the two sat in the car for a few moments to see if anyone would come to the rail and greet them. Realizing no one from the ship was curious about their presence, the two officers threw up their hands, got out of the car, marched up the ramp into the cargo deck. At that point, a seaman stopped them by the time they reached twenty feet inside the door.

"What do you men want?" he asked as he gestured them to stop.

"Good afternoon, Sir. I am Officer Black and this is my partner Officer Paulo. We wanna speak to the Captain, please."

"Is he expectin' you?" the seaman asked.

"Well, no, not exactly," Paulo said.

"Then why do you want to see him?" the seaman questioned.

"It's about a missing person report."

"Oh, I see. Ya found a body, huh? Floating in the river, maybe? Ya know who he was? Ya think ya know which ship he came from?" the crewman blurted out as he nervously fidgeted with his hands and refused to make eye contact.

"I didn't say we found a body. Didn't say the body was floatin' in the river. Didn't say the body was a he or she. You sound like you might know something about this."

"Oh, I didn't mean to say 'he', Sir. I'm just used to callin' everyone 'he'," the crewman backtracked.

"Never mind. Take us to the Captain, now," Jerry insisted.

"Okay, so you didn't say anything about a body. But ya wouldn't be here if you hadn't found one," the crewman rattled on and immediately turned his back to them. "Follow me."

The three walked the length of the cargo hold, climbed three sets of metal stairs to the officers' quarters, and approached the Captain's cabin. Following a hard knock, the Captain flung the door open and glared at the two policemen.

"Well, well, Gentleman, what brings you onboard?" the captain asked with a twisted smile on his unshaven face.

"We are following up on a missing person incident and wondered if you are missing a crewman?" Jerry asked.

"You guys get right to the point, don't you? How recently?"

"Oh, in the past few days, perhaps." Jerry responded.

"Nope, all of our crew is accounted for," he assured the officers.

"You mean they are all present?" Paulo tried to clarify.

"That's what I said. You speak English?" the Captain snarled.

"Don't be a smart aleck, Captain. And your name is?"

"Captain Franco, John Franco."

"Okay, I guess that will do for now. Thank you for your time,

Capt'n," Jerry said.

"Wait. Tell me 'bout this missing person. What do you know about this person? Why did you decide to come here?" the Captain quizzed.

"Oh, well, we don't know much yet, except we found a body floating in the river a few days ago, right across from this ship and wondered if he might have . . . ."

"Come from here? No, no," the Captain interrupted. "As I said, everyone is here. Check the other ships. You're wasting your time here."

"Yes, we are checking other possibilities. Thanks again," Officer Black said. "Oh, by the way, for your information the man was shot. It's a murder case now. We're looking into that, too. Good day."

The Captain turned to his mate and ordered him to escort the police off his vessel. As they walked through the interior passageways of the ship, Jerry tripped over a large plastic bag marked 'trash' that partially blocked the aisle. Some of the contents spilled onto the deck.

"Oh, geez! I'm sorry I'm so clumsy. Wasn't paying attention. Here, I'll put these clothes back in the bag," he said apologetically to the crewman, immediately leaned over, and began shoving everything back into the bag. In the process, he could not help but notice the contents— several shirts, a couple pairs of trousers, shoes, underwear, socks, a jacket, a small framed picture of a pretty *seniorita*, and a document labeled 'Ramos Hernandez'. Paulo stared at the document for a second before the crewman snatched the paper from Paulo's hand and pushed him down the passageway.

"I'll take that. This is ship's trash," he said nervously and placed himself between Paulo and the trash bag. "I'll clean it up later. Let's move on," the crewman insisted as he forced the two to continue on to the exit ramp.

When Jerry and Paulo climbed into their cruiser on the dock, Jerry opened the conversation. "Did you make a note of the captain's name, Captain John Franco . . . and the name of the ship?"

"I got Franco's name but I didn't see the name of the ship," Paulo replied.

"That's all right, I got it. It is the *Coral Sun Ray*. I saw it on a placard on a bulkhead near the officer's quarters. And did you see the expensive cars in the cargo hold?" Jerry asked.

"I saw a dim outline of cars in the darkness, but I couldn't tell what kind they were."

"Well, they seem to be pretty high class cars for a ship's crew." Jerry said with curiosity.

"Oh, that's no big deal. I've heard shipping companies pay their crew pretty well. Or maybe they are delivering them to someone. Anyway, I don't care about the cars. It's none of our business," Paulo acknowledged.

"Yeah, you're right. Well, I guess we came up with another dead end. No leads here," Jerry said relieved that the day's work was finally done.

"Yep, but I sure did want to give that guard a smack in the face. Let's go back to headquarters."

At a prearranged time, Jason sat down in front of the short wave radio on board the *Southwind* and called Maisy. He made two attempts before Maisy answered.

"Oh Jason, I am so glad to hear your voice again. Are you okay?" she asked.

"Yes, of course. How are you coping today?" Jason asked cautiously.

"Jason, I . . . I . . . I have very bad news." There was a long period of silence.

Jason broke in, "Maisy, I'm so sorry. Can you tell me what happened?" Jason asked fearing the worse.

"They found my parent's boat. It was floating, half submerged, on its side about twenty miles offshore and . . . and . . . I just can't deal with this anymore." Maisy started crying and turned off her microphone.

Jason then knew what she was trying to say. His worst fears became a reality as his mind filled with the horrible thoughts of the death of her parents.

"Maisy, I understand. I want to help you," Jason said trying desperately to find the right words.

"The funeral was three days ago. It was terrible, and . . . and . . ." Maisy started crying again.

"Maisy, listen. I know how you feel. I'm so sorry for you and your friends. I want to see you. I am coming to Moxey Settlement soon, over."

There was silence. "Maisy . . . Maisy . . . come in, Maisy," Jason pleaded in the microphone.

"Jason, I'm sorry. I feel so bad," Maisy sobbed.

"Maisy, did you hear me say I am coming to Andros to see you?"

"Yes. Oh, I want you to come here. I would be very happy to meet you. You have been so helpful, but you are so far away, over."

"Don't worry about that. I am planning to sail there in my sailboat, but I have one concern. I studied the sailing charts for Andros, and it appears that the Moxey channel is almost blocked with coral reefs. In fact, the water between Coakley and Moxey is full of shallow reefs. Is that right?"

"Yes."

"My sailboat has a deep draft, and the sailing guides warn not to sail in these waters without local knowledge. If I sail to Coakley Town instead which is just 35 miles north of you, could I take a water taxi to Moxey Settlement?

"You could hire someone to take you in a small boat, but I can catch the mail boat to Coakley Town and meet you there. It runs once a day," Maisy said. "I think that would be better."

"Wonderful. I have to work out the details, but I am thinking about leaving Wilmingtown in two weeks. To help with the sailing chores, I am bringing two friends with me. It should take a week to make the trip. I'll stay in contact with you by radio every day, over."

"Thank you, Jason. You are so kind," she said.

"Keep your spirits up and I'll call you same time tomorrow, okay?"

"Yes, that will be great. Have a good evening, Jason."

"You, too. Bye."

Spending the weekend on board the Southwind, Jeff, and Jason studied the navigation charts and plotted their course to the islands. Jason glanced at his watch and discovered to his surprise that it was 1:30 in the morning, and with that realization, he decided to call it quits for the evening and went to bed. Still wide-awake, however, Jeff looked over his shoulder at Lori who was asleep in a chair in the main cabin. Putting his hand up to his chin, he got up from the chart table, slipped quietly over to Lori, and placed his hand gently on her forehead. Like magic, Lori's eyes opened.

"Sweetheart, I'm not ready to turn in yet. Let's go for a little boat ride in the dinghy up the river . . . you know, a moonlight cruise. It's quiet, no wind, the moon's full, just you and me," Jeff whispered to Lori. She stared at Jeff for a few seconds, closed her eyes again, and fell asleep. Jeff waited a few minutes and then shook her arm gently.

"Lori, wake up. I'm serious. It's a perfect night for a little boat ride. Just think, the entire world's asleep and we can float quietly in the night, unnoticed and enjoy the peace on the river."

"What? Are you crazy? Is it morning already?" Lori asked still a bit foggy.

"Yeah, I'm crazy."

"You mean I slept all night in this chair, didn't even crawl in bed?"

"Well, sort of," Jeff said.

"What time is it? It's still dark outside." Lori asked as she began to wake up.

"It's, uh . . . 1:30."

"1:30! You are out of your mind? A boat ride at 1:30 in the morning?"

"Sure. Why not?" Jeff insisted. Then he went to the door of Jason's cabin and whispered, "Hey Jason, are you still awake?"

"Yes," he mumbled.

"You don't mind if we take the dinghy out, do you?" Jeff asked.

"That's fine. Have fun," Jason responded.

Lori tried to turn over and throw the covers back over her head, but the chair would not yield.

"Ow, my arms and legs are so stiff!" she sighed.

"You see, getting up and going for a short boat ride would loosen up those stiff muscles and give you the exercise you need. Then you can go to sleep in a real bed," Jeff rationalized.

Lori stared at him like it really wasn't happening, a bad dream, then she sighed. "Okay, give me a moment to wake up. You get the dingy ready," she muttered. Then she laid her head back down on the pillow, pulled the blanket over her head, and fell asleep again.

Jeff climbed into the cockpit, grabbed two life jackets, a flashlight, binoculars, a couple of oars, and tossed them in the dinghy. He lowered himself down the swim ladder into the boat, sat down in the back, and waited.

"Hey, Lori. Come on. Let's go," he shouted from the dinghy.

There was no response in the cabin. Jeff hollered a second time. Finally, he carefully moved forward to the bow and climbed back on board the *Southwind* to get her going again. Seeing the lump under the blanket, he gave her a poke.

"Okay, okay, I'm awake," Lori complained.

"Good, let's go. I'm not moving until you get up," Jeff insisted.

After a couple of minutes Lori stumbled out of the cabin and shuffled down the ladder with her blanket still wrapped around her. Jeff held her hand while she awkwardly plunged into the dinghy. After making adjustments to the outboard motor, Jeff pulled on the cord twice to get the fuel flowing through the carburetor to start the engine.

Surprisingly, Lori managed to untie the bow from the *Southwind* and toss the rope by her feet. Then Jeff steered the dinghy quietly up the dark river and headed toward the opposite bank where a ship was moored along a decaying wharf and pilings.

Now fully awake, Lori admitted, "You're right. This is a beautiful night." She snuggled closer to Jeff and put her arm around his waist. "Look at that full moon . . . how it reflects all across the river."

"See. I told you it is a special night," Jeff added.

As they approached the ship, they noticed several cars parked on the dock and a couple of men talking to each other. Curious as to what was going on, Jeff steered the dinghy around the stern of the vessel where he could get a closer look at the loading dock. Lori picked up the binoculars and focused on the dock.

"What do you see?" Jeff asked.

"Well, nothing much, just three cars and a couple of people talking."

"Let me see the binocs," Jeff insisted. He adjusted the focus and watched intently as the men drove the cars up the cargo ramp and into the ship's hold. "Obviously they're shipping cars somewhere."

"Yeah . . . maybe. But I only saw two. If they're shipping cars, wouldn't dozens of them be out there ready to be loaded?" Lori questioned.

"I don't know. Maybe those are the last two. Let me look again in the binocs." Jeff watched the activity for another minute. "I think one of the cars was a black BMW and I don't remember what the other car was. I don't believe it was a BMW. You would think all of the cars would be the same kind. Who knows what they are doing?" Jeff conceded as he set the binoculars down on the seat.

But Lori was fighting a losing battle for sleep. She wrapped her arms around her knees, plopped her head down on them, and exclaimed, "It's two in the morning, for God's sake! Let's go back to the *Southwind* and go to bed. I don't want to sit here all night and watch people load a ship with stupid cars."

"Okay, okay. I agree, it's not important."

Jeff swung the dinghy around and headed back to the marina. He looked back at the stern of the ship and then muttered to himself, "*Coral Sun Ray.*"

"Did you say something?" Lori asked.

"That's the name of the freighter. I saw it on the stern."

"Oh, God. Let's just get back to the *Southwind*," Lori pleaded.

He glanced at a small floating dock adjacent to the stern of the freighter. "Now that's weird. See that small boat tied to the dock. Jason told me that the boat that stopped by the marina in the middle of the night and searched the *Southwind* with a searchlight had a damaged bow. That boat has a damaged bow. It must be the same one." Lori did not respond. She was asleep again with her head on her folded up knees.

"Oh, well . . ." He paused. "I just thought it was interesting."

Jeff guided the dinghy slowly through the calm, black water toward the marina while Lori remained motionless. When he docked the boat behind the *Southwind,* Lori wasted no time climbing up the swim ladder with the bowline in hand and tying it to the railing. By the time Jeff finished his chores securing the outboard motor and putting away the oars and life jackets, Lori was already curled up in the bunk fast asleep inside the cabin.

At six-thirty, Lori suddenly sat up in bed and began screaming, "No, no, don't do it!"

Jeff rolled over and looked at Lori. "What's the matter? You look horrible."

"I was having a nightmare. I can't get that body out of my mind. He was about to grab us and kill us."

"It's just a dream. Everything is okay. No one is here," Jeff reassured her.

"Yeah. But it was scary," Lori said.

Lori looked out the port window at the fist rays of the morning sun already dancing across the ripples in the water. She shoved her hand against her forehead to try to calm her dreadful, swirling reminders of the body bumping against the rudder.

"I know. It's tough. But you'll get over it." Jeff thought for a moment, and then added, "Look, let's think about our trip to the Caribbean . . . just the three of us, away from the hassle of this rat race, relaxing among the quite coconut coves, doing some diving, just enjoying life." Jeff forced a big smile and his eyes sparkled as he looked into Lori's troubled eyes.

"I'll try," she sighed.

By the time Jason, Jeff and Lori finished breakfast in the cockpit under the shade of the Bimini cover, Lori had recovered and began talking about their sail south. During the course of conversation, Jeff told Jason about the damaged boat they saw next to the freighter.

"Well, we know where the boat came from, but I still don't know why they were snooping around the marina in the middle of the night," Jason said.

"Changing the subject, I'm curious. How old do you think Maisy is? You seemed to have fallen for her, yet you don't know anything about her," Jeff asked.

"Ah, I was waiting for you to ask me that question. Her voice sounds like she is young, perhaps in her twenties. But I wanted to find out, too, so I asked her in a diplomatic way. She told me on the radio that she was twenty-four. And she is not married," Jason added cheerfully. "She wants to go to college in Nassau, but she has no money and now her life has turned upside down."

"Well, this is going to be an intriguing voyage in many ways," Jeff concluded.

Lori added her two cents to the conversation, "Are you sure your auto body shop isn't going to crash while you're away for a month?" Her tone suggested that she really expected it would.

"It might. But they wouldn't dare do anything foolish. I am their job security. If they screw up . . . well, this is a silly conversation. Just don't worry about my company. At that moment, Jason's cell phone rang.

"See, your shop's already in trouble. They're calling for help," Lori laughed.

Jason smiled as he picked up the phone. "Hello?" There was no answer. "Hello," Jason repeated. Still there was still no answer. "Humph. Must be a wrong number."

"Fortunately, for a professional writer like you, Jeff, you can go anywhere and still write, right?"

"Sort of."

"And what about you, Lori?" Jason asked.

"No problem. My boss will let me go. He can hire a temporary secretary while I am gone. He's easy going. He'll understand," she said confidentially.

"Perfect," Jason said and raised his arm in triumph. "We're off to the tropics," he shouted with excitement.

Chapter 3

Grand Theft

On the south side of Atlanta in a rough neighborhood, a middle-aged man sat with a young blond woman in a dimly lit booth in the back of the Tiki Bar. The man's arms and chest were covered with tattoos, and he was dressed in worn jeans and a black shirt with a skull and cross bones stenciled on the front. Across the table from him, the girl twirled strands of her bleached hair with her finger, and then pushed it over her shoulders and let if fall to reveal her skimpy tee-shirt. The two talked quietly out of earshot of two men sitting on bar stools at the counter and the bar tender. It was almost midnight.

"So, Miss Sassy, how's the underworld treatin' ya?" asked the man, named Gunner.

"Underworld bull crap! I ain't no part of the underworld, you rat fink! If it wasn't for me, you'd be outta a job. So, watch your mouth," Gina fired back.

"Settle down, Sis. I wasn't trying to get your hackles up," Gunner said as he placed his hand on top of hers. "When's our next job?"

Ignoring him, Gina stared off in the distance then guzzled down her gin and tonic in one shot. For a few seconds the shock of alcohol flooding her throat astounded her. She set the glass down and looked at Gunner.

"There's a year old Mercedes convertible in a city-parking garage on Fifteenth Street, third deck up. The owner parks it there every day. I checked it out. She arrives around 8:30 in the morning and leaves around 4:45 in the afternoon. My scanner found the door lock and ignition activation codes, so we can open the door and start the engine. This one's a piece of cake. It's an easy catch."

"Good. When do we make the hit?" Gunner asked.

"Tomorrow morning, 9:30. The garage should be quiet by then. I'll be your lookout as usual, and I'll beep you on our walkie talkie if I see anything suspicious," Gina responded.

"This one's way overdue. I'm getting' low on cash, and I need this job to pay off a debt," Gunner said.

"Right. See ya tomorrow," Gina said as she awkwardly squeezed out of the booth and stumbled her way toward the door. Gunner raised his arm to wave goodbye but she never looked back.

The following morning, Gunner stepped off the city bus on Fifteenth Street and walked into the parking garage. He leaped up the stairs two at a time to the third level and found Gina sitting in a small black car near the doorway to the stairs. She held a newspaper in front of her face pretending she was reading it. Gunner walked over to passenger side door of her car and tapped on the window.

"Well, surprise to see you here," Gunner joked. "You just seem to be everywhere."

"You're not funny, jerk. Get in," she snapped.

"Loosen up, Poopsie Pie. This is gonna be as smooth as swallowin' your gin down your throat. Where's the car?" he asked.

"Over there, next to the outside wall, the Mercedes convertible," she said as she pointed out the front window.

"Ah yes. There she is. This gem is an easy 500 bucks in my pocket."

"I have been watching the activity in the garage awhile. This parking level is filled, and no one has been around. So, let's go for it," Gina ordered.

When they reached the Mercedes, she pulled out of her pocket the scanner, pushed a button, and turned the scanner-tuning knob. Several car door locks clicked in the immediate vicinity followed ten seconds later by the doors on the Mercedes. Quickly Gunner pulled on the front door handle and jumped in.

"Yes, we're golden. We got this one." Gunner waved in delight. He got out of the car, opened the hood and short-circuited two terminals in the engine compartment with a wire and alligator clips. To his delight the engine started. "Way to go, baby," Gunner hollered and patted his hand on the fender. Climbing back into the car, Gunner reached in his pocket and placed a ten-dollar bill on the dashboard to pay the parking attendant, and then quickly backed out of the parking slot. Gina followed him in her car down the ramp to the exit. As he approached the ticket booth, he opened the window and held out the money to the waiting attendant.

"Morning, Sir. Couldn't find my parking stub. Looked everywhere. But I came in this morning. What do I owe ya?" Gunner asked.

"Well, you'll have to pay a full day's parking for a lost ticket," the attendant explained.

"That's okay. How much?"

"Seven dollars."

Gunner handed him the ten-dollar bill. "Keep the change, buddy. Have a good day." Gunner pulled into the street and sped off to the warehouse five miles away.

Fifteen minutes later Gunner pulled up to a door of an old wooden building on a deserted back street. He got out, unlocked the door, opened it and drove in. Gina followed close behind. The large storage area was dimly lit as they drove to the back corner of the building, and then gunner removed all personal items belonging to the owner from the car.

"Well, that was easy. Good job," Gina said to Gunner as she climbed out of her car.

"Yeah. Now I've got to get on the road soon and head east before they issue an all points bulletin on this hot rod," Gunner said. "Yep. I'll contact Capt'n Franco and let him know you're comin'," Gina said.

"Thanks. Here's some of the owner's stuff. Get rid of it. I'm ready to load up," Gunner urged. "Move the truck over to the loading ramp while I finish cleaning out the car."

Gina hopped into the driver's seat of a large, white, panel truck and drove it out into the alley. The sun illuminated the sign painted on the sides as she backed it into the loading pit.

WILLIE'S DISCOUNT APPLIANCES
Serving the Southeast

Gunner lifted up the rear door of the truck and drove the Mercedes inside all the way to the front. Meanwhile, Gina, maneuvering a forklift, loaded large, empty, cardboard boxes labeled 'Refrigerators', 'Washers', 'Dryers' and 'Ranges' into the back of the truck to conceal the car.

"There. That'll do it. See ya in a few days," Gunner said as he waved goodbye to Gina, climbed into the front seat, and drove down the alley to the street. He turned right and headed east toward the North Carolina coast.

On board the *Coral Sun Ray*, the Captain's phone rang.

"Hello?" Captain Franco answered.

"John?"

"Yes."

"Gina here. Gunner's bringin' a Mercedes to you tonight. It's just a year old and a good one."

"Okay. We can handle five more cars before we head south in two weeks, "Captain Franco said.

"We could probably get you a couple more, and then we have to lay low for awhile until things cool off. What about Dingo and Merinda? How are they doing?" Gina asked.

"Very well. They have two comin' in tonight from Miami and Tampa," John said.

"Fantastic. We'll try to get you two more before you head for the Caribbean. I'll stay in touch." Gina said.

Captain Franco hung up the phone and paged Rafael on the ship's intercom to come to his cabin. A few minutes later Rafael knocked on the cabin door.

"Come in," the Captain insisted.

"Yes, Captain. You paged?" Rafael asked.

"Juan, we have three cars coming in tonight. Just wanted to let you know. Be ready for them, okay?"

"Yes Sir" No problem," Rafael agreed.

"Here's a list of the cars," the Captain said as he handed Rafael a piece of paper.

"Okay. We'll be on the lookout for 'em."

"One more thing. About Ramos. You may have heard that two kids in a ragtop sailboat across the river found Ramos' body a few days ago, and the police stopped by here recently asking questions. We know nothing about a body or Ramos. Get my drift, Rafael?" John warned.

"Yes Sir, Captain. We know nothin.'" Rafael repeated.

"Excellent."

Rafael left the Captain's cabin and went down to the cargo hold. He called Carlos, his deck hand, to his office. "Carlos, Franco tells me we have three more cars coming in tonight. We are getting close to our twenty-six car limit, aren't we?"

"Almost," Carlos said.

"Good. Keep me posted about the deliveries tonight."

"Sure thing," Carlos assured.

Gunner drove his truck east on Interstate 20 toward Augusta. It was mid-afternoon when he approached the South Carolina State line and saw the truck weigh station sign ahead. As he pulled over into the truck exit lane, he encountered six trucks ahead of him moving slowly but at a steady pace. When Gunner pulled up to the scales, the South

Carolina State Trooper signaled him to pull over into the inspection lane instead and wait for an inspector. A few minutes later, the inspector appeared at his window and asked to see the truck registration papers, manifest and his driver's license. Gunner had them ready on the seat beside him and handed them to the inspector.

"What's this all about? I never had to go through an inspection before," Gunner said to the officer.

"Well, we have a bulletin alert to be on the lookout for stolen cars in the southeast. This one was issued an hour ago regarding a stolen black BMW from Atlanta, so we hafta check all trucks traveling the Interstate. We have patrol cars on the road looking for the cars, too. Well, I see you are carrying appliances, huh?" he questioned.

"Yes, Sir, makin' deliveries to stores in North Carolina. Refrigerators, stoves, you know, the usual household appliances."

"I see. Mind if I have a look inside?" the inspector asked.

"Go ahead; I'll open up the back for you." Gunner hopped out of the front seat, nervously walked to the back, and opened the door. "See, as I said, just appliances."

"Looks like you have a full load here," the inspector said.

"Yeah. We don't like to make partial shipments. Full loads keep our costs down," Gunner said.

The inspector read the labeling carefully on the large cartons jammed up against the back door. "Okay, you're good to go. Paperwork looks correct, too. Have a good trip," the inspector said as he handed the registration and manifest papers back to Gunner.

Three hours later, Gunner arrived at the North Carolina State line on Interstate 95 northeast of Florence. He pulled off the freeway again and entered a North Carolina State weigh station. Gunner stopped the truck next to the officer standing on the tarmac.

"Good evening, Sir. Where did you come from?" the inspector questioned Juan.

"Atlanta."

"Carrying any weapons, hazardous materials, livestock?"

"Nope."

"Okay. You're cleared," the inspector said. He stamped an official inspection document and handed it to Gunner.

Darkness had already set in at the Yarrow Shipyard when Gunner turned off the river road onto the dirt lane leading to the dock. The truck's headlights lit up the guard shack ahead, and by the single light hanging from the ceiling inside the shack, he could barely make out the silhouette of the guard sleeping in a chair next to the window. Gunner stopped in front of the gate and waited. When it became obvious the guard was not coming out to challenge him, he got out of the truck, walked onto the porch and kicked the door hard.

"Hey! Get off your fat butt you lazy scoundrel!" Gunner growled. The sudden intrusion caused Jago to jerk violently and fall off his chair. Holding his hand on his head, he looked up at the door and saw Gunner's snarling teeth glaring through the door windowpane.

"Oh. It's you. I didn't see you come in. I . . . I was daydreaming," Jago said sheepishly.

"Bull. You are two sheets to the wind again and off in never-never land. I've got a good mind to haul you onboard and let the Captain deal with you. He don't like no screwballs who nap on the job. Bad for business," Gunner snarled as he walked up to Jago and grabbed him by the collar. "Understand, hollow head?"

Jago yanked Gunner's hand away from his collar and kicked him against the wall. "No one calls me 'hollow head'. Not even a street rat like you," Jago shouted, as he held up his fists ready to punch him in the stomach.

"Ha, ha, ha," Gunner laughed. You couldn't kill a flea on the back of a southern hound dog, old man. Now get out there and unlock that gate before I have you keel hauled. I don't have time to mess with you." Jago zigzagged cautiously past Gunner and out the door to the gate while Gunner watched in the doorway. When the gate opened, Gunner climbed in the truck and drove through to the dock.

Rafael stood on the main deck, leaned on the railing, and watched the activities along the Wilmingtown riverfront until he spotted Gunner on the dock. He walked to the loading ramp and waved to him to drive up, and when Gunner reached the top of the ramp, Rafael stopped him at the doorway.

"Hey old buddy, how's the famous car thief?" Rafael joked.

"Doin' great. Where do you want me to unload this million dollar jewel?" Gunner asked.

"Take a right and go aft until you reach the bulkhead. I'll get someone to help you unload when you get there," Rafael said.

"Hey Juan, get the lift and take care of the load that just came in," Rafael shouted to his deck hand who was drinking coffee in front of the office at the opposite end of the cargo hold.

"Yes Sir, boss."

Gunner walked into the galley of the ship and grabbed a cup of coffee. In twenty minutes, the car was off loaded and the dummy crates reloaded into the truck. Then Juan parked the lift and headed to the crew's lounge for a break while Rafael caught up with Gunner in the galley and sat down with him to chat.

"All right, buddy. You're all set."

"Thanks. See ya on the next trip," Gunner said as he crawled into his truck, backed it out of the parking place in the ship's cargo hold and drove down the ramp.

Thirty minutes later, two more trucks arrived from Miami and Tampa with another load of a stolen Audi and a Lexus.

"Ah, they're beautiful, ain't they?" Rafael said to Juan as he patted the Audi on the hood.

"You bet. But sitting here with a ship full of expensive cars makes me . . . ."

"Scared?" Rafael interrupted. "You poor little kid. You really are a rookie, ain't ya? Been on board now, what is it, a whole two weeks, wow!"

"Yeah, but I'm no rookie. I know some things about ships," Juan said proudly.

"Really? Tell me all you know. I have a few seconds," Rafael dug in.

Anger suddenly overcame him and Juan jumped up and reached for Rafael's shirt collar. Rafael quickly jerked aside to avoid Juan's hand.

"You scum. No one calls me a kid!" Juan shouted.

Impatient with Juan's foolishness, Rafael kicked him in the stomach and shoved him against the bulkhead. "Look, Punk. You're a rookie on this ship, understand? I'm your boss and I'm the one in charge of the cargo, not you. And I can call you whatever I want. If you keep your head straight and your mouth shut, you just might make it to the end of this cruise. And one more thing, the Capt'n and I have been mates for years. He believes what I say. And if I say you're no good, you're no good. Got it?" Rafael threatened, backed off, and let him crumple to the deck.

Juan remained speechless and hunched over with his hands over his head. He looked up at Rafael for a moment, then stood up and headed for the crew's quarters.

The following week, Captain Franco sat in his cabin looking over the list of cars he had on board. He walked over to a calendar taped on the bulkhead and circled May 18, the date of departure for the islands. Then he reached in the cupboard and grabbed an empty cup, refilled it with stale coffee brewed eight hours earlier and picked up the ship's phone.

"Jon, could you come to my cabin, please? I want to talk to you about our departure next week."

"Aye, Capt'n. Be right up," Jon acknowledged.

In a few minutes, Jon, the ship's engineer, knocked on the Captain's door.

"Come in, Jon. Have a seat. It looks like our cargo is 'bout topped out. I believe we may have room for a couple more cars, and I expect that to happen in a few days. So, I want to depart for the Caribbean on May 18, next week. How's our fuel oil situation?"

"I have a truck coming tomorrow to top off the tanks. We are half full now, but I already anticipated we'd be leaving soon, so I already made the arrangements," Jon said.

"Excellent. How 'bout other provisions—food, supplies? Are we ready to go?" the captain asked.

"Yes, I have taken care of everything, except for the food. I wanted to wait until I got the word from you on our exact departure date to stock up. So, I'll arrange to get the food on board in a couple of days, "Jon agreed.

"Excellent, that'll be all then," the captain said.

"Uh, Sir. There is one thing I have been meanin' to ask you. What happened to Ramos?" Jon asked. "His personal belongings are still here, but he suddenly disappeared."

"Yes, he left us."

"Well, I figured that, Sir. But why? He told me he wanted to join our crew and work as a deck hand when we picked him up in Tampico, Mexico . . . and then, bang, when we returned to Wilmingtown, he vanished."

"Yep," the captain responded.

"So. Is that all there is to it? Jest 'yep'?" Jon questioned.

"Ramos promised to pay us the usual fee if we brought him to Wilmingtown and smuggled him into the country along with the other immigrants we had on board. He told us he did not have the money at the time he came on board in Tampico but would get the money from a friend when he arrived in Wilmingtown. However, a day before we reached the Cape Fear River, he decided he wanted to join us and work as a ship crewman to pay off his debt to us."

"Ah. Let me guess. He couldn't get the money. He really didn't have a friend to bail him out and there were no jobs for him to do on the ship," Jon surmised.

"You got it," the Captain said.

"But he really didn't want to work on the ship either. He just wanted to buy some time until he could escape . . . which meant a free ride to freedom."

"You got it," the Captain repeated.

"So, what finally happened to Ramos?"

"Well, one of our crew saw Ramos running down the ramp onto the dock to escape two days after we arrived in port. The crewman, whom I shall not name, yelled at him to stop. Ramos shouted back, 'I'm free, I'm free' and kept running. A shot rang out. Ramos fell on the edge of the dock and slid into the river. I ordered a search party to find him and fish him out, but we could not locate him. So, he's gone. But, as I said, the official word is that we have no info on a Ramos. We don't know anything about him. He's never been on board. Understand?"

"Certainly, Sir. You have my word on it," Jon promised. "I don't suppose you can tell me who shot him?"

"I suppose not."

"Very well, Sir. I'll get back to my duties. I'll keep you posted on the supplies."

"That'll be good."

Jon left the Captain's cabin and returned to the engineering office pleased that he no longer had to deal with Ramos.

The night before Jason, Jeff, and Lori were to depart for the Caribbean, Jason sat in the main cabin of the *Southwind* and listened to the marine forecast on the radio:

"Coastal forecast for the area from Cape Lookout south to Charleston out thirty miles, winds east at twelve knots diminishing to eight to ten knots after 7:00 tomorrow morning. Seas three to five feet decreasing to two to four feet after sunrise. Skies clear to partly cloudy. Forecast valid for the next twenty-four hours. Extended forecast for Sunday through Wednesday, winds steady at ten knots from the east swinging to the southeast on Tuesday. Seas two to four feet. Skies partly cloudy."

"Perfect," Jason mumbled. "Hey, Jeff, did you hear that?" he hollered.

"Yes I did," he replied happily. "Goin' to be a great day for our launch."

"You bet. And I have gone over everything on our checklist. Looks like we are ready. Can you think of anything we forgot?" Jason asked.

"Uh, no," he pondered. "Did you talk to one of your shop workers about picking up your mail?"

"Yes, he is going to call us on the short wave radio if there are any emergencies or if something needs to be taken care of immediately," Jason replied. "How 'bout you?"

"All set. Well, I guess we're ready then."

Jason mulled over his charts once more.

"What luck! The tide will be goin' out when we get underway tomorrow. We'll be flying down the Cape Fear River to the inlet at eight to ten knots ground speed," Jason shouted. He then looked at his watch.

"Hey, it's almost 7:00 o'clock. Our reservation at the restaurant is 7:15. Time to celebrate our adventure, our last good meal," Jason joked.

"What! What's wrong with my cooking? I'm supposed to be the galley cook," Lori squawked.

"Just checkin' to see if you were listenin'" Jason said.

"Okay, I'm ready to go eat," Lori said.

They locked up the hatch, climbed over the railing onto the dock and headed for Jason's car in the parking lot. Fifteen minutes later, they walked into the River View Restaurant.

"Hi guys. So, tomorrow's the big day, huh?" the host said as he greeted them in the lobby.

"Yep. Want to come along?" Jeff teased.

"Love to. Give me a few minutes to throw a couple of shirts in a duffel bag and I'll be ready."

"Yeah, that's all you need." Lori laughed. "Everyone's just wearing shirts, nothin' else."

"Stop that! You're crude! Don't believe her," Jeff nudged Lori in her side.

"Aw, come on. Where's your sense of humor?" Lori said.

"Follow me, folks, I have a perfect table for you three right by the window. See, I fixed up a table complete with a clean, white table cloth and a candle."

"Amazing. You have made some changes. I mean, look at this, clean tablecloths. Wow!" Lori cracked.

"Hey, be nice," Jeff interrupted and poked Lori gently with his elbow.

After they sat down and looked at the menu, Jeff looked out the window at the ship moored across the river. The pier was lighted and two cars were sitting on the dock.

"I see the *Coral Sun Ray* is still here and working.

"It's too far away. I can't tell what they are doing," Jason exclaimed.

"I can't either, really. I just saw a car drive up the ramp to go inside. Can't tell what it is. Oh well. Who cares?" Lori said and continued to look at the menu. The waiter returned to their table with pad and pencil in hand.

"Okay guys. What'll it be tonight?"

At 5:00 o'clock the following morning, Jason turned over in his bunk and looked at the clock on the bulkhead. He rose up and stared out the port into the darkness across the river. On the eastern horizon he could just see a hint of a sunrise reflected in the sky. Now fully awake he decided to get up and start preparations for their south sea adventure. Lori and Jeff were still asleep, so he decided to let them rest a little longer since he knew the first day at sea was going to be challenging for them. As soon as he rolled out of bed and quietly plopped his bare feet on the carpet, however, Jeff threw open his cabin door and shouted, "Good morning, Jason. I heard you get up."

At the same time, Lori turned over in her bed and asked, "Where're you going, Jeff?"

Jeff turned around and responded, "I thought you were sound asleep. I have had enough sleep, so I'm getting up. Jason is already up."

"Me, too. I've been awake for the last half-hour. Gettin' anxious, I guess." She shoved the covers off, hopped out of the bunk, dressed and headed for the galley to prepare breakfast.

"Good monin', Capt'n Jason. Today is the big day! I'm ready! Yahoo!" Lori cheered.

"Yeah. And I checked the weather. We're good to go."

After a quick breakfast, Jason removed the covers from the jib and mainsail, Lori secured the dinghy to the stern, and Jeff started the engine. The charts lay on the seat cushion next to the helm, the radio's frequencies set, and the items inside the cabin secured for the voyage. Finally, Jeff stood on the bow and untied the lines from the dock while Jason untied the stern lines and manned the helm.

"Okay, all lines are free," Jeff shouted back to Jason.

Jason eased the throttle forward and the *Southwind* slipped away from the dock and into the river channel . . . on a voyage never to be forgotten.

Chapter 4

Southbound

Jeff unfurled the jib and raised the mainsail while Jason hauled in the jib and main sheets on the starboard side to capture the fresh breeze from the southeast. Quickly the sails billowed out with a loud snap, and the *Southwind* lunged forward toward the inlet at Southport fifteen miles downstream.

A mile north of Southport and nearing the mouth of the river, the light breeze clocked around to the southwest. With the outgoing tide, the river current in their favor, and the wind 30 degrees off the port bow, they raced through the brackish water with white foam spraying off the bow. By noon, nothing but the open sea lay ahead of them. Jason checked the marine forecast again to confirm the sea and wind conditions for the remainder of the day and evening. Off shore, the winds were blowing from the south-southwest at ten knots, seas three feet and forecast to remain that way for the next twenty-four hours.

Steering a course of 215 degrees, Jason guided the *Southwind* along the marked channel through Frying Pan Shoals at the mouth of the river. Not far away, they could see waves breaking over the shallow, shifting sandbars on both sides with depths as little as two feet in some places. Reaching the Cape Fear sea buoy four miles off shore by 1:15 in the afternoon, Jason altered course slightly to the southwest to 220 degrees to take them fifteen miles off shore of Cape Romain. Jason engaged the autohelm while Jeff eased up on the port main and jib sheets to maximize the efficiency of the sails for the afternoon's run down the coast.

The seas were as predicted with two to three foot swells rolling in on *Southwind's* starboard bow. The period between the swell crests lengthened and gave the boat a gentle, manageable ride as they sailed further out to sea. Every thirty minutes Jason plotted their position on the chart using the GPS and distant landmarks while Lori curled up in the cockpit with a book. Knowing sleep was a precious commodity on a sailboat, Jeff took advantage of the calm seas to take a nap in the cabin before his turn at the helm began.

Later that afternoon, Jeff took over the cockpit watch duties while Jason went below and turned on the short-wave radio.

"This is the *Southwind* calling Miss Maisy, over." He waited several minutes and then repeated his call. "This is the *Southwind* calling Miss Maisy on Andros, come in please." Again, there was silence. Jason tried a third time, "Hello, Miss Maisy. This is Jason on the *Southwind*. Can you read me, over?" The airwaves continued to be quiet.

After several more minutes transpired, he heard her voice, "*Southwind, Southwind*, are you there?"

"Yes, Maisy, this is Jason, can you hear me okay, over?"

"I hear you loud and clear," she replied with a hint of cheerfulness in her voice.

In his cabin on board the *Coral Sun Ray*, Captain Franco walked away from the chart table and picked up the ship's telephone. "Now hear this. This is the Captain speaking. All hands report to my cabin immediately."

Below decks, the crew stopped their chores and hustled to the officer's quarters. Within minutes, everyone assembled around the large green table in the Captain's cabin.

"Gentleman, the day has arrived. We have met our quota of automobiles on board. I want to get underway for the islands this afternoon. Jon, are you ready?"

"Aye, Sir," the chief engineer replied.

"Good. Rafael, how 'bout the vehicles? Are they secured?"

"Yes, Sir, everything is ready to go," the cargo master said.

"And Ming, do you have the charts we need to get to the islands and Mexico?"

"Yes, Sir, we're all set."

"Excellent," Captain Franco said with a smile." He placed his pipe in his mouth and added, "Then I want everyone to make plans to head out to sea by three o'clock."

"Roger," the crew resounded in unison.

The meeting disbanded and the crew headed their separate ways to their duty stations. Jon radioed the tug operations to request assistance leaving the dock and a river pilot for guidance down the Cape Fear River. Ming hustled to the bridge, laid out the charts, and plotted the course to the islands from the mouth of the Cape Fear River. Later that day, the tugs tied onto the bow and stern and pulled the ship away from the dock and into the center of the river channel. At the same time the river pilot walked on the bridge and took command of the ship.

By seven that evening, the *Coral Sun Ray* passed the Cape Fear River sea buoy. The pilot disembarked, and the ship headed out to sea. Carlos, one of the deck hands, took over at the helm and steered the ship south along the coastline toward the islands, while Ming Chi plotted the ship's position every hour in the chartroom using radar and the GPS system.

With a brisk southwest breeze, Captain Franco stood on the port wing of the bridge, his eyes fixed on the rolling sea before him. He reached in his pocket and pulled out his pipe and a tin of tobacco. Then he filled his pipe and lighted it behind his cupped hand to shelter it from the wind. Managing to bring the tobacco to a glowing red with a few strong puffs, the warm, aromatic smoke blew aft past his face as he held the pipe in his mouth for several minutes contemplating the events to come in the islands in less than a week.

Captain Franco looked into the pilothouse and ordered, "Ming Chi, come here. I want to talk to you."

"Aye, Captain. I'll be right there, Sir." In a matter of seconds, Ming Chi stood beside the captain.

"Ming, I would like to see the course you plotted for us to Andros and your expected time of arrival, please."

"Yes, Sir. I was already working on that. I'll have the calculations done in about twenty minutes, Sir," Ming said.

"Good. If I am not here, I'll be in my cabin. Just knock on my door."

"Aye, aye, Sir."

As promised, Ming knocked on Captain Franco's cabin door twenty minutes later.

"Come in," the captain ordered.

Ming walked in with his arms loaded with charts and plopped them down on the large green table in the center of his cabin. With pencil in hand, he traced the routing for the captain. Captain Franco studied the penciled route for a few minutes and then pointed to a spot on the chart north of Andros.

"See this area along the north coast of the island. There are many uncharted coral heads here . . . nasty enough to sink us if we hit one of them. I suggest we steer a course to the Northwest Channel Light on the northern tip of Andros and then turn to 150 degrees to clear Morgan's Bluff. We must stay at least five miles off shore heading southeast once we round the northern end of Andros." Captain Franco pointed along the northeast shoreline of Andros and continued, "Paralleling the East Coast of Andros is a barrier reef over 140 miles long. There are only a few openings for us to get through. Based on my experience, we can stay out of harm's way going this route. Also, the harbor entrance at Coakley Town is surrounded by the same barrier reef as you can see on the chart. It is best if we sail through the cut at hide tide. With a full load on board, we need at least sixteen feet of good water. The channel to the dock has been dredged to eighteen feet. Have you looked at the tide tables for that area for the time we expect to arrive?"

"Not yet, Sir, but I will do that immediately." Ming Chi admitted.

"Okay, keep me posted," the captain requested.

In the engine room, Jon finished making final adjustments to the propulsion systems for the extended voyage at sea and then climbed to the main deck to get some fresh air. He leaned on the railing, took a deep breath, and watched a frigate bird soar above his head along the port rail. Shortly thereafter Juan emerged from the crew's quarters and joined Jon on deck.

"Good evenin', Sir," Juan said cheerfully.

"Hey," Jon snorted.

"Looks like smooth sailin' out there, doesn't it?" Juan said.

"Depends. May be a lull before a storm," Jon said. "The sea's always changin'. If it's calm now, just wait."

"Well, I meant it looks good now," Juan backpedaled.

"You ain't been at sea long, have you? First cruise, huh?" Jon asked.

"Yes sir," Juan admitted.

"So, we hafta to deal with a rookie on board! Ain't that a crock of bull!" Jon complained.

"I'm a quick learner. Say, I been wantin' to ask you somethin'. Where're we goin'? I heard the Capt'n tell everyone that we're heading for the islands, but what islands? No one talks to me. Seems to be a big secret or something.' Doesn't make sense. I'm one of the crew, I should know what's goin' on," Juan pleaded.

"No one talks, eh? Maybe they don't like no rookies. Ever think of that?"

Juan rolled up his fist and leaned toward Jon in a threat of anger.

Reacting quickly to his intimidation, Jon grabbed Juan's collar, "Don't even think of bustin' me, shrimp. You'll be at the bottom of the sea in no time. Git my drift?"

"Yes, Sir. But, I ain't no dummy. I know we have a cargo full of expensive cars. I figured we were transportin' them to Latin America for customers who moved there on business or somethin'. Isn't that right?"

"Keep thinkin' that," Jon replied.

"You don't know either!" Juan sneered.

Jon grabbed Juan by the collar again and whispered in his ear, "Look, punk, nobody questions me about what I knows or don't knows. Understand, bonehead? I've been engineer for this old steamer for fifteen years. I knows everything about what we are doin'. You're a deck hand. You don't need to know what we're doing. Just do your job cleaning the decks."

"I don't clean decks!" Juan muttered. "I help wherever I am needed."

"Like I said, go clean the decks."

Juan's face grew a bright red with rage. He stared into Jon's eyes and clinched his fist again ready to swing but thought differently when Jon turned his back on him. Jon quietly left the rail and headed aft toward the crew's quarters while Juan stood silently looking out to sea until his temper melted into loneliness, then into despair.

There was a knock on the captain's door. "Yes?" the Captain replied.

"It's Ming Chi."

"Come in."

Ming laid down a handful of charts on the table and pointed to the area just north of Andros. "I plotted a new course around Andros to the east side, clear of the reefs. And I checked on the tides. We may have to wait three or four hours off shore for high tide. It depends on when we arrive."

"Of course. We'll have to go slowly through those coral mine fields anyway and keep a sharp lookout for color changes in the water when we approach the channel."

"Roger on that, Sir."

"That'll be all. Thank you, Ming," the Captain said.

Close to midnight, Rafael rolled over in his bunk and looked at the clock on the bulkhead. He had fifteen minutes to relieve Carlos on the helm to begin his watch. Quickly throwing on a shirt, pants, and shoes, he splashed cold water on his face and headed topside toward the bridge. As he climbed the ladders to the upper levels, he met Juan heading in the same direction.

"Well, surprise to see you roaming the streets late at night," Rafael remarked.

"Good evening, Sir. I was on my way to the bridge. I am supposed to observe and learn how to steer the ship as an apprentice."

"I see. Well, you're in luck. You'll have the best trainer on board—me. I'm the one in charge of the bridge for the midnight to four watch."

When they arrived in the pilothouse, Rafael relieved Carlos from the helm and sent him off to the crew's quarters to get some sleep.

"Okay, Juan, come take the helm." Juan grabbed the wheel and held tightly. "Now, maintain our present course of 230 degrees using the compass in front of you," Rafael ordered.

Juan glued his eyes on the compass needle. He watched the course heading begin to drift slowly to the right. When the compass indicated 235 degrees, Juan abruptly spun the wheel several full turns to the left to get back on course. The bow began swinging quickly to the left rapidly passing 230 degrees, then 220 degrees. At that point, Juan quickly spun the wheel four turns to the right. Again, the ship responded and swung to the right, passing 230 degrees in the other direction, continuing on to 245 degrees, and then 260 degrees before Juan could reverse the turn.

In the crew's quarters, Jon tossed restlessly in his bunk and decided he could not sleep. He left the crew's quarters and strolled across the deck toward the stern to catch some fresh air. When he arrived, he noticed the ship making a snake wake in the moonlight behind the stern. Puzzled, he hustled forward across the main deck and climbed the ladders to the bridge. "What the hell are you doing? Are you drunk?" Jon shouted to Juan.

"Hey, don't scream at him. He's jest learnin'," Rafael shouted as he threw up his arm to prevent Jon from grabbing Juan.

"Well that explains it. It's the idiot at the wheel," Jon snarled. "I thought I told you to stick to cleaning decks."

Juan's head became so inflamed that it was all he could do to hold onto the helm and not retaliate. To keep the peace, Rafael motioned to Jon to step out on the port bridge for a talk in private.

"Listen, I know Juan is a rookie. And this won't be the first time he screws up. But I think the best way to teach him the ropes on this ship is to let him get so fouled up he'll never forget it. We're at sea, so if he drives like a drunken sailor briefly, so be it. Let him wallow in his own blunders. He'll get it eventually, the hard way. Trust me. He's sweatin' like a hog in August right now. I'll rescue him in a minute."

Jon laughed and punched gently Rafael's shoulder "Okay, I trust you, man,"

"I thought you'd get a kick out of this. So, I'll get us back on course as soon as you leave," Rafael promised.

"Goodnight, my friend." Jon left the bridge and retired to the crew's quarters. Then Rafael approached Juan.

"Havin' fun, my boy?" Rafael taunted him.

"What's wrong with this steering? The ship won't stay on course. I'm trying to steer 230 degrees, but this crappy ship won't do what I am telling it to do," Juan said in frustration.

"You think it's the ship's fault, eh?"

"I don't know what to think. All right, so it's my fault. What am I doin' wrong?" Juan conceded.

"You're over-reacting. You hafta make small corrections. Turn the wheel a quarter turn and wait for the ship to react. If that's not enough, turn a quarter turn further and wait for a response. Give the rudder and ship time to react. Remember, this is a 200-foot hunk of metal. It's a monster. You can't expect it to jerk around like a hot rod on a racetrack. Just cool it. Ease onto the course. I'll tell you what, I'll get us back on course, and then you can try it again," Rafael explained.

"You're the only shipmate on board who has been willing to teach me something. Thanks," Juan said.

"It's simple. You hafta prove yourself. You see, they hate rookies. I mean they *really* hate rookies. You're a target for their jokes. Learn quickly and soon they'll be nice to you. But each time you fall down, they will laugh in your face. And don't pick a fight with anyone. Guarantee you'll lose, and they will not rescue you. This is no place for punks. It's up to you to prove you can handle the job. That's my advice. But don't expect me to bail you out. I have my own reputation to keep."

"I got it" Juan said. "By the way, can you tell me what we are doin' with these cars and where we are goin'?" Juan asked.

"Sorry, I can't. Just keep your eyes and ears open. You'll figure it out in due time. That's all I can say," Rafael exclaimed.

Shortly after two in the morning, the *Coral Sun Ray* overtook the *Southwind* a quarter of a mile apart, both heading south, both unaware of the other vessel.

In the small harbor of Coakley Town, the coconut palms swayed freely in the tropical trade winds blowing from the southeast and a light chop lapped rhythmically against the empty bulkhead at Ringo Industries. Walking along the wharf, Sanchez turned toward the office half a block away, leaped up the five steps to the front door and rushed inside.

"Ah, Sanchez, you are here. When is the *Ray* due in from Wilmingtown?" Jack Ringo asked.

"Thursday. In four days,"

"Good, we need more work. How many cars do we have left to convert?"

"Three, Sir. But they should be finished in a couple of days and ready to ship to Mexico on time," Sanchez assured him.

"Make sure they are."

"Yes, Sir," Sanchez acknowledged nervously knowing that this was going to be a difficult challenge.

"Oh, by the way, I was told today that there is a hole in the chain-link fence in the back of our property. Get it fixed now. If I see a stranger snooping around our operations, I might be tempted to blow his head off," Jack warned. "Understand?"

Sanchez nodded, then left Jack's office and walked into the warehouse where the auto shop operations were underway. Steady noises of hammering, grinding, and drilling permeated the dimly lighted work area, and along the back wall in a paint booth, a one- year old Lexus was being repainted a metallic blue. Sanchez chased down the foreman and reminded him that all three unfinished cars must be completed by Friday morning for shipment.

"But, Sir, that's impossible. There're not enough hours in the day to do this," the foreman complained.

"Get it done or you'll be walking the beach wondering what hit you," Sanchez snarled.

"Hey, don't you threaten me," the foreman shouted and raised his fist in Sanchez's face.

Sanchez ignored the foreman's warning.

"Just get out of here," the foreman whispered under his breath as he turned away from Sanchez.

Sanchez slammed the office door and headed to the center of the small village of Coakley Town a block away. He walked into Mango's, his favorite bar, sat down at a cozy, rustic wooden table and ordered a rum punch, his favorite soothing tropical drink. With the frosty drink in his hand, he casually observed an attractive, young blond sitting alone at a table near the back wall. She was staring out the open window. He watched her for a while, got up, and ambled over to her table.

"Mind if I sit down and join you, Ma'am?" as he pulled a chair out

from the table and plopped himself down without waiting for a response.

"Looks like you just did. Do I really have a choice?" she challenged.

"Yes, I could leave," Sanchez offered.

"But you obviously intended to invade my space. So, now that you are here, who are you?"

"Sanchez."

"All right. What do you want . . . besides me?" she asked.

"Oh, I just want to be friendly. You look lonely. Haven't seen you before. Your name is?" Sanchez asked.

"Is that important?"

"Well, I was hoping you were a nice, pleasant girl to match that pretty face of yours, but I guess I was mistaken."

"You got that wrong. I am nice. Name is Francesca," she finally confessed and extended her hand toward him.

Sanchez shook her hand and continued the conversation. "What brings you here to Coakley?"

"I'm looking for Capt'n Franco," she said. "You know Capt'n Franco?"

"Yes, but he's not here. Won't be here for a few days yet."

"I figured that much. The dock's empty. But I know he'll be here soon. I hafta to see him as soon as he arrives."

"Why is he so important?" Sanchez asked.

"It's a private matter. What's your job here?"

"Uh, it's a private matter," Sanchez responded with a wry smile.

"Touché," she said. "So I guess we've made full circle in our conversation." She immediately stood up and looked at Sanchez. "Maybe I'll see you again sometime." She held out her hand again to say goodbye. They shook, and then Francesca turned her back and walked out the door.

Sanchez finished his rum drink alone and then left Mango's two sheets to the wind. He walked along the pier, paused, and looked out the entrance channel toward the sea as if he expected the *Coral Sun Ray* to appear suddenly over the horizon. The sun began to set behind him and the streets of Coakley Town became deathly quiet.

Chapter 5

Bimini Challenge

When the sun rose above the watery horizon the following morning, Lori was already in the galley making pancakes and hot coffee for breakfast. She was an accomplished cook and was delighted to take over those chores on board the *Southwind*. Jeff manned the helm keeping an eye on the three-foot seas, the wind, the sails, and the occasional ship traffic running north and south to break the monotony. Jason made a note of the latitude/longitude coordinates from the GPS receiver and announced that they were fifteen miles off shore from Hilton Head Island.

Suddenly Jeff noticed that the depth sounder was reading zero, and he called Jason to the cockpit to check it out. Jason switched the instrument to the knot log mode and it still read zero. He checked the wiring behind the instrument and traced the connections to the sensor unit above the keel, but the electrical connections seemed intact. He pounded on the readout unit with his fist but to no avail.

"Well, mates, we have a problem. I can't fix the sounder, and it is critical for navigation when we reach the islands. We have to find a place to get it fixed right away before we reach the Bahamas. For one thing, there's an enormous import tax on imported boat parts if we fix it there. But the real problem is the treacherous barrier reefs surrounding the islands that could ruin our day without information from the depth sounder. Let's look at the chart to see the closest town, inlet, and marina from our current position."

Lori brought the chart to Jason and the three looked it over.

"We're just off shore from Port Royal Sound. There is a good marina in Beaufort, South Carolina on the Beaufort River just up the sound about five miles. I vote we divert to Beaufort." Lori and Jeff agreed. "Okay, Jeff, turn right to a course of 340 degrees. That should take us into the sound." Jeff turned the rudder while Jason adjusted the jib and mainsail sheets. The wind and rolling sea were now behind them off the port quarter and that caused the *Southwind* to swing back and forth thirty degrees. With each oscillation, Jeff attempted to correct the heading but discovered he only made the situation worse.

"Just hold the helm steady, don't fight it," Jason advised Jeff. "Let the bow swing back and forth by itself. It should average out to the same course we want, 340 degrees. Watch how far it swings to each side and make sure the average is still the course we want. This is a test to see how good a seaman you are," Jason laughed.

Three hours later the *Southwind* entered Port Royal Sound and the swells diminished. Shortly thereafter Jason spotted the entrance to the Beaufort River, and he steered the *Southwind* upstream to the town. To take advantage of a following wind, Jason slacked the mainsail sheet and moved the jib to the opposite side for a wing on wing effect. The speed increased half a knot but they still fought an opposing current in the river.

Around noon, they arrived at the marina, and Jeff secured the sails while Lori hopped over the railing onto the dock and secured the bow and stern lines.

"Jeff, we might as well top off the fuel tank while we are here. I know it won't need more than a gallon or so, but let's take advantage of being in port. Lori, you can check on our ice supply while I find a mechanic to fix the sounder" and with that they departed in different directions to do their assigned tasks.

During her search for ice, however, Lori became keenly interested in people boarding a horse drawn carriage under the shade of a live oak tree next to the marina. Fascinated over the thought of a carriage ride, she ran back to the boat to tell Jeff about it. At the same time, Jason returned to the boat with a mechanic.

"How long do you think it will take to get that thing fixed?" Lori asked Jason.

Before Jason could respond the mechanic said, "Oh, I think I can have this done in hour or so."

"Good. Then we're in for a special treat," Lori said leaping for joy. "We're going on a carriage ride. Jason, you can come, too, unless you have to stay here with the mechanic."

"No, I don't need any help. Go ahead and enjoy the ride," the mechanic intervened.

Lori ran ahead and asked the carriage driver to hold up for three more riders. Cathy held the reins patiently as they clambered into the carriage and then she introduced them to Molly. Molly was a high-spirited, excitable horse that failed to cope with the hectic traffic congestion, noise and crowds in the historic district of Charleston several months ago. Fired from her job, Molly was transported to Beaufort and now seemed more relaxed, standing under the live oak trees in the quiet waterfront park. Cathy assured them that this was not going to be a hold-onto-your-hat wild adventure.

"Giddy up," she said calmly and Molly casually trotted down the street toward the center of town. In a dreamy state of mind, Lori, Jeff, and Jason thought of the early days when life was perhaps simple and peaceful in this charming coastal town. Leaving the serenity of the park, Molly turned onto Bay Street and clip-clopped her way to the downtown historic district a few blocks away while passing 19th century homes on both sides of the street.

"Folks, as early as 1520 the Spanish visited the area, and in 1527 the Spanish attempted to establish a colony here but failed. Then the French tried their hand at a settlement in 1562, but it also did not survive. It was not until the early 1700s before Beaufort became a stable town," Cathy rattled on with her canned speech.

Suddenly, Molly stopped in her tracks. They had reached the heart of the downtown area just behind a parked tractor-trailer truck with its diesel engine roaring and black smoke belching from a stack above the cab. Despite Cathy's coaching and whispering sweet nothings in Molly's ear, Molly stood firm. With her ears back and occasionally twitching from side to side, Molly refused to move another foot forward.

"Is this the end of the tour?" Lori asked Cathy.

"No! Just sit tight. I'll get Molly going here in a moment," Cathy said frustratingly.

"Maybe Molly is afraid of big trucks," Lori suggested. But Cathy ignored her remark.

"Come on Molly, let's go," Cathy urged as she snapped the whip against her tail.

Trying to decide which would be worse, an attack from the truck or punishment from Cathy, Molly suddenly bolted forward and galloped past the vehicle. Lori, Jason, and Jeff held tightly to the railing as Molly picked up her pace and raced out of control toward a red light at a busy intersection. When they reached the intersection crosswalk, Molly stopped with a jarring jolt that sent Lori and Jeff lunging forward off the seat and almost over the rear of the horse before Jason grabbed them and pulled back. Cathy was not amused.

"I'm so sorry, folks. Is everyone okay?" she asked as she looked around.

No one complained. "I'll have to admit that on a tour earlier today, Molly covered the tour in half the time that it normally takes."

"I believe it," Jason said wiping his forehead with his handkerchief.

The light turned green and Molly calmly proceeded across the intersection to the next block. Then Molly stopped again. Just ahead, a construction worker was breaking up concrete on a sidewalk with a jackhammer. When he recognized the frightened look on Molly's face, he gently put the hammer down and walked away out of sight. After a little coaxing from Cathy, Molly continued with the tour. Once Molly left the congestion of downtown and reached the quiet historic neighborhoods, she settled down and became an honorable and respectable tour horse that she was supposed to be. Thankful that a real disaster had been averted, they returned to the waterfront park and disembarked. Lori felt sorry for Molly and she walked around the carriage, stood in front of her and gave her a gentle pet on the nose.

"Good job, Molly. You're gonna make it, kid. Just hang in there," she said with a smile and a bit of optimism. Molly perked her ears ups and looked at Lori in her eyes. "You know what? I think you understand," she said to Molly.

At the marina, the mechanic finished the repair job and all climbed aboard and made ready to set sail. By late afternoon, they sailed out of Port Royal Sound into the open sea and headed south toward Andros Island. Jason set the sails and course to take advantage of the favorable conditions as the crew settled back to their routine chores. We should arrive at the north end of Andros in about four and a half days at our current pace," Jason informed the crew over the dinner table. "But first we are going to make a brief stop in Bimini to clear customs and immigrations."

"Sounds great. I'm glad the sea is calm. You seem confident this wonderful weather is going to continue all the way to Andros," Lori said pleased with their progress.

"Well, we've been lucky so far. But it's possible we could run into a few days of rough weather before we arrive," Jason explained.

"Aha, there's a hint of doubt in your voice," Lori said as she suddenly showed a look of concern.

"Don't worry; this boat can handle a lot of rough weather. At least we will not have to deal with a hurricane," Jason said.

"How about checking the weather forecast again," Lori insisted now worried.

Jason agreed and went below to listen to the radio. A few minutes later, he returned to the cockpit. "The weather looks okay for the next several days. But I'll keep checking to pick up any changes," Jeff assured his crew.

"I'm not afraid of bumpy weather. Let it come. I think it would be a thrill ride, just like the ride with Molly," Jeff said.

"Will you shut up! Don't wish disaster on us," Lori begged.

Jason checked their position on the GPS and marked it on the chart. They were now fifteen miles off the northern coast of Florida and had made excellent progress. But by 8:00 in the evening, the wind diminished and *Southwind* slowed to 3.5 knots. For the rest of the evening, the wind and sea conditions remained calm causing the boat to slow down even further to an unimpressive 2 knots.

In the wee hours of the next morning, Jeff was at the helm and had to make minor course adjustments on the autohelm to counter the effect of a current set toward land. By 5:00 o'clock, he could see the glow of the sun on the eastern horizon. An hour later, it was time for Lori to take over the watch, but Jeff was not tired and offered to extend his watch so that Lori could fix another super breakfast.

"Good morning, Capt'n," Jeff greeted Jason as he crawled out of bed.

"Morning'. How was the night watch?" Jason asked.

"Fine. Well, almost fine. The mast running light quit sometime during the night, but I thought it could wait until morning to be fixed, so I didn't wake you up."

"You should have gotten me up right away. It is critical for night navigation. I'll go check it out now," Jason said, a little annoyed.

Jason traced the electrical circuits behind the switch panel and found the cause of the failure was a broken wire that had fallen across the terminals of the mast light switch. Jason reconnected the wire to its proper terminal and then turned to Jeff and said with a snicker, "You're lucky I didn't send you to the top of the mast to change the light bulb. That's the job for the rookie crew you know." Jeff ignored Jason's sarcasm, turned his head, and looked out to sea.

At mid-morning, Lori spotted ten dolphins five hundred feet ahead, and soon they swam alongside the *Southwind's* bow for ten minutes before disappearing off the stern. By noon, the wind clocked around to 160 degrees and increased to fifteen knots straight down the bow forcing them to turn to a heading of 130 to recapture the wind in the sails on the starboard tack. Jason realized now that they would have to tack down the coast of Florida. Later the wind freshened to twenty knots from the south with seas building to six feet. With the *Southwind's* speed pushing greater than five knots and a constant salt spray coming across the bow, the main deck and into the cockpit, Jeff was forced to put on foul weather gear while Lori and Jason battened down the hatches and reefed the mainsail to stabilize the ride.

By early evening, they were twenty miles off Cape Canaveral, but the brisk winds continued to blow out of the south-southeast at twenty knots whipping up seas to 6 to 7 feet. Jason decided to lower the jib and put up the storm jib with the help of Jeff at the helm and Lori working the halyards and sheets. Then he reefed the main down two feet to make the ride tolerable. With sail adjustments completed, Jason remained at the helm while Lori and Jeff attempted to get some sleep.

Morning arrived with wind and seas showing signs of abating and ship traffic north and south becoming more numerous as they approached the coastline of Palm Beach, Florida. At Jason's request, Jeff turned the helm to the left to steer straight for the west coast of Bimini. When they reached the Gulf Stream, the wind settled to a steady eleven knots from the southeast.

"Wow, look how clear the water is . . . just all of a sudden," Lori remarked.

"Yep, that's the beginning of the Gulf Stream. It's like someone painted a line in the ocean. Now that means we have a northerly current to contend with. So we'll have to steer a course of 170 instead of our intended course of 155 to counter the current. The width of the Gulf Stream at this point is about twenty-five miles. We should be clear of the stream in five or six hours," Jason said.

"You're so smart!" Lori retorted.

"Experience. That's what it is. I've been doing this for awhile," he assured her.

Jason was at peace with his surroundings as he watched a few puffy pink clouds float overhead just as the sun sank below the horizon over Florida. The Florida coastline was now a memory. They were alone in sea of vast emptiness . . . three sailors trusting that the *Southwind* would safely carry them to their destination, three sailors dreaming of what might lay ahead, three sailors anticipating meeting Maisy for the first time.

Jeff learned some navigational skills and continually plotted the boat's position on the charts using the GPS. Suddenly the depth alarm sounded. Jeff stared at the gage and saw it rapidly change from infinity to 50 feet . . . 34 feet . . . 27 feet . . . 14 feet . . . 6 feet. Then the alarm began a double beep signaling danger of grounding. Jason crawled out of the cabin into the cockpit and looked at the gage. Instantly he recognized what was happening and retreated into the cabin unconcerned. However, Jeff and Lori were concerned.

"Jason! How can you walk away from this problem? What is happening? We are going to run aground!" Jeff shouted.

In fear of sinking, Lori rushed into the cockpit, grabbed her life jacket, and then looked at the depth sounder again. It was screaming and hovering at 5.0 feet. The draft of the *Southwind* was 4.5 feet "Oh my God! We are going to crash into a reef or something!" she screamed.

"No we're not," Jason said boldly. "Look at where we are on the chart. The water depth is more than 500 feet. There are no reefs here."

"Then why is the depth sounder proving you wrong," Lori insisted.

"The depth sounder is sending a sonar-like pulse out from our keel and it is bouncing off the thermal layers in the Gulf Stream as if the layers were solid objects," Jason began. "The water is warmer in the Gulf Stream than elsewhere. Ten minutes later the depth sounder stopped beeping and the gage read infinity again. Jason turned to Lori, nodded, and tipped his hat to her.

"Smarty!" Lori said in response.

Jason looked at his watch. It was time to call Maisy on the radio, and he sat at the chart table and tuned to the short wave frequency. "Calling Miss Maisy, calling Miss Maisy. This is the *Southwind*, over."

"Hi, Jason," Maisy responded almost immediately.

By 8:00 o'clock that evening, Jeff estimated their position to be mid-point in the Gulf Stream. The northerly set had reached its maximum velocity and Jeff eased up on the correction course to the right to compensate for the decreasing northerly drift.

The overnight sail across to the Bahamas went well, and at 5:30 the next morning, Jason caught sight of the lights of North Bimini six miles ahead on the horizon. "There is something about the first sight of land after a long night at sea that calms the soul," Jason remarked. Half-hour later they approached a radio tower on a bearing of 085 degrees and continued their way toward the island. Jeff spotted the shallow sandbars that mark the entrance to the Bimini Harbor as he stood on the bow to look out for reefs and sand. Soon *Southwind* made its way into the harbor and turned north to the anchorage next to the Customs

House.

"According to my Bahamian guide, the customs office does not open until 8:30, so we'll have to anchor in the harbor until then," Jason advised.

They cruised into the anchorage area and Jeff raised the yellow quarantine flag to the base of the spreader. Jeff freed up the anchor on the bowsprit after Lori lowered and stowed the sails. With the engine running, Jason eased the *Southwind* over a sandy spot in the harbor and shouted to Jeff, "Okay, lower the anchor."

With a heave Jeff threw the anchor ahead of the bow, while Jason backed the boat down to allow the boat to pull on the anchor rode and dig into the bottom. In a few seconds, the boat came to a stop.

"Welcome to the Bahamas," Jason hollered and raised his arm in delight. "Bimini used to be a hiding place for pirates, wrecking gangs, blockade runners, rum-runners, and drug smugglers and in modern times, people running from the US law. Now much of the place lies in ruins." Jason looked at his watch. "We still have an hour to go before Customs opens up. Then we'll weigh anchor and tie up at the dock next to the Customs building. Meanwhile, I'm going to study the charts to Coakley Town."

Soon, Jason pulled up the anchor and motored over to the Customs dock. In a matter of minutes, they secured the *Southwind* to the dock and remained onboard until the office opened. But it was not until 8:45 when the inspector arrived in his beat-up, rusty Jeep. Finally, the inspector motioned from his office door for them to come ashore. Jason presented him with their documents, declarations, itinerary, and passports.

"What was your last port of departure?"

"Beaufort, South Carolina," Jason said.

"What is your destination?"

"Coakley Town, Andros," Jason replied.

"Are you carrying any drugs, weapons, alcohol, spare boat parts, or food?"

"No."

The inspector stamped the paperwork and then announced, "That will be fifty-six dollars for overtime charges."

"What! No way!" Jason said.

"You arrived here before 8:30 am. I saw you come in. Anyone arriving before we open for clearance is charged overtime fees."

"Wait a minute," Jason said angrily. "We did NOT get off the boat except to tie the lines until you signaled for us to come ashore at 8:50. We were flying the quarantine flag as required so there was no attempt to hide the status of our arrival. Finally, you were *not* here until after 8:30. You were late, Sir!" Jason argued visibly upset.

"That will be fifty-six dollars for overtime fee," he calmly repeated.

The Customs official refused to look at Jason. Their options were limited since he was withholding the one document that was essential for them to continue their journey in Bahamian waters—the Cruise Permit. The inspector sat patiently waiting for the cash to come across the table. Realizing that the situation had reached an impasse, Jason said, "I'll have to give you a check. I do not have the cash to spare."

"No, I need cash."

Jason stood his ground and repeated that it was a check or nothing. The official finally agreed and Jason gave him a check made out to the Bahamian Customs. He handed Jason the cruise permit and Jason returned to the *Southwind*. "Okay guys, we got it. Let's get out of here quickly before they decide to hit us up for more fees." Jason started the engine, Lori untied the lines from the dock, and they headed for the open sea again. In a matter of minutes, they cleared the barrier reefs and sandbars and turned south for Andros.

Chapter 6

Rough Seas

Officer Black rushed into the Captain's office. "Sir, I have been batting my head against the wall for the past week trying to figure out this case about the body we found in the river. We keep running into dead ends. Officer Paulo and I were talkin' about it this morning. Something bothers us. While we were aboard the *Coral Sun Ray*, I tripped over a trash bag in a passageway. I started to clean up the mess when I noticed a couple of interesting items - an official document with the name 'Ramos Hernandez' on it and a picture of a pretty Spanish girl. Just at that moment the crewman who was with us grabbed them from my hand and abruptly pushed me away from the bag. He insisted that we move on. He said it was just trash, but we noticed it was full of personal items. I wonder. . . ."

"You wonder if it had something to do with the body we found in the river?" the Captain interrupted.

"Well, maybe or maybe not. It's a real long shot, isn't it? It's just that he suddenly acted . . . well nervous, like he was hiding something. He was very determined to keep us from seeing what was in the trash bag."

"I think you need stronger evidence than that, Jerry. It sounds like that was simply coincidence, but keep on the lookout for anything suspicious," The Captain urged.

"Yes Sir." Jerry acknowledged. He left the Captain's office and headed straight down the hall to see Paulo.

"Hey, old buddy," Jerry hollered as he slapped Paulo on the shoulder. "I spoke to the Captain just now. He thinks our theory about the trash bag is full of holes. 'Probably a coincidence' he said."

"Are you surprised or disappointed?" Paulo asked.

"You know the answer to that. Okay, maybe he's right. Maybe that trash bag isn't goin' to move us ahead on this case. Have you come up with anyone reporting a missing person, yet?"

"Yeah, one, but it doesn't match the description of the body."

"Man, I hate failing. We're supposed to come with the answers, and all we are doing is drawing blanks," Jerry said.

"And stumbling over trash bags," Paulo laughed.

"All right, it's not funny," Jerry snapped.

"Listen, it's only been a week. Sometimes these cases take a real long time . . . perhaps a year. How long have you been on the force?" Paulo asked.

"A month. Okay, so I'm still learning. I just hate failing."

"Roger on that," Paulo acknowledged.

Jerry left Paulo's office and walked slowly down the hall feeling helpless. He looked at the clock on the wall. "Still an hour to go before my watch ends," he thought. Then he suddenly broke out into big smile and rushed over to the dispatcher's office.

"Listen, I have to check on a lead. I'm going over to the Yarrow shipyard. You can call me on the radio if you need me." He hustled out the door and hopped into his cruiser, and fifteen minutes later pulled off the highway onto the dirt road that led to the Yarrow Shipping gate and guardhouse.

"Crap! What luck, the ship is gone!" he mumbled to himself and banged his hand on the steering wheel. But he continued on to the guardhouse and stopped. Jago slowly got out of his chair, walked down the porch steps and ambled over to the cruiser.

"Now what do you want?" Jago asked.

"I came to talk to the ship's Captain again. I have a few more questions," Officer Black said.

"You're blind, aren't ya? Do ya see a ship out there? Now tell me occifer, where do ya see a ship? Are ya havin' hallucinations?"

"You're a real smart aleck. I didn't know the ship was not here until I drove in the driveway. When is the ship coming back?

"Who knows? Maybe never," Jago said with a wide smile. "So obviously, you are wastin' your time and mine. I suggest you just turn that little bumper car right around and hightail it outta here."

"Wow, what a stinkin' attitude! You have to be hiddin' somethin'."

"Hey, occifer, I was doin' fine until you showed up. I told ya I can't help you. The Captain ain't here . . . period. I know nothin' more. Now git." Jago turned his back, walked onto the porch, entered his office, and slammed the door shut.

Jerry gritted his teeth together, slammed down on the gas pedal, and tore down the dirt road toward the highway leaving a thick dust cloud behind. When he stopped at the highway, the dust caught up with him and smothered his cruiser. Coughing and cursing, he rapidly rolled up his windows but not until the dust settled on the inside of his police cruiser. When the air cleared, he noticed a large trash bin nearby. Out of sight of the guardhouse, he drove his car next to the bin, got out and began sifting through the trash. He pulled a large plastic bag from the bin that contained clothing and personal effects. Suspecting that this was the bag he had tripped over in the ship's passageway, he dumped the contents on the ground and began examining the items carefully. He searched through the pockets of the clothing and found notes about meeting the *Coral Sun Ray* in Tampico for transportation to Wilmingtown and a note about difficulties in paying the smuggling fee to the ship's Captain. Then he found what he was looking for – the document that identified the person as Ramos Hernandez as well as his picture. Jerry stared wide-eyed at the picture and quickly shoved the clothing and papers in his cruiser, cleaned up the trash on the ground, and sped off to the police station with a silly grin on his face.

The following morning Officer Black hurried into the police Captain's office with a handful of papers and a bag of old clothes. "Good morning, Captain. I've got some hot stuff here . . . it's about the *Coral Sun Ray* and the missing person we found floating in the marina."

"Yeah? Let me see," the Captain said with renewed interest.

Jerry handed the collection of papers and bag to him. "I found these in the trash bin at the Yarrow Shipping operations where the *Coral Sun Ray* was docked. The papers and picture were stuffed in the pockets of some old clothes I found in the trash bag. It's the same clothes and picture I saw in bag I tripped over in the passageway aboard the *Coral Sun Ray*. With the picture and name, this identifies the body we found in the river and it links him with the ship. Furthermore, this implies that the ship may be involved in smuggling immigrants to Wilmingtown from the port of Tampico, Mexico," Officer Black said with confidence.

"This may offer some clues about the body in the river, but it doesn't offer evidence of an immigrant smuggling operation going on here," the Captain said. "Keep on the case. We need something more concrete to link the ship with immigrants."

"But Captain, this is solid evidence. Ramos was an illegal immigrant?" Jerry insisted.

"Really? Show me evidence of that and your claim that the ship is bringing in others?" the Captain questioned.

"Okay, Sir. You win. I'll try to get more evidence." Jerry conceded.

Jerry left the Captain's office discouraged and headed to Officer Paulo's office. He sat down and told his friend what had happened and what he found in the trash bin yesterday afternoon at Yarrow Shipping.

"Paulo, old buddy, the Captain was pleased I found information on Ramos, but he doesn't buy my accusation that the *Coral Sun Ray* is involved with the importation of illegal immigrants," Jerry said.

"Well, he's probably right. Why don't you get a search warrant and really dig into their operations if you think there is something funny going on there?" Paulo suggested.

"Oh man, that would mean I'd have to deal with that idiot at the guardhouse again. What the heck, it's important. I'll get to it right away," Jerry said with renewed enthusiasm.

Later that afternoon, Jerry got the search warrant and requested his pal, Officer Paulo, to accompany him back to the Yarrow shipyard.

"Well, Paulo, here we go again. Are you ready to deal with our nice, polite friend again?" Jerry asked sarcastically.

"He ain't no friend of mine. In fact, you may have to put handcuffs on me to keep me from smacking him in the face," Paulo laughed.

"I know what you mean. Well, here we are. It'll be interesting to see how much garbage he throws at us with this warrant in our hands," Jerry said as they pulled onto the dirt road leading to the guardhouse.

Jerry parked the cruiser in front of the gate adjacent to the shack, and they walked onto the porch. There was no activity at the pier and no one seemed to be in the guardhouse. While Jerry knocked on the door, Paulo peeked through the window and saw the guard lying motionless in a stuffed chair. Jerry knocked harder and Paulo hollered through the window. The guard stirred and opened his eyes. Startled, he jumped up and came to the door but did not open it or unlock it.

"I thought I told you guys to beat it. You are not welcome here. Now scram!" Jago yelled.

Jerry plastered the search warrant against the door window in front of Jago's face. "See this. Now open up immediately, old buddy," Jerry ordered.

"Forget it. There's nothin' here. Now scram," Jago responded.

"If you don't unlock this door, we'll have to break it down. We're here on official business," Jerry insisted again.

Jago stood in front of the door in silence for a moment. Then he reached for the doorknob and unlocked the door. Jerry and Paulo rushed in and handed Jago the search warrant.

"What are you looking for?" Jago asked.

"We want to look through the files and records of the *Coral Sun Ray*. Just relax, we won't be long," Jerry said. "Has this ship been to Tampico, Mexico?"

"Couldn't tell you. I don't run the ship," Jago said.

"Of course you don't, but you do work here. You do know where the ship goes, unless you are stupid. Are you stupid?" Paulo grilled him.

"They don't tell me nothin'," Jago said.

Meanwhile, Paulo continued to search the files when he suddenly found the document he was looking for. The ship had been in Tampico and while there picked up twelve immigrants and smuggled them into Wilmingtown. Paulo kept silent about his discovery but took pictures of the document with his camera and made some notes where he found the evidence in the files. "Okay, Jerry, I guess we can leave now."

"What were you takin' pictures of?" Jago asked nervously.

"Oh, just some paperwork. We'll get back to you if it's important," Paulo insisted.

The officers left the guardhouse, drove slowly down the dirt road to the highway, and headed straight for the police station. "I think we struck gold, Paulo. I suspected the *Coral Sun Ray* was importing illegal immigrants into the U.S. all along, and now I have proof."

"Yeah, I know. I had a hunch they were up to something. I'm very suspicious of Jago, too. He knows more than he's telling us," Paulo said.

"Obviously he knows something about those cars we saw on board, too. They were expensive wheels," Jerry said.

"So? People ship cars all over...even to Mexico. There's probably a dealer in Mexico that sells those luxury cars in that country. Nothin' wrong with that."

"Nope . . . unless they were stolen," Jerry speculated.

Three miles ahead of the *Coral Sun Ray,* the Northwest Channel Light was visible above the horizon just north of Andros Island. Captain Franco stood on the port side of the bridge looking ahead through his binoculars. A stiff easterly breeze blew the smoke from his pipe into his nose and eyes, forcing him to turn his head away from the wind, remove the pipe from his mouth and stuff it into his pocket.

"There it is," he remarked as he pointed ahead across the bow. "Can you see it?" he asked Carlos who manned the helm.

"Aye, Captain, I've got it in sight."

"Good, steer for the light. We want to keep it close to our port side as we pass it. Then turn to a course of 160 degrees. There will be a barrier reef on our starboard side all the way to the northern tip of

Andros. It should be clearly visible. Make sure you keep the reef in sight."

"Aye, Captain."

"I'm going down below to talk to Jon. I'll be in the engine room if you need me, Carlos."

"Yes, Sir, Capt'n."

Captain Franco left the bridge and descended the ladders until he reached the bowels of the ship. He found Carlos in the engineer's office.

"Good afternoon, Capt'n."

"Afternoon. As you probably know, we are nearing the northern tip of Andros. We should be near Coakley Town by this evening. We'll anchor and head into port tomorrow morning. I would like to off load the hot cars tomorrow, load up the new cars and head to Tampico by early the next day. I know we normally have enough fuel to carry us through."

"Well, Sir, we do have enough fuel, but I was countin' on staying in Coakley for a few days. We have a shaft bearing that is running hot and needs replacing. I can get it done in Coakley, but it will take a couple of days. I didn't say nothin' because we always stay in Coakley several days anyway," Carlos said.

"Carlos, you are aware that any engineering concerns must be reported to me immediately, aren't you?"

"Yes, Sir."

"Then why are you tellin' me this now? When did you know about this problem?" the Captain growled.

"Just this afternoon, Capt'n. I was gonna tell you soon, but you beat me to it," Carlos said.

"You make me nervous. I don't know whether to believe you or not."

"Oh, it's the truth, Capt'n. I wouldn't lie to you, Sir."

"Okay, I'll believe you this time," the Captain conceded. I have urgent business to tend to in Mexico that requires me to get this vessel there as soon as we can. Can't you throw more lubricating oil in the bearing housing or wrap it in a water cooling jacket?"

"No, Sir. The bearing has cracked. There is too much friction. Soon it will shatter and the propeller shaft will have to be shut down. I'm prayin' we can make it to Coakley before we're dead in the water."

"Very well, I'll contact Ringo and tell him the news," Captain Franco said. "Keep me posted of any changes."

"Aye, Sir."

Franco, angry over the news of his crippled ship and a growing distrust of his engineer, returned to his cabin. He threw himself in his chair and stared at a picture hung on the bulkhead of Coakley Town harbor with coconut palms casting shadows over white sandy beaches. Then he left his cabin for the radio room and called Ringo Operations.

Meanwhile, Jon left his office and climbed below into the engine compartment. He felt the propeller shaft again.

"Ouch! Man, you can fry an egg on that," he hollered shaking his hand and blowing on it frantically.

He immediately called the bridge and advised the helmsman to reduce the speed to one third in attempt to lessen the heat stress on the bearings. Then he advised the Captain. An hour later, Jon rechecked the shaft. It had cooled somewhat, but he was convinced that repairs had to be made in Coakley Town. *The Coral Sun Ray* slowed to seven knots creating a gentle wake in its track. Ming Chi recalculated the ship's progress to the harbor entrance. He called the Captain to break the news.

"Captain, this is Ming. I have plotted our course to the harbor entrance at the slower speed and have determined we'll arrive around 7:00 in the morning, and the tide will be in our favor at that time. So, we can proceed directly to the pier in the harbor and not have to anchor outside."

"Good, Ming. I kinda figured that would be the case. Thanks for confirming it. Just make sure we clear the reefs along the way. It's like a mine field out there close to shore."

"Will do, Sir," Ming acknowledged.

Heading south a mile off the west coast of Bimini, the *Southwind* sailed in calm seas and gentle winds while following the reef line from South Bimini on their port side for twenty miles. Lori took advantage of the fair weather and caught up on some reading in the cockpit while Jeff manned the helm and Jason looked over the charts in the cabin.

By noon, Lori took over the helm responsibilities when they reached Gun Cay and then turned southeast toward the northern tip of Andros Island. Lori cranked the wheel around to port and steadied the *Southwind* on a heading of 120 degrees. An hour later, the waves began to foretell a change in the weather. A long counter swell was emerging from the northeast, and Jason knew there were signs of a rough ride ahead, but he kept quiet. Jason took over the helm duty around 4:00 o'clock as the winds gradually shifted to the east-southeast and freshened to twenty-five knots causing the seas to rise. An hour later, the *Southwind* heeled twenty-five degrees to starboard and plunged ahead into seven-foot seas with a roar. Lori was in the galley holding onto the counter rail tightly with one hand while trying to decide what to do about cooking dinner.

"Jason, what the hell is going on? I don't like this!" Lori screamed from the galley.

"We've got some weather to contend with ahead."

"You're telling me!" Lori shouted. "How long is this gonna last?"

"It should calm down by morning. Remember, I said the boat is capable of handling this. Just hold tight, and don't come out in the cockpit without a safety harness and line tied to you," Jason warned. "Hey Jeff, check the weather on the radio will you please? The last time I listened there were no storms predicted, just some wind."

Jeff turned on the radio and tuned in the forecast for the northern Bahamas. The weather service announced that there was an amendment to the forecast. Jeff turned up the volume so that Jason could hear it in the cockpit.

"*A weak low pressure system had formed off the northern coast of Cuba and was causing a wind shift and increase in velocity along the southern Florida coast and the northern Bahamas. Winds were forecast to become thirty to thirty-five knots from the east-southeast with seas building to ten feet by midnight. Conditions are expected to improve by morning around sunrise as the low continues to move rapidly west. Winds will diminish to fifteen to twenty knots and shift from the east-northeast by daybreak. Conditions will continue to improve by tomorrow afternoon with seas subsiding to five to six feet.*"

Jason called Jeff for help on deck. "Jeff, I have to lower the jib and reef the main. Take the helm for a few minutes, please. Try to maintain a course of 120." Jeff donned a harness, crawled into the cockpit, and attached himself to the railing with a safety line. He held the wheel tightly while Jason attached his safety line to the rail and inched his way forward on his belly to the bow. The bow heaved into the air and then soared down the other side of the swells with such abruptness that Jason became airborne briefly and had to grab the railings to keep from being thrown overboard. Only when the boat reached the bottom of the sea trough and started its rise up the next swell could he let go his grip for a few seconds to lower the jib and secure it to the deck.

"We're gonna lose the *Southwind*," Jeff screamed.

"No we're not!" Jason hollered back. "This boat is doing fine. It can tolerate much worse conditions than this. Don't panic! *Southwind* is handling this very well." The boat continued to crash ahead at 6.5 knots.

Thoroughly soaked by the time half the tasks were completed, Jason crawled back to the cockpit, took a moment to catch his breath, then worked his way to the foot of the mast and tied himself to it with a safety line. He lowered and reefed the mainsail while the *Southwind* continued to fight the seas not willing to give up. A little while later, a strong gust of wind roared through the rigging and ripped an eight-inch hole in the mainsail at one of the reefing points. Jason summoned Jeff back into the cockpit

"Here, take over the helm while I lower the mainsail completely and raise the storm jib," he ordered.

Repeating the grueling process of crawling along the deck to the bow, Jason managed to complete the challenging job in less than ten minutes. With a minor adjustment in the course, Jason was able to ease the *Southwind's* ride with less violent rolling and pitching motions.

"There, that should make everyone a little more comfortable with just the storm jib. You are getting initiated to real sailing now, Jeff," Jason said and gave Jeff a big pat on the back. Jeff did not respond. His hands were frozen to the wheel in fear as he stared at the oncoming mountains of water.

"Try to relax. We're gonna be fine. This will all be gone by morning. You can call yourself a real sailor now," Jason assured him.

"Yeah, I guess I can call myself a sailor now," he replied.

The weather continued to deteriorate to thirty-knot winds and ten-foot swells as the sun sank below the horizon. But the seas continued to aim for the bow forcing *Southwind* to cut through the blue water with vengeance.

Jason went below to comfort Lori for a moment while Jeff manned the duties in the cockpit. He found her in her cabin wedged in her bunk with pillows and rolled up blankets and a look of terror in her eyes. Jason leaned over her and gave her a long hug and a kiss on the cheek.

"We are going to be fine, Sweetheart. I have been in much worse sea conditions than this. The *Southwind* is a tough boat. It can handle this very well. The only weak link is the crew and if we don't give up, we'll make it through with flying colors. I'm *not* giving up, you're not giving up, and Jeff is not giving up. So, we are going to be okay. In a few more hours, the conditions will improve and the uncomfortable ride will be over. Hang in there a little longer," Jeff said as he held her hand.

Lori forced a brief smile on her face and grabbed Jason's other hand as if to say thanks. Then she closed her eyes.

Jason returned to the cockpit and relieved Jeff at the helm. "Go below and try to get a little sleep. I think Lori would like to have your company."

The swells were now breaking at the crest as the seas aimed for *Southwind's* bow causing the vessel to dig in its heels and shoot airborne like a bullet and crash against the oncoming swells. Volumes of blue water flowed over the bow and rushed across the deck into the cockpit.

In the cabin, Lori made a valiant attempt to prepare sandwiches for dinner, but she was fighting a losing battle of seasickness. Finally admitting defeat, she ran quickly to the head, slammed the door shut, and fell down on her knees in front of the toilet.

"Poor girl, I feel so sorry for her," Jeff hollered to Jason as he listened to her throw up from inside the cabin.

"Yeah, I know what she's going through. However, she'll get over it soon. Motion sickness doesn't last long. Her body will adjust to the motion. She'll be better in the morning," Jason assured him. "Try to get some sleep before your midnight watch at the helm. We'll leave Lori alone. I'll take her watch tonight. Let her get some rest. I suggest we make tonight's watches two hours long since the weather is so rough. We'll all be better tomorrow morning."

"Sounds good to me. It's hard work keeping my feet spread out to maintain balance while holding on to the helm and maintain a steady course," Jeff said.

"You're right, and the autohelm is useless under these conditions. Now get some sleep," Jason ordered.

"Thanks. I feel okay, but I will try to get an hour sleep, however." Jeff said.

Jeff rolled into the quarter berth with Lori who was moaning with her hands over her head. She had wedged her back against the bulkhead with her knees bent against the opposite bulkhead to keep from being tossed back and forth. He tried to close his eyes and force himself to fall asleep, but Lori's groaning and the noise of the boat crashing through the swells outside kept him awake for more than an hour. Finally, he rejoined Jason in the cockpit.

"You're back too soon," Jason remarked.

"Are you kidding? I'm wide-awake. Besides, Lori is keeping me awake. I'd rather stay here and keep you company," Jeff said.

"How's Lori doing?" Jason asked.

"She's miserable, but she'll survive," Jeff responded.

"Oh I know she will. Poor Lori," Jason sighed and patted Jeff on the shoulder. "I wish I could help her, but. . . ."

The seas continued to rage the remainder of the night, but by daybreak, the weather showed signs of improvement as promised. Jeff was at the helm again when Jason emerged from the cabin.

"Still hangin' in there?" Jason asked.

"Yep, I'm doing okay," Jeff said assuredly.

"Great. How about some breakfast?" Jason asked. "Hungry?"

"Sure, sounds good to me. Is Lori awake?"

"No. I'm letting her sleep while she can. Besides, I doubt she'd be in the mood to fix breakfast right now. I'll make my famous pancakes for the two of us if you can manage the helm a little longer," Jason said.

"Yeah, I'm good here. But I could use some coffee right now," Jeff requested.

"Comin' right up," Jason said while gripping the railing with one hand.

Jason retreated to the galley, made some coffee, and handed it to Jeff in the cockpit. Then he returned to the galley and whipped up his famous pancake batter. At midpoint in the process, however, he paused and climbed up to the cockpit to make sure that Jeff was comfortable under the heavy sea conditions. Suddenly, *Southwind* took a thirty-degree roll to port causing the bowl of batter in the galley to fall off the counter top and spill onto the carpeted deck below. And to make matters worse, his charts received some of the gooey mess on the tabletop. Hearing the racket, Jason quickly retreated to the galley to witness the batter sloshing back and forth on the carpet and his charts. Refusing to waste his morning's masterpiece, he quickly rounded up a couple of dish sponges from under the sink, sopped up the batter from the charts and carpet, squeezed the sponges into the hot frying pan, and cooked the pancakes. A few moments later, he proudly served the pancakes to Jeff in the cockpit.

"Man these are the best cakes I've had this morning," Jeff laughed.

"Yeah, they are good aren't they?" Jason responded with a smirk on his face. And then he added, "They're special."

Following breakfast, Jason decided to mend the mainsail now since the wind and sea conditions had improved. While he searched the sail locker for the mending materials, Lori stumbled out of her cabin and approached Jason.

"Feeling better?" Jason asked.

"Yes, but don't talk to me about eating breakfast unless you want it right back slightly used. I might have some saltine crackers, but that's it." She stared at Jason rumbling around in the sail locker. "What are you doing?"

"We had a little rip in the mainsail last night and I am going to sew a patch on it," he said.

"Can I do it?" she asked.

"Sure. Do you really feel up to it?" he asked.

"Yes, I think I'll be better if I do something outside," Lori said.

"You're right. Here, take these and I'll show you how to get started."

They climbed into the cockpit and onto the top deck where the mainsail was tied to the mast. Jason pulled the sail down into the cockpit and showed her how to make the mend. By noon, the seas and winds had settled into a gentle breeze out of the southeast, and Jeff was relieved that they beat the odds of a challenging sea the night before.

Later that evening, the Northwest Channel Light was clearly visible five miles ahead. Jason looked at his stained chart to verify the course through the channel and adjusted the heading ten degrees to the right. Fully recovered from her bout with seasickness, Lori was eager to take her turn at the helm. From the east, a light trade wind settled in creating long gentle swells moving from port to starboard under a starry night and a few fair weather clouds. Lori kept looking at the heavens and was amazed how many billions of stars there were in the sky. Meanwhile, Jason adjusted the jib and mainsail sheets to maximize *Southwind's* speed to five knots and activated the autohelm. Half-hour later they rounded the Northwest Channel Light and Lori changed course to 160 degrees to clear the northeast tip of Andros Island.

The following morning at first light, under a gentle trade wind from the east, the Southwind sailed smoothly four miles off shore from Morgan's Bluff on the northeast tip of Andros. The closer they got to Andros the higher Jason's adrenaline levels rose as he thought about Maisy. He looked at his watch and realized that they should arrive in Coakley Town in just a few hours. After breakfast, Lori sat on the bow and watched the colorful reefs pass beneath the keel in the crystal clear waters ten to twenty feet below. Jeff sunbathed on the bow with her while Jason steered the boat to Coakley Town. Several dolphins swam half a mile behind the Southwind, and it wasn't long before the pod caught up to the boat.

"Jeff! Are you awake? We have visitors!" Lori exclaimed. "Look behind us."

By the time Jeff raised up to look, the dolphins were alongside. Jeff leaned as far out as he could over the rail to try to touch them when they came up for air, but they were always just out of reach. However, one dolphin came close enough to spray Jeff in the face that prompted a shriek of laughter from Lori. The dolphins danced in front of the *Southwind* as if to show them the way to Coakley Town. At the same time, a mile ahead and on the right, Jason spotted a line of waves breaking over reefs running close to the shoreline.

"See the white water breaking ahead. That is the beginning of the barrier reefs that extend along the entire East Coast of Andros. It'll be easy navigating from here to Coakley Town using that reef line as a reference. All we have to do is keep those reefs a mile or so to starboard and plot our positions using landmarks along the coast."

"Hey, can I do the navigating and plotting? I want to learn how. Will you teach me, Jeff?" Lori asked.

"Sure. Come with me. We'll get the charts, binoculars, compass, and notepad and go for it," Jeff said.

Jason looked at his watch again. "We should be in Coakley Town by 11:00 o'clock." He was now getting visibly anxious to see Maisy. "Just a few more hours and I'll be able to hold you, kiss you, and. . . ."

"What did you say? You talkin' to me?" Lori shouting through the cabin door.

"Huh? Uh, no, I was just talking to myself," Jason said.

Chapter 7

Rendezvous at Coakley Town

By mid-morning, the *Coral Sun Ray* reached the flashing white light buoy marking the entrance channel to Coakley Town. Captain Franco stood on the starboard side of the bridge with binoculars in hand coaching Carlos at the helm on how to avoid the treacherous reefs on both sides of the narrow, shallow channel.

"Keep her steady on course 240. You can see the reefs ahead. Stay dead center of the channel. We only have a few feet clearance below the keel. There's no room for error," the Captain warned.

"Aye, Sir, steady on course 240."

"There's a shoal on the south side just as we enter the harbor. It has been dredged for us to slip through with only a foot to spare," Franco warned again. "You'll see our dock on the port side just before the bridge."

The ship slipped slowly at two knots past the entrance channel marker. Then the Captain ordered, "Come right to 245 degrees."

"Aye, right to 245," Carlos repeated and turned the wheel a quarter turn clockwise. "Steady on 245, Captain," Carlos announced.

"Thank you."

Captain Franco leaned over the edge of the bridge railing to get a better view of the reefs ahead. Suddenly he noticed a chunk of coral break loose and swirl to the surface next to the bow. "Blow me down!" he shouted. "We did it again . . . chiseled away at that nasty coral head at the edge of the channel."

"Aye, Sir," Carlos uttered. "Just followin' your orders, Sir."

"Turn left to 235," Captain Franco ordered. Carlos swung the wheel to the left.

"Steady on 235, Captain," Carlos said.

Less than a minute later the Captain order, "Turn right to 240." Carlos acknowledged. "All engines stop," the Captain ordered.

As the *Coral Sun Ray* slipped quietly into the small harbor of

Coakley Town, Rafael stood on the bow with a shot line to throw onto the pier for Sanchez to catch. At the stern, Juan was ready with a line to throw to Jack who was waiting at the other end of the dock. The Captain gave the order to reverse all engines one-third as the ship nudged gently against the dock. "All engines stop," he shouted into the pilothouse. "Heave bow and stern lines to shore," Captain Franco hollered through his megaphone to Juan and Rafael on deck. When the lines were secured, Rafael opened the side hatch and lowered the car ramp onto the dock.

"Well done, Carlos. We'll be here for a few days. You can take a day of R&R if you wish. Be back onboard by Saturday," Franco ordered.

"Thank you, Sir," Carlos said.

The Captain left the bridge and went below to speak to Jon about the shaft-bearing problem. When he reached the engine room, he found that Jon had already begun to dismantle the bearing housing. "I see you're not wasting any time. I'm going to ask Jack for assistance as soon as I go ashore," Franco said.

"That would help. I already have spare bearings. It's just a matter of taking this apart and removing them. I just hope the shaft has not been scored. I can't replace the shaft without putting the ship in dry dock," Jon explained.

"I know that," the Captain said. "Keep me posted."

"Of course."

Captain Franco freshened up in his cabin, walked down the gangway and headed for Ringo Operations. Along the way, however, Francesca approached him on the road near the dock.

"Excuse me, Sir, are you Captain Franco?" she asked.

"Maybe, who are you?"

"I'm Francesca . . . from Santa Marta, Colombia. You don't know me, but I know you. Do you have some time? I need to talk to you about your operations. It's in a lot of trouble. How 'bout joinin' me for a drink at Mangos. My treat," she insisted.

"I'm afraid I have an urgent appointment at the moment. Can I meet you there in an hour?"

"Yes, that'll work. See you at Mangos," Francesca confirmed. She turned and walked into town while Franco headed for Ringo's office.

The steamy, tropical humidity forced a steady drip of sweat from Franco's face as he walked in the sun down the pot-holed street and across the short bridge to the operation's headquarters two blocks away. Wiping his face with his grungy handkerchief, he climbed the three steps onto the porch and barged through the door. Jack sat at his desk, smoking a cigar and waiting for him.

"Welcome to Paradise, old man," Jack said.

"Yeah, Paradise," Franco repeated. "As I mentioned over the radio, we've got to fix the bearings in the propeller shaft. Jon thinks he can fix it, but I know he's gonna need help. Can you spare a couple of your men to go over to the ship and see what can be done? I want to get underway Saturday."

"I can spare one man. I have to finish up the last few cars for you to take to Tampico," Jack replied.

"And I have twenty-six for you to off load. How many do you have for me to take south?" the Captain asked.

"Eighteen," Jack said. "Come on out to the floor, and I'll show you what a fantastic job we've done to alter these cars. I'd like to know what you think. Okay?"

"Sure," Franco agreed. They walked into the warehouse where fifteen, shiny, like new cars were lined up at the door ready to roll onto the ship. Jack led Franco to the back of the warehouse to see several mechanics finishing the last three cars.

"We're getting ready to paint these this afternoon. We'll load them all Friday afternoon. What do you think?" Jack asked.

"They look great. We should get top dollar for them in Mexico. Good job, Jack."

They finished the tour and returned to Jack's office where they continued their conversation about the current operations and what's expected down the road. Then Captain Franco noticed the clock on the wall. "Hey, I need to hustle back to the ship to see how the repairs are going. I'll check back with you later," Franco said. He left Jack's office and headed straight for Mangos instead.

Francesca was sitting alone at a table in the back of the bar next to a large open window. A wooden fan swirled the tropical air overhead as she sipped her rum punch and stared at the coconut palms a few feet outside the window. With her back to the front door, Captain Franco came up silently behind here and grabbed a chair.

"Oh, you startled me," she said as she jumped slightly in her chair. "I'm glad you were curious enough to check me out."

"My pleasure. So, what brings you to this remote tropical jungle?"

"Business . . . importing, exporting business," she said.

"So, you said you're from Colombia?" the Captain asked.

"Yes, but before we get started, what'll you have to drink?"

"Their specialty, the rum punch."

"I should have guessed that. Hey waiter, bring another punch, please," she hollered. The waiter nodded.

"So, what business do you have that's so urgent to corner me in Coakley Town? Why do you think I'm in trouble?"

"It's your operation in Tampico. You need to know what's goin' on," Francesca said.

"Really? How do you know what we are doing in Tampico? Who are you? Why are you telling me this?" the Captain asked.

"I have a close friend in Tampico who knows what's going on."

"So? Why are you here? What do you want?" Franco asked.

"The local authorities in Tampico are highly suspicious of what your operations are doing at the port. At the moment, the police have been unable to find any hard criminal evidence, but they are determined to find something. A Tampico undercover agent has been assigned to infiltrate the operations to uncover suspected criminal activities. And knowing the Mexicans, they will find what they are looking for. They're planning to search your ship and investigate your crew when you arrive."

"Why are you telling me this? What's your role?" Franco asked with a hard stare into Francesca's eyes.

"I live in Santa Marta, Colombia and have a lot of influence with the underground there. The black market for high-end cars is hot in Columbia, much bigger than in Tampico or anywhere else in Mexico for that matter and we want your business in Colombia . . . before you get hijacked and shut down in Tampico. You need to get out of Mexico immediately. I can set you up in Santa Marta as a partner that will make you rich. The Santa Marta government won't touch us. They're scared. You can have free run there," she urged.

"Sounds like a bribe! I don't pay bribes," he said angrily and abruptly stood up from his chair to leave.

"Sit down!" she demanded. "I'm not finished. It's not a bribe. I want to head off destruction of your operations. You're in trouble, and if you join our team, we'll protect you and make you more money than you dreamed of. . . ."

"You are trying to hijack my business. You are not going to order me around!" the Captain shouted.

"Shut up and listen to me," Francesca demanded and cut him off in mid-sentence. Your days are over in Tampico," she warned.

"You're a fool! You're lying!" the Captain hollered and stood up again to leave.

Francesca leaped up, grabbed the Captain by the arm, and shoved him back down in his chair. "You'll find out when you get to Tampico. Then it'll be too late," she threatened. "The authorities will swarm your ship and crew like fire ants. You don't have a chance. It's a sting set up waiting for your arrival. The Mexicans can be mercenaries."

Captain Franco turned away from Francesca and put his face in his hands. After rubbing his forehead for a moment, he looked back at her.

"How much do you want?" he asked angrily.

"I don't want your money now. I want to be your partner in Santa Marta. Twenty percent of your dealings."

"What? I'm no idiot! That leaves me with nothin'!" he yelled.

Their outrage immediately attracted the attention of the bar tender and the three other patrons sitting in front of the bar. They stared at the Captain and Francesca for a few seconds.

"Now you have everyone here staring at us. Good job, Captain. Shall I stand up and announce who we are and what we are doing?" Francesca said.

"All right, I'll be quiet. But I still say you are a fake," the Captain said simmering down from a rage to anger.

"Well, let me tell you, Mr. Hardhead," Francesca began. "Your math is faulty. You make more than twenty percent but suit yourself. Go on to Tampico and get thrown in jail. Don't come crying to me. Remember, justice in Mexico moves slowly. You'll be locked up for months before you get a chance to talk and defend yourself. That'll put an end to everything," she responded with arrogance. "You are the one in trouble, not me. You better listen to me. Skip that port and go straight to Santa Marta. I've already set things up for you. We're waiting for you to arrive."

"I need to think about this. How long are you goinin' to be in Coakley?" he asked.

"As long as you are," she said. "This is an urgent matter. It is a win-win situation for both of us. I'll wait."

"Meet me here tomorrow afternoon at three o'clock," the Captain said. "Oh, thanks for the drink."

"Anytime," she said with a smile and a wink in her eye. Captain Franco hastily exited the bar and headed to his ship. Francesca raised her glass of hurricane punch toward the bar's open window while watching him hurry down the dirt road toward the *Coral Sun Ray*. "Here's to Santa Marta, you fool," she murmured to herself.

The following morning around 10:00, Jason looked through his binoculars at the flashing white light near Long Cay marking the entrance channel to Coakley Town. On both sides of the marker, he could see white waves crashing furiously over the reefs.

"Okay guys, I have the channel in sight," he shouted as he pointed fifty degrees off the starboard bow. Jeff and Lori strained their eyes to see just as Jason handed over the binoculars to them.

"Wow, that's a lot of surf action going on there," Jeff noted. "This is going to be a challenge avoiding those coral reefs."

"Yeah, but if you look carefully, you'll see a small break in the white water between the reefs. That's our channel. It'll be narrow, but the charts indicate twenty feet of good water. We'll just have to pay close attention to the color of the water as we go through the passage," Jason cautioned. "I am counting on you and Lori to be lookouts. Remember, brown or black water means dangerous shallow reefs and rocks ahead. Breaking waves also means rocks and reefs ahead. Blue or dark green usually means deep water. White means sandy bottom. The whiter it is the shallower it is. There is an art to reading the color of the water in the Bahamas, but I'll help you."

With a fresh easterly trade wind, the *Southwind* slipped rapidly toward the channel and prompted Jason to release the mainsheet and capture the wind in the mainsail from astern. Simultaneously Jeff let up on the jib to allow it to billow out adding another knot toward Coakley channel. When they reached half a mile from the marker, Jason turned on the engine and let it idle just in case they encountered a cross current that might slam them onto the reefs as they made their way through the passage.

The waves crashed over the reefs just one hundred feet on either side as they slipped through the passage to the entrance to the harbor. When they entered the tiny harbor, Jason briefly spotted the coastal freighter tied to a small pier ahead. Busy with getting the *Southwind* settled in the harbor and moored to a dock, he didn't notice the name of the ship on the stern.

"Okay, Jeff, haul down the jib. I'll stay at the helm and steer us around inside the harbor until we have the sails secured. Lori, take care of the main, please." There was a unanimous, "Aye, aye, Captain."

In a few minutes, all sails were down and secured and Jason maneuvered the boat to the dock on the north side of the channel. Lori leaped over the railing with the bowline in hand and tied it to the dock cleat, and Jason tossed the stern line over to her seconds later. *Southwind* had arrived.

"Whoopee!" shouted Jason.

"Yeah, we made it. What a crew! " Jeff said and he gave Lori a big hug.

Jason looked at his watch. It was almost 11:00 o'clock.

"What great timing. In just three hours, Maisy will be here on the mail boat. Man, I feel like I'm in heaven," Jason said as he exploded with a burst of excitement.

Meanwhile, Lori ran over to the dirt road, dropped to her knees, and kissed the ground. "I love sailing, but I'm so glad to have my feet on solid ground," she hollered and threw her arms in the air.

"Does that mean you are not sailing back?" Jeff asked.

"Maybe . . . maybe not. I'll probably feel differently tomorrow. Right now I am thankful to be here."

When Jason shut off the engine, the sounds of a tropical island became readily apparent to the crew—the street noises in the village of Coakley, the warm tropical breeze whistling through the palm trees, the surf crashing over the rocky reefs nearby. Jason hustled into the cabin to freshen up and start preparations for lunch with Lori's help. Feeling a great relief from a week of sailing, Jeff collapsed on the bench in the cockpit, sat motionless, and absorbed the tropical ambiance. In twenty minutes, they gathered under the shade of the cockpit cover and ate their first meal in the harbor of Coakley Town, Andros Island.

After lunch, the three left the boat and hustled into a general store nearby.

"Good day, Ma'am," Jason greeted the clerk. "Does the mail boat dock here from Moxey Settlement at two o'clock?"

"Well, depends. Sometimes it comes at noon, sometimes at two; sometimes it comes at five, and sometimes it comes next day. Depends," she said casually.

"Depends on what?"

"Depends on the weather, depends on how much mail, goods, passengers want to come this way. If boat don't have enough things to bring, it waits 'till next day. Like I say, depends," she repeated.

"Is it comin' today?" Jason asked with concern. He paused and then added," I know . . . 'depends.'"

"You got it, Sir."

Jason's face showed a hint of anxiety. Lori walked over to Jason and put her arm on his shoulder. "Hey, don't worry. Maisy said she would be here at two. So, she'll be here at two o'clock. She must know the boat schedule. Don't listen to this clerk. She couldn't care less. She just works here. Let's go outside and wait for Maisy at the dock. Enjoy the outdoors."

The three strolled across the dirt road to the harbor and sat down on the edge of the dock with their feet dangling over the side. Jeff stared at the freighter moored across harbor.

"Jason, wasn't the name of the freighter we saw on the Cape Fear River the *Coral Sun Ray,* the one loading cars in the middle of the night?" Jeff asked.

"I think so, why?"

"Take a look at that freighter across the waterway. Check out the name," Jeff insisted.

"Good grief. That's it!" Jason said wide-eyed. "What is it doing here?"

"This is weird. That ship could have sailed anywhere in the world, but it ended up here in Coakley Town . . . with us," Jeff said.

"Yeah. I wonder what is going on in Coakley." Lori added.

"Maybe we'll find out, but not now. I have a date with Maisy," Jason insisted as he looked at his watch again and then paced down the dock toward the entrance to the harbor hoping to spot the boat coming through the channel.

Lori leaned over to Jeff and whispered, "I sure hope Jason is not going to be disappointed. He has no idea what Maisy looks like or anything about her. She could be an overweight homely looking girl for all he knows."

"Shhhhhh. Don't be pessimistic. Give him a chance. Maisy could be as beautiful as a movie star," Jeff said quietly.

"Movie star? Here?" Lori laughed.

"Not so loud. You know what I mean . . . a pretty little island girl. She could be, right?"

"We'll soon see," Lori acknowledged. She looked at her watch. The boat was already twenty minutes late.

Jason returned to Jeff and Lori sitting on the dock. "Where is that boat?" he hollered to anyone who might be within hearing distance. Then at 2:25, he caught a glimpse of a boat about a mile away entering the channel entrance. He ran into the store again and asked the clerk," Is that the mail boat comin'? And please don't say 'depends' again."

The clerk slowly walked to the door of the store and looked toward the harbor entrance. "Could be," she said.

"It has to be, right?" Jason insisted.

"Yes, probably. Expectin' a package?"

"You bet, a fabulous package from Moxey Settlement."

"A part for your boat?" she asked with a hint of curiosity.

"Not exactly, but she's a very special package," he said.

"She?"

"Uh, yes, it's a long story. I have to run and meet the boat. Thanks." He rushed out the door and shouted, "The boat's comin,' the boat's comin.' This is it. Yahoo!" The three stood on the dock and watched the boat intently as it inched its way through the channel toward the harbor. Soon, the captain maneuvered the mail boat close to the dock while Jason scanned the passengers standing on the deck for any signs of who might be Maisy. He spotted a beautiful, tall, thin, well-tanned girl with long blond hair standing next to the starboard rail looking toward him. His eyes fixed on her as he thought . . . could this be her? Could he be setting himself up for disaster if he were wrong or joy if he were correct? His heartbeat fluttered. Then he knew. She waved at him. "Oh my God. It is Maisy," he muttered to himself. He waved back and shouted, "Maisy?"

"Hi Jason," she hollered back.

Jason's excitement overwhelmed him, as he rushed to the edge of the pier and grabbed one of the tie lines to speed up the docking process. A dockworker yelled, "Sir, we'll take care of that, please put the line down." Jason complied. He stood impatiently while the boat captain lowered the gangway and let four passengers off the boat. Maisy was last, and as soon as she left the ramp, she ran into the arms of Jason and gave him a big hug.

From a distance, Lori and Jeff looked at each other and then Jeff remarked, "Well, I'll be. What luck! She *is* a queen."

"Ah, don't be too quick. She looks good on the outside, but what's the rest of her story?" she cautioned.

"Who cares? This is a great start," Jeff added.

"Men!" Lori laughed.

"Finally we meet. This is an exciting day for me. You are prettier than I thought," Jason said to Maisy as he looked into her cheerful blue eyes.

"Thank you. What did you think I looked like?" she asked with great curiosity.

"Never mind. It's not important now," he said.

"You're not so bad either. I have been looking forward to seeing you. Seemed like forever, didn't it?" she said.

"Yeah."

When Jeff and Lori joined Maisy and Jason, Jason introduced them.

Jeff shook hands with her and Lori placed her hand around her shoulder.

"Jason told me a lot about you guys," Maisy said.

"Oh, are we in trouble already?" Lori asked.

"No, no. He said nice things."

"Let's head over to our boat," Jason suggested. "Jeff and I will help you with your things. The four headed down the road a short distance to the dock where *Southwind* was tied, and along the way, Maisy reached out and held tightly to Jason's hand. They climbed aboard and entered the cabin below.

"Well, this is our little home. There are enough beds for the four of us. I assume you can stay a few days," Jason said hopefully.

"Yes, I can stay as long as you are here," she said and gave Jason another hug. "I like it. You have all the comforts of home. It's a beautiful boat."

"It is except in a storm," Lori complained.

"In a storm? What do you mean? Did you run into a storm sailing here?" Maisy asked.

"Tell her, Jason. Tell her how horrible it was," Lori challenged him.

"Not now. I'll put your things in the guest cabin. Lori and Jeff are sleeping in my cabin, and I'll sleep here in the main cabin."

"Perfect. I'm easy to please," Maisy said.

Captain Franco strolled into Mangos for his rendezvous with Francesca and saw her sitting at the back table sipping a rum punch.

"Have a seat, partner," Francesca greeted him.

"You are being presumptuous, aren't you?" he said as he pulled up a chair and sat down.

"Maybe . . . maybe not," she replied. "You'll come around and see my side, partner."

"Stop calling me 'partner'!" he said becoming irritated. "We have a lot of talkin' to do. Have you seen our operations here in Coakley?" he asked.

"No, but I know what is going on here," she said.

"Well, let's go meet Jack anyway. He's our boss in Coakley and he'll show you around," Franco insisted.

"If you insist."

Captain Franco led Francesca down the street to Jack's office and went inside.

"Whoa. Who's this?" Jack hollered as he jumped up from his chair.

"Relax; I want you to meet a friend, Francesca. She says she can set up a business for us in South America, so I thought you would show her our operations here."

Jack looked at her with suspicion and reluctantly shook her hand.

"I see. Where did you run into her?" Jack asked.

"She was here waiting for me to show up," Captain Franco said.

Jack looked at Francesca. "How did you know the ship was coming here?"

"I have my contacts," Francesca said. "I want to. . . ."

"Look, Jack, what Francesca is doing is my business," Franco interrupted. "I told her you would give her a tour and then she and I are going to talk later. She's safe."

"Okay, if you say so," Jack acknowledged uncomfortably. He then led the two into his shop.

"Wow, I'm impressed. Where did you get all of these expensive cars?" she asked.

"What? I thought you knew what we were doing," Franco said.

"Oh, yes, I mean what State did they come from?"

"Does it matter?" the Captain asked.

"No, of course not, just curious," she said.

"We have car thieves working for us all over the East Coast. They're professionals. Know how to avoid getting caught. Then we alter them, disguise them, and fix them up here in Coakley. No one bothers us here. And the locals don't ask questions. They need our support for the village. Helps their economy if you know what I mean."

"Then you take them to Tampico and sell them," she added.

"Correct."

"But the police in Tampico are highly suspicious of what you are doing, and they think you are doing more than dealing with stolen cars," she volunteered.

"Oh, you mean the smuggling operations to the U.S.?" the Captain asked.

"Yes, how's that going?"

"That's a big money maker. We usually smuggle ten to twenty people into the U.S. through Wilmingtown on each cruise. Wilmingtown's a sleepy port, a small town. It's easy to get these into the country without detection. You must know about that, too," Franco said a little puzzled.

"Yes, of course. I just wanted to know how you felt personally about the immigration business. It seems to be profitable to you, then."

"Yeah. We couldn't run this operation on just stolen cars," he said.

After the brief tour, they returned to Mangos and sat down again at the back table.

"Okay, tell me the details about your proposed market in Colombia?" he asked still not convinced.

"Of course. I plan to notify my operations in Santa Marta tonight and by the time you arrive in port, the cars you load up here tomorrow will already be sold by the time you arrive in port. Cash could be waiting for you when you tie up to the pier. Furthermore, I guarantee that at least twenty immigrants will be ready to come aboard for your return to the U.S. with cash in hand. Columbia is a hot bed for immigrants trying to get to the U.S. I told you I would take care of you. After all, it's my business, too, remember . . . partner?"

"I never agreed to be your partner. You're really stuck on that, aren't you?" Franco said.

"You'll come around, partner."

"You're thick headed!" Captain Franco repeated and pounded his fist on the table. "For the last time, stop calling me 'partner.'"

"Okay, what are you trying to tell me, Captain?" Francesca rolled her eyes in front of his face to intimidate him.

"All right, I'll let you in. We'll go on to Santa Marta," Franco finally agreed. "You had better be right or I'll have your head."

"Good. You're doing the right thing," she said as she stood up and shook hands with him. "I'll call my contacts in Santa Marta right away and fly to Colombia tomorrow. Have a safe voyage, Capt'n. Call me when you are a day out of Santa Marta. Here's my card. See you in port in a week or so." The Captain shook his head in disbelief and watched her walk out of the bar.

When Francesca disappeared into the village, Franco sat back down in his chair and ran his hands through his hair trying to figure out how his operations got so screwed up. Nearing a state of despair, he got up and hurried to his ship to check on the progress of the shaft repairs. He climbed up the gangway and made his way down into the engine room, but en route, Juan stopped him in the passageway.

"Uh, Captain, there's an urgent message for you in your cabin. It's from Tampico. I didn't read it, Sir. I just know it came from Tampico."

"Thank you, Juan. I'll look at it as soon as I talk to Jon." Franco continued down the ladders to the engine room where he found Jon and one of Jack's coworkers putting the cover back on the propeller bearing housing.

"Good news, Capt'n. I think we got it fixed. If you have a few minutes we'll give it a test to see if the propeller shaft turns without getting hot. I have doubled up the dock lines to make sure the ship stays put."

"Well done, Jon," the Captain said.

After a few bolts were tightened, Jon signaled the bridge that a test was about to be started and for him to be advised if the ship moves or lines break during the test. Soon, Jon eased forward on the throttle and watched the shaft turn slowly. Carlos called from the bridge and said that the dock lines tightened but were holding. Jon increased the speed of the shaft a little more and let it run for ten minutes. Then he felt the bearing housing. It remained cool.

"I think we got the job done, Capt'n," Jon said with a smile.

"Good, let's plan to load the ship tonight and get underway tomorrow. I checked the tide and we'll be able to get through the channel by mid-afternoon."

"Aye, Capt'n, tomorrow afternoon's okay. We'll be ready," Jon acknowledged.

"Oh, by the way, Jon, we have a change in our itinerary. We're goin' to Santa Marta, Colombia, instead of Tampico. There's trouble in Tampico, and we have been advised to forget that port for now. I think we'll do better in South America anyway," the Captain assured Jon. I'll advise Ming to plot a course to Santa Marta."

"Sounds okay with me," Jon answered.

"How's our fuel situation for sailing to Colombia?"

"We have enough to cruise for twenty five days," Jon said.

"That's plenty. It should take less than a week to get there," Franco said.

"Aye on that, Captain."

Captain Franco left the engine room, made his way to his cabin, and closed the door. An envelope lay on his table marked "Urgent." He quickly picked it up and ripped it open.

Captain John Franco—Urgent! The Tampico Police have been interrogating our men daily about our operations. They suspect we are importing stolen cars from the U.S. and possibly other crimes. I have denied everything, but they think I am lying and want to put a stop to our operation. The police are poised to pounce on your ship and crew when you arrive. Don't come to Tampico until things cool down. Chico.

Franco crumpled up the note and tossed it in the trash. He walked to the port window, stared at the channel entrance toward the sea, and then paced in his cabin for a few moments with his hand on his chin. He returned to the table, sat down and jotted down a response to Chico.

Thanks for the warning. Just met new business partner who is operating in Santa Marta, Colombia. Tipped me off about Tampico. Am diverting to Santa Marta. Underway tomorrow. Will keep you posted. Captain Franco.

He folded the paper, stuffed it in his pocket, and headed to the radio room where he gave the note to the radio operator. "Send this right away to Tampico," he requested.

The Captain left the radio room, climbed down the ladders to the main deck and walked down the gangway to the dock. He looked back at his ship for a moment and then headed for Mangoes. The bar was empty when he strolled through the door, and he plopped himself down at the back table next to the large, opened window. The bartender approached him.

"Afternoon, Capt'n. You're here again I see."

"Got a lot on my mind. Need some time to think. How 'bout a stiff drink?"

"What, no rum punch?" he asked.

"No, give me somethin' that'll make the hairs stand up on my chest," the Captain insisted.

"Okay, Capt'n. I'll mix up a glass of our Hurricane Blaster. It'll make you want to take cover before you finish the first glass."

"Good . . . and hustle," the Captain urged.

"Yes, Sir, comin' right up."

Franco leaned back in his chair and watched the brisk tropical breeze twist the leaves on the coconut palms in a disorderly manner outside the window. The same chaotic turmoil churned and twisted his thoughts. He began sinking into a state of anxiety over the apparent dismantling of his operations in Tampico and the uncertainties in Santa Marta. He needed a place to hide, to retreat, to stop the torturing in his mind.

"Hey, hurry up with my drink," he shouted across the room.

"I had to open up a new bottle of rum, it's comin'," the bartender apologized. A moment later, he brought over a tall, frosty glass topped off with a fresh slice of pineapple stuck to the top edge. "There you are, Sir, the Hurricane Blaster. Drink it slowly, or we'll have to carry you out and bury you," he warned.

"Blimey, don't tell me how to drink! I've been around this island before you popped out into this world." With that, he took several huge gulps of the explosive concoction without taking a breath. His head turned several shades darker red as he gasped for air. He tried to stand up while holding tightly to the edge of the table, but could not hold himself erect before plunging down in his chair again. Still trying to catch his breath, he pounded on his chest in desperation. Suddenly, he took in a large volume of air, and his natural color began to return to his face. "Man, that's good stuff," he complimented the bartender.

"Yeah, but take it easy. Just sit for awhile before you take another drink," he urged.

The Captain started to reprimand him for his advice again, but changed his mind and turned his head and stared out the window in silence. Soon he slouched over the table and rested his head on his arms as the outside world began to shut down around him.

Moments later, Jason and Maisy walked into Mangos and sat down at a table near the Captain in the back of the bar.

"That guy must be one of the local drunks. He really looks out of it," Jason remarked when he glanced at the Captain. "Do you know him?"

"No. Maybe he's taking an afternoon siesta," she suggested.

"Yeah, or just plain drunk. He looks like an old sea captain. I wonder if he's from the *Coral Sun Ray*?" he asked her.

"Uh, could be, but I don't care," she said.

"Maisy, I'm sorry about your mother, father, and brother." Jason reached out and held Maisy's hand. "The funeral must have been very tough for you."

Her lips quivered and a tear trickled down her cheek as Jason spoke, but she squeezed Jason's hand tightly, regained her composure, and said, "Thanks for caring and for your help with the search party. I miss them terribly and I'll never recover completely, but I have to move on with my . . ." She stopped talking in mid-sentence and glared out the window. Jason reached for a paper napkin on the table, leaned over to her, and wiped another tear from her face.

"Thanks. You're sweet," she said as she looked into his eyes. "Only one in a million would have sailed a thousand miles to see me. That's something very special. You are something very special," she admitted.

"Maybe I think you *are* worth it," he said.

"It's more than 'maybe', isn't it?" she thought.

"Yes. When I heard your voice on the radio and learned what was happening to you, I decided I had to come here. I had to meet you."

Jason paused and Maisy kept her focus on his eyes. Then she leaped from her chair and rushed over to Jason causing him to stand up. She put her arms around him and gave him a kiss. He responded by holding her even tighter and returned her kiss.

"Let's go for a walk," he suggested. She nodded her head in agreement. They left Mangos and headed down Coakley's main street to the beach. Jason found a coconut palm in the sand near the surf, sat down, leaned against it, and pulled Maisy to him. She sat in the sand and snuggled close to him. The two watched the surf gently roll onto the sandy beach then slip back to sea repeatedly, and they held each other closely, kissed and talked about their adventures on and off the island. A seagull circled over head, shrieked and flew out to sea. They remained embraced for more than an hour. As the sun began to sink low in the western horizon, Jason and Maisy headed back to the *Southwind* to join Lori and Jeff sitting in the cockpit under the Bimini cover.

"Well, look at the two love birds," Lori remarked.

"You might be right," Maisy said as she gave Lori a poke on her shoulder.

"Of course she's right," Jeff added. Jason just smiled and looked at Maisy.

After dinner, the four sat in the cockpit while Maisy shared her life experiences living in the Bahamas. By eleven o'clock, Maisy and Lori's heads were nodding, and at Jeff's suggestion, the four plunged into the cabin, climbed into their bunks and turned out the lights. Jason then slipped into Maisy's cabin, put his arms around her and gave her another goodnight kiss. Soon the only sound that could be heard aboard the *Southwind* was the hypnotic roar of the surf crashing over the reef less than a mile away.

Nearly two in the morning, however, the quiet solitude of the harbor was abruptly interrupted. Jason woke up when he heard an enormous splash next to the stern of the Southwind followed by a gush of water landing in the cockpit. He quickly rummaged around in the cabin for a flashlight and in the process created enough commotion that Maisy woke up and joined him. Then they heard a smack on the surface of the water near the stern.

"What's going on out there?" Maisy asked sleepily.

"I don't know, but I am going to find out," Jason said. "Come on, let's take a look."

Quietly crawling into the cockpit with their heads low, they peaked over the railing at the darkness across the harbor. Searching the water with the flashlight, they found nothing.

"Wait, see those bubbles leading away from the boat," Maisy pointed out. "It's a dolphin."

"Yeah, I think you may be right." Jason said.

Minutes ticked by without any more signs of activity. Suddenly, out from the blackness of the quiet harbor, the dolphin soared above the railing next to the cockpit and drenched Jason and Maisy to the skin.

"Wow! What a show," Maisy screamed.

"And a shower," Jason added as he wiped the salt water off his face.

Hearing the racket, Lori and Jeff emerged from the cabin and joined them.

"You guys are sure making a lot of noise up here. And look at you two . . . out for a midnight swim?" Lori jibed. "What's going on?"

"Just stay right where you are. You'll find out what's happening in a few seconds," Maisy said. "Here, lean over the rail and watch closely," she insisted.

As Maisy hoped, half a minute later the dolphin resurfaced and blew a stream of water into Lori's face.

"Gotcha, didn't he?" Maisy said and they all laughed . . . except Lori.

Jason scrambled into the cabin and fetched towels for everyone.

"Is this Sea Adventure after hours, or what?" Jeff chuckled.

"Yes it is, and the best part is that it's free," Maisy exclaimed.

That was the last they saw of the dolphin. With the excitement still racing in everyone's minds, it was another hour before they could go back to sleep.

Chapter 8

Ringo Industries

The early morning rays of the sun wove its way through the swaying coconut palms, spilled into the cabin of the *Southwind* and woke Jason up. He turned to face Maisy sleeping beside him, and after a moment of thought decided to let her sleep. Now fully alert, he became aware that the hypnotic sound of the distant surf he heard last night was gone and was replaced by activity on the *Coral Sun Ray* across the narrow harbor. Curious, Jason leaned over Maisy and peeked through the porthole to check it out. Two BMW's moved along the pier and disappeared behind the ship, which immediately brought flashbacks in his mind of the same activity in Wilmingtown.

"Something weird is going on over there," he muttered to himself.

"What? Did you say something?" Maisy said sleepily as she turned over to face Jason.

"Oh, I thought you were asleep. I was just talking to myself," he said.

"I heard you say 'weird.' What's weird?" she asked.

"Well, I was watching cars being loaded aboard the ship across the harbor. They were doing the same thing in Wilmingtown. It blows my mind to run into the same ship in remote Coakley Town almost a thousand miles away working with the same kind of cars . . . expensive ones like BMWs and Lexus, not pieces of junk. What's so special about Coakley? Are there car dealerships here?"

"Of course not," Maisy said. "The nearest place is Nassau . . . a long way from here."

"So, why is this ship in Coakley?" Jason asked.

"I don't have a clue," Maisy said. "I do know that other ships have come into this harbor and unloaded and loaded cars. I remember seeing one ship with a Canadian flag on its mast. So whatever is going on here must support a pretty good car business. The weird thing is that everybody knows everybody on the island, so it's nearly impossible to keep secrets here. Yet the cars and ships are a mystery."

"Well, I think this is more than just a coincidence. I can't stand it any longer. I have to know what's going on," Jason demanded. "If they are selling them, why not go to Nassau where the customers are? I have a bad feeling about this operation. I mean who would guess this little island village to be full of cars like these. I don't see BMW's and Lexus' driving around the dusty streets of Coakley."

Maisy and Jason joined Jeff who was already eating breakfast at the galley table. When Jason mentioned what he saw across the harbor, Jeff rationalized, "There could be a paint shop or special repair shop here. You've heard of companies farming out certain jobs of assembly work to businesses overseas because the labor is cheaper."

"Oh, come on, Jeff. These are BMW's and Lexus's. The manufacturers are multi-billion dollar companies. They have their own assembly plants and paint shops on-site."

"And elsewhere," Jeff insisted.

"No way. They would never send a handful of cars all the way to Andros for a paint job. That would make no sense. Get realistic! I'm in the car repair and restoration business, remember," Jason said.

"Okay, you may be right," Jeff conceded. "So, what do you think is going on here?"

"I don't know but I intend to find out. I'll start bugging people in the village. Somebody here knows about this," Jason insisted.

"Good idea," Maisy agreed. "But we have all tried and told to mind our own business."

Maisy began preparing breakfast for the rest of the crew, and a few minutes later Lori woke up and strolled into the galley.

"Good morning everyone. Well, look at you. I thought I was the cook aboard this rag top and here you are fixin' breakfast," Lori said to Maisy as she patted her on the shoulder and laughed.

"Be my guest," Maisy responded.

"Oh no, please continue. I welcome any help I can get."

"I thought I would treat everyone to a Bahamian breakfast," Maisy offered.

"Wonderful," Jason said. "What's a Bahamian breakfast?"

"Ha. It's a surprise. Just gather together in the cockpit, and I'll have a tropical breakfast served in about ten minutes," Maisy said.

The three headed up the ladder under the Bimini top and sat down. Lori was restless with anticipation, but as promised, ten minutes later Maisy carried a tray of tropical fruit diced to bit size, chunks of white coconut meat, Bahamian bread with fruit preserves, and a pot of hot coffee. She handed the tray to Jeff.

"Here, pass this around," Maisy said with a big smile on her face.

Lori stood up and clapped and Jason shouted, "What a girl! Thanks, Maisy," "Where did get all of this tropical fruit?" Lori asked.

"I had it in my backpack when I came aboard. I brought it from home.

When Maisy returned to the galley, Lori leaned over to Jason and whispered, "You have to be the luckiest guy in the world. What a find! I must admit she's a charmer . . . and cute too. And what manners! She has had some excellent upbringing.' She wants to please everyone." Jason smiled.

Lori volunteered to clean up the breakfast dishes and galley but Maisy insisted she help, too. An hour later, the cleaning chores were completed.

"All right guys, I have to find out what the *Coral Sun Ray* is up to in Coakley. Maisy, is there anything you can tell us about this?"

"Well, as I mentioned before, people have been hush-hush about this. Everyone on the island has been suspicious about Ringo for a long time. The thugs running the show, however, are mean and have threatened to kill several people who have tried to pry into their business," Maisy said.

"Well, that does it. We are not going to go snooping around and get shot. The decision is made," Lori blurted out.

"Just a minute. Let Maisy finish," Jason said.

Maisy continued, "The locals just keep their distance and don't ask questions. We all have noticed the expensive cars going back and forth, but we figured it was just a shop for special custom projects with cheap labor. But I have always wondered why it would be cheaper to ship cars here for repair and then ship them back."

"Exactly," Jason said. "It's not cheaper. Something else is going on. Anyone willing to join me for a sleuth adventure?"

They all agreed, except Lori, but Jeff took her aside, climbed onto the dock and left Maisy and Jason alone for a few minutes. Shortly, they returned and Jeff announced, "Lori has changed her mind. She's coming with us."

The four climbed over the railing of the *Southwind* and walked quickly down the street toward the general store. When they passed the mail boat dock, Jeff grabbed Jason's shirtsleeve.

"Hey, look over there." Jeff pointed to a small motorboat tied to a piling along the dock. "I recognize that boat. It has a dent in the port bow. That same boat came into our marina and shined a spotlight on the *Southwind* in the middle of the night. It belongs to the *Coral Sun Ray* across the harbor. Let's go check out the ship first. Maybe we can con them into giving us a tour," Jeff exclaimed.

"Man, the suspense is building up. I vote we find out what they are doing with these cars first. I saw one of them coming from a building down the road next to the bridge. Then we can check out the ship," Jason suggested. They agreed with Jason's plan.

When they approached the cement block warehouse on the outskirts of the village, they discovered the windows boarded up, no company identification on the outside walls and a high chain link fence surrounding the backside of the property. There was a single, wooden door in the front of the building with two stone steps leading to the entrance. Jason leaped up the steps and knocked on the door while Jeff, Maisy, and Lori stood from a distance at the edge of the road. When no one responded, Jason knocked a second time. There was still no answer.

"How about we walk around to the back? There must be a gate to let the cars through. Maybe we can get in there," Maisy suggested.

They followed the fence to the rear of the building until they came to a large gate, but it was locked with double padlocks.

"Let's follow the fence around the whole property. Maybe there is another gate," Jason suggested.

They continued toward the back of the property, but their progress became difficult as they encountered heavy vines, thick tropical shrubs, and prickly cactus.

"Ow," Lori screamed as a cactus thorn stabbed her in the leg. She looked down and saw blood trickle down to her ankle, which prompted Jeff to reach in his pocket, pull out a handkerchief and blot the spot to stop the bleeding.

"Still hurt?" Jeff asked.

"It stings a little, but I'll be okay. Let's move on," Lori insisted.

"Yeah, just watch your step. It's nasty through here," Jeff said.

"Tell me about it," Lori said and attempted to laugh. As the progress became more difficult, however, Lori hollered out, "Why are we doing this? I'm getting nervous about going any further. We are trespassing and that's illegal."

"Because I want to know what's going on here. I don't think this is an honest business, and it's obvious this operation is connected with the ship. You saw the cars going back and forth from the ship, and you saw that speedboat that snooped around our marina in the middle of the night," Jason said.

"But what if something jumps up and bites me in this jungle?" Lori asked.

"Like what?" Jeff asked. "Cactus?"

"No, you goof. Like a thirty-foot python."

"There are no pythons in the Bahamas," Maisy reassured her.

"But there must me some slithery creature here that just can't wait to have us for lunch," Lori rationalized.

"Will you stop complaining," Jeff ordered. "Keep moving, nothin's gonna have you for lunch."

"All right then. I have another question. Why doesn't this place have a company name? All businesses have their name on their building or a sign in front. There's nothing here. That's a red flag right there," Lori continued.

"Precisely. That's why we are investigating this secretive, mysterious, illegal, red flag operation," Jason said.

"Oh God! I knew I shouldn't have signed up for this cruise," Lori cried. "First it was this little 'bumpy ride' as you called it at sea when it was really a hurricane we went through and almost died, and now we are heading for certain death because of your uncontrolled curiosity."

Jeff let out a huge puff of air while everyone else looked the other way and ignored her. Finally, the jungle growth became so thick next to the fence that their progress came to a halt. Jason hollered back and told them to hold up a few minutes while he attempted to clear away some of the brush. Now struggling on their hands and knees through heavy vines, they finally reached the point where the fence turned ninety degrees to the left. Rounding the corner, they slowly trudged ahead climbing over more cacti and vines until they reached a hole in the fence close to the ground.

"Aha! An open door just waiting for us to enter," Jason said with delight. I knew if we were persistent, we'd find a way to get in."

They squeezed through the hole on their chests and entered the back lot. Jason then saw a weather-beaten wooden sign bolted to the back wall of the building that read *Ringo Industries*.

Several new cars were parked in back, and just beyond they noticed the back door open to the shop. Hurrying across the yard and around the cars, they stopped short of the door to assess their progress so far. Jason signaled to be quiet. Cautiously they entered the warehouse where they spotted several workers painting a Jaguar in the far corner of the building.

"Hello, anyone work here?" Jason shouted in a loud voice that could be heard across the entire shop floor.

"That was stupid. Of course they work here," Lori grumbled and punched Jason gently in his side.

"Okay already. I was just being polite." Jason said in defense.

"That was dumb, too. They are criminals. You don't be nice to criminals," Lori chastised.

"All right you guys, stop it," Maisy pleaded.

The painters immediately looked up and saw the four standing inside the doorway. Immediately one worker ran into the front office while another came over to intercept them.

"How did you punks get in here? This is private property. We don't like no visitors here," he threatened.

"Well, Sir, we were curious about what you do here and wondered if you give tours of your shop?" Jason asked in a sarcastic manner. "Looks like a classy operation to me . . . you know, working on such expensive cars. We don't see these driving around the streets of Coakley. Where did you get them?"

"You dirty little pests! It's none of your business where we get them. Now get out before I blow your heads off," he demanded. Then he turned around and shouted to one of his co-workers standing nearby, "Jingo, come boot these brats out the front door."

But before Jingo could escort them out of the shop, the operations manager threw open the office door and rushed onto the shop floor.

"How did you get in here? I have a good mind to have you arrested for breaking and entering," Jack threatened.

"We did not break in," Maisy corrected him. "We just walked in through a hole in the fence; and besides, there were not any no-trespassing signs on the property. So, if you want us to leave, we'll just leave peacefully, thank you anyway." Maisy grabbed Jason's arm and yanked him toward the warehouse door, "Come on, Jason, obviously we are not welcomed here. Let's go."

"Wait! Not so fast," Jeff interrupted. "Now that we are here, I want to tell you that we saw the *Coral Sun Ray* loading these cars. . . ."

Lori nudged Jeff and whispered, "What are you doing? Let's get out of here while we still have our skins."

"Shut up! It's none of your business what we do here," Jack yelled getting very irritated.

Jeff's temper was boiling over now and refused to listen to Lori.

"You brought these cars from Wilmingtown. We saw you loading them up in the middle of the night. It's more than a coincidence that the same kind of operation is going on here. You must be involved in some kind of stolen car operations. I bet these cars are not intended for sale in the Bahamas, are they?"

Lori nudged Jeff harder and pulled on both him and Jason toward the doorway to get out of there.

"Hey, Jingo, grab her before she escapes," Jack shouted. "I told you to shut up!" Jack screamed as Jingo rushed to the door and blocked their exit.

"No, I want to know where you got these cars and where you are taking them," Jeff insisted. "And one more thing, I noticed a speedboat docked by the *Coral Sun Ray* that was the same one in Wilmingtown snooping around our boat at 2:00 o'clock in the morning. You must know something about that, too." Jeff shouted as his anger hit the roof.

Finally, Lori felt compelled to fight back and fuel the fire, "I bet you crooks had something to do with that body we found floating in the Cape Fear River. Maybe that body came from your ship out there. Maybe that body was someone who used to work here. Maybe we should have you arrested. Where *did* you get these cars, steal them off the streets in the States?" Lori was beet-red with anger.

This time Maisy grabbed Jason's arm and tried to pull him out the door, "Please, let's get out of here. This is getting out of control. Forget the tour," Maisy shouted.

In a fit of rage, Jack pulled out a gun from his pocket and pointed it at Jason and Maisy. "Just hold it right there! You brats are going nowhere. Sanchez, grab some rope and tie them up. They know too much, and I'm gonna turn them over to Franco. He'll get them off the island and dump them at sea." Immediately, Jason latched on to Maisy and tried to make a run for the door, but Sanchez rushed ahead of them and blocked their path.

"One more outburst like that, you fools, and there will be only two of you left, understand? I've killed before, and I can do it again. That's the last warning you are gonna get!" Jack threatened.

Sanchez gathered up rope from his workbench and tied them to two posts near the center of the shop floor. Meanwhile, Jack returned to his office and called Captain Franco.

Now that the four were left alone, Lori became hysterical and started screaming, "I don't want to die. Jason, it's all your fault. I hate you for this!"

"I had no idea we would stumble into a hornet's nest! Don't' you think I want to live, too? I'm not stupid!" Jason shouted.

"You're lying. You always push the limit. You wanted to be a super spy and plunge right into this. You just had to answer that 'mayday' call in Wilmingtown, didn't you? Now our time has run out. Now we're going to be killed!"

"Stop it, you two!" Maisy interrupted. "We are doomed only if we panic. We're smart and we'll figure a way out . . . alive, but we must keep our heads on straight. If he wanted to shoot us, he would have done it already. He had his chance. Obviously, he has other plans. Let's see what he is going to do next. We'll find a way to escape if we all work together and look for an opening when they make a mistake. That's when we make our move."

"Thanks, Maisy," Jason said.

"Oh, that's easy for you to say, Miss Maisy. You're dreamin.' You are livin' in never-never land. You're as hopeless as Jason is. So, what's your magic plan since you claim to be so smart?" Lori snapped.

"I don't have a plan yet. And besides, we have to think this through together, not just me. I said let's wait and see what is going to happen next before we figure our escape plan."

Lori simmered down to just a whimper and wiped her tears on her shirt sleeve. Twenty minutes later Captain Franco and Rafael burst into Jack's office so fast that the doorknob broke when the door slammed against the wall.

"What the hell is going on here?" Franco shouted.

"We have four drop-in guests from your home port in Wilmingtown. They think they know what we are up to. I want you to take them with you and dump them at sea. Get them off the island," Jack insisted.

"Rats! Where are they?"

"Come with me. They're tied up on the shop floor," Jack said.

They left Jack's office and rushed into the warehouse where the four were still tied to the posts. When Jason saw the Captain come through the doorway, he whispered to Maisy, "Look at that man with the gray beard. He's the drunk we saw at Mangos whom I suspected was from the ship."

"Yeah, you're right," Maisy acknowledged.

"Well, what do we have here, a bunch of scum butts, right?" the Captain bellowed. "Looks like you fell into a trouble hole and can't get out."

"Yeah," Rafael echoed. "I recognized your ragtop sailboat across the harbor. You are the ones who found Ram. . . ."

"Shut up, Rafael!" the Captain yelled as he slapped Rafael across his head.

"So, that's who you are," Jason said suddenly. "You are the one who was sneaking around the Wilmingtown marina at two a. m. with a flash light. That body came from your ship, didn't it?"

"Body? What body?" the Captain asked.

"You know what body I mean," Jason said.

"That's not important!" the Captain shouted.

"Oh yes it is. It was one of your crew, right?" Jason pushed on.

Then Jeff piped in "And what are doing with those cars? They were stolen, weren't they?"

By now, Rafael and Franco were ignoring the questions. "Okay, Jack. We'll take these creeps as guests to our ship," the Captain said. "Jack, I need your help escorting them on board."

"Sure thing, Captain," Jack said.

Rafael, Jack, Sanchez, and the Captain untied them from the posts and led them out the back door of the warehouse. Twice Jason tried to wiggle free but Jack reminded him that his loaded gun was still in his pocket and that it would be a lot easier to deal with three prisoners then four. A few minutes later, they pushed and shoved their way up the gangway of the *Coral Sun Ray* and headed toward the officer's quarters on the second level. Captain Franco kicked the prisoners into a vacant cabin and locked their door.

Lori grabbed Maisy's shoulders, shook her, and shouted angrily, "So, now what's your fabulous plan, smarty pants? We are prisoners on a death voyage destined for who-knows-where!"

Jason rushed over to them and ordered, "Stop it, Lori. Leave Maisy alone. She didn't create this problem. We have to remain calm and think about how to get out of this alive.

"They are taking us somewhere. Now we have some time to think of a plan together, in private," Maisy added.

"You're so cool, Maisy. I vote that you be our leader through this crisis," Jason suggested.

"No, we are in this together. We are equal. Everyone's ideas count," Maisy countered. "We should agree that if we have to vote on a plan, we follow whatever the majority vote is. Okay?"

They nodded their heads in agreement. Jason looked out the porthole and saw the *Southwind* tied to the dock across the harbor, which caused him to choke up. He tried to hold back his tears, because he feared that he might not see his boat again. For the next hour, Jason, Maisy, Jeff, and Lori sat in the cabin and speculated what might happen next and where the Captain was taking them. Jason looked out the port again and noticed that the ship was moving. All four glanced out the porthole and watched the ship turn around in the harbor and pass by the *Southwind* docked across the harbor.

"We're heading out to sea!" Lori shouted. "I need to get my stuff off the sailboat!"

"Yeah, don't we all. Maybe we're going back to Wilmingtown," Jeff hoped. "Jason, call for help on your cell phone!"

"Don't have my cell phone. It's on our boat," Jason replied.

"Great. Now what are we going to do?" Jeff asked.

"Let's see which way the ship turns. If we are going back to Wilmingtown, that would be some help," Jason said.

"That would make no sense," Maisy said. "Why would they bring cars from Wilmingtown to Coakley, load them back on board, then turn around and go back to Wilmingtown?"

"You're right. We're not likely going back to Wilmingtown," Jason agreed.

They watched the harbor channel buoys pass one by one until they reached the last one marking the entrance to the harbor. Then the ship made a sharp right turn.

"Well, guys, forget about Wilmingtown. We just turned south," Jason said sadly.

"What's south of us?" Lori asked.

"The rest of Andros Island and the southern half of the Bahamas Islands. After that there are Cuba, Mexico, Central America, and South America," Maisy said.

Jason sat down and did some calculations based on his estimates of the ship's speed and distances. He figured out approximately how many days it would take to reach Cuba, Central, and South America.

"Okay guys, I have a plan," Maisy said enthusiastically.

"Finally," Lori said sarcastically.

"The crew has to take care of us. I don't think they're going to dump us at sea. They are taking us somewhere and probably are going to deal with us at some foreign port."

"How can you be so sure of that?" Lori asked.

"I am not sure of anything, just a hunch, but we have to keep thinking positively. If they wanted to kill us, it would have been easier to do it in Coakley and not on board. They went to a lot of trouble to capture us and drag us on board."

"But if they dumped us at sea, that would be no trouble and there would be no trace of us," Lori countered.

"I still think they are determined to take us somewhere," Maisy insisted.

"Keep talking. What's your idea?" Lori asked.

Maisy continued, "This ship is not stopping any more on Andros Island. There are no more deep-water ports on the south end of the island. I don't think we are going to Cuba either, because that is a hostile country to America and the Bahamas. So, I suspect we are heading to Central or South America or maybe even Mexico to unload these cars on the black market. And if that's the case, we're gonna be on board for awhile. Meantime, maybe we can befriend a member of the crew to help us."

"Why would any crew member want to help us?" Lori asked. "What's in it for him? That would betray the Captain. Is that the same as mutiny? A crew member's not going to risk his life for mutiny."

"Well, we need to come up with a strong incentive for a crew member to betray his ship mates," Maisy said. "Maybe we could promise him that if he is willing to help us escape, we can report the criminal operations to the authorities and claim he helped us escape and arrange for the capture of the criminals. He would not be thrown in jail with the rest of the crew because of his role in destroying the criminal operation, and he would receive a reward for breaking the case."

"Wow! That's a long shot fantasy. You're a dreamer," Jeff said.

"Hey, at least it's a plan. So, what's your plan, Mr. Jeff?" Maisy snapped.

"Uh, well, I don't have one yet," Jeff conceded.

"Right, then it's time for a vote. Unless we can come up with something better, I vote we go for Maisy's idea," Jason suggested. They all agreed.

Just before sunset, their cabin door was unlocked and Juan stood in the entranceway.

"Good evenin' ladies and gentlemen. The Captain has ordered you released while we are at sea. You are free to roam about the ship for awhile," Juan said.

"Hey, that's very kind of you, mate. What's your name, Sir?" Jason asked.

"Juan."

"Juan, what do you do on this ship?" Jason asked.

"I do most anything that needs to be done. I'm a deck hand."

"How long have been aboard?" Jason asked.

"Not very long. They call me a rookie. But it's a good job, most of the time." Juan volunteered.

"Well, thanks for helping us. You are a good seaman," Maisy added.

"Thanks, ma'am. Say, you're kind of cute. What's your name?

"Maisy."

"Where are you from?" Juan asked with a gleam in his eye.

"Andros. I was raised on the island."

"Ha, a local. Don't see many of them," Juan said with heightened interest.

"Oh, there are a few of us left. Thanks again for helping us. By the way you're not bad looking either."

Juan smiled at her, turned around, and walked down the passageway leaving them in the cabin with the door open.

"Brilliant, Maisy. I bet you already have a game plan for Juan," Jason said anxiously.

"As a matter of fact, I do," Maisy said. Then she moved closer to Jason, gave him a hug and whispered, "Jason, trust me with Juan. It's our best shot to get off this ship alive. He's a rookie and seems vulnerable for a little personal persuasion, if you know what I mean."

"All right, go for it, Maisy. So, what's your plan?" Jason asked.

"I don't have the details worked out yet, but did you notice he said something interesting. He said his job was a good job 'most of the time' meaning there is a hint of bad times. If we play up his bad experiences, he might be more willing to help us escape and gain his freedom, too. I'm gonna wait for him to come back to me. I've set the bait. Let's see if he takes it," Maisy said.

"But what if he doesn't?" Jeff asked.

"Then I'll have to sweeten the pot," Maisy laughed.

"Oh my God. I don't want to hear it," Lori piped in.

"Well, one thing is for certain. We must make him think I don't have a boyfriend." Then Maisy looked at Jason and said, "I want to refrain from showing any close affection toward you in his presence for awhile."

"Wow. That's going to be tough for you two," Lori added.

Chapter 9

Prisoners at Sea

In Wilmingtown, Officer Black rushed into Paulo's office.

"That guard at Yarrow Shipping is haunting me to death. I am positive he knows more about the *Coral Sun Ray's* operations than he is telling us. He's stubborn as a mule. I want to bring him in for further questioning. We have to find a way to force him to talk. Grab your hat and let's hit the road," Jerry ordered.

"Great. I've been waiting to get that old toad ever since we first confronted him," Paulo said.

The two officers raced down the highway, crossed the Cape Fear River Bridge, and squealed to a stop at the entrance to Yarrow Shipping. After pausing for on-going traffic, Jerry swerved sharply onto the dirt road and turned on his flashing lights. When they stopped in front of the locked gate, Jerry got out of the cruiser, walked onto the porch and banged on the door. He paused for a few seconds for a response, and then knocked harder.

"I hate to tell you this, pal, but I don't think anyone's in there," Paulo said.

"No way. They wouldn't abandon this operation," Jerry insisted.

Jerry stood still for another half a minute. Finally, he retrieved his flashlight from his pocket and strolled around to the back of the shack. He peered through the back window but could not see anything. Disappointed, he returned to his cruiser. Just when Jerry closed the car door, however, Paulo noticed the window shade inside the guardhouse move slightly to the left leaving a one-inch crack in the window.

"Wait! Jerry, I think I saw something move inside." Paulo jumped out of the car and ran onto the porch. He banged on the door and yelled, "Open up. This is the police. We want to talk to you. I know you are in there, now open up!"

Half a minute passed with no response. Finally, Paulo stepped back several feet and slammed his shoulder against the door with such force that the door flew open and crashed inside leaving a dent in the wall. Jerry stood alone in the room with his gun pointing in front of him and froze in his tracks to listen. Suddenly he heard something fall on the floor in the next room. Holding his loaded gun steadily in front of him, he pressed himself against the wall adjacent to the interior doorway and waited. He heard nothing more. Slowly he peered around the corner and looked into the dark abyss and then slid his hand along the inside wall next to the doorjamb until his fingers felt a light switch. After a quick flip of the switch, he ducked behind the wall again and waited. Still not detecting any movement, he cautiously looked inside the room and scanned the area from corner to corner.

"All right, I know you're in here. I'll give you thirty seconds to come out alive or I'll blast this place apart," Paulo shouted.

The closet door on the opposite side of the room opened slowly and Jago stepped out in clear view of Paulo. "I figured you'd be here, Jago," Paulo said.

"What do you want this time? The ship is not here," Jago said.

"Yes, I know. Why are you hiding? We want to talk to you at police headquarters. Come along."

"I'm not hiding anything." Jago insisted.

"We suspect Yarrow Shipping is smuggling immigrants into this country from Mexico and we think you know what's going on," Officer Black said.

"And maybe you could tell us about Ramos Hernandez," Officer Paulo added.

"Don't know nothin''bout a Hernandez. You hafta talk to the ship's Captain," Jago said. "I'm just a security guard. They don't tell me nothin'," Jago said.

"Oh yeah? Your files say otherwise. And we found some interesting things in the trash bin. You're lying. You know what's going on. Now get in the car," Paulo insisted as he poked his gun in Jago's side. Jerry drove the police car down the dusty road, onto the highway and high-tailed it to police headquarters. The cruiser pulled into the parking lot of the station, and the three walked briskly into the building to Captain Jenkins' office where he was taking a sip of coffee when they rushed into his office.

"Well, what have we here?" the Captain asked, already knowing who Jago was.

"Captain, this is Jago, the security guard at Yarrow Shipping," Jerry said.

"I see. Sit down, gentlemen, please," the Captain said. "All right, guys, tell me what's going on."

"Yarrow Shipping seems to be involved with bringing in illegal immigrants to Wilmingtown, and we brought Jago in for further questioning. We found some documents in his security office and in the trash bin that support our suspicion. We think Jago knows what is going on," Officer Black said.

"I see. Well, Jago, first question is, do you work for Yarrow Shipping or a contract security company?"

"I don't have to answer that question," Jago said defiantly.

"Okay, we could lock you up until you are ready to cooperate," the Captain warned. He repeated the question.

"Yarrow Shipping," Jago responded.

"Does Yarrow Shipping operate any other ships beside the *Coral Sun Ray*?" the Captain asked.

"Nope," Jago volunteered.

"Just the *Sun Ray*?" the Captain repeated.

"You don't hear too well, do you?" Jago sneered.

"Where is the ship now?" the Captain continued.

"I don't know," Jago said.

"Okay," the Captain said.

At that moment, Officer Black handed some papers to the Captain, who then shuffled through them. He retrieved a document about Ramos. He showed Jago the paper. "Do you recognize this person?" he asked Jago.

"Never saw him," Jago said.

"All right. Do you men have any questions then for Jago?" the Captain asked.

"Yes," Officer Paulo said eagerly. "In digging through your files, we discovered you and your operations may be involved with the importation of illegal immigrants from Mexico. And one of those persons was found floating in the river with a bullet hole in his head. We have evidence that that person came from the *Coral Sun Ray*. You agree with that?"

"Since you claim to know all of the answers, you can answer that question for yourself." Jago said with an intimidating grin.

"You're a sassy old crank, aren't you?" Officer Paulo grumbled and sat back down in his chair.

"Yes Sir, I am indeed," Jago acknowledged.

"Get him out of here!" the Captain ordered. "We don't have

enough evidence to hold him. Jerry, keep me informed of any new information about this case."

"Yes Sir, Captain. We'll hop to it," Jerry said.

As soon as they left his office, the Captain finished the last few sips of his coffee, packed up his briefcase, and left the station . . . for Yarrow Shipping. It was rush hour and traffic was backed up on the Cape Fear River drawbridge. He sat motionless in a double line of traffic just a mile from the crossing, and he thought about turning on his siren and flashing red lights, but there was no place for him to move. In frustration, he pounded the steering wheel with his fists. Ten minutes crept by before he could move forward two car links. Five hundred feet from the bridge, he suddenly saw the flashing lights from the drawbridge, the gates come down and the roadbed lift up. Realizing now that this was going to be a very lengthy affair waiting for a ship to pass beneath, he managed to turn around and head back to the other bridge five miles away in hopes of beating the ship heading down river.

It, too, had traffic backed up, but at least the cars were moving. Stewing all the way across the bridge, he managed to make it to the other side of the river and head down the highway toward Yarrow Shipping. He passed the main entrance to the shipyard and proceeded down the highway to the next road on the left. There were no signs at his turn off, just a single lane dirt road that led to the river. Trying to avoid as many potholes as he could, the Captain joggled his way up to a small, unmarked shack next to the riverbank, and he bolted out of his car and ran inside. Sitting at a desk and talking on the telephone was a gruff, unshaven man in his mid-fifties. On the other side of the room was a young blond in a mini-skirt and low-cut tee shirt lounging in a stuffed chair.

"Hey, the police Captain just walked in. I gotta go. I'll talk to you tonight," Jake said quickly and promptly hung up the phone. H stood up and walked over to greet the Captain. "Charlie, how in the world are ya?"

"So, so. Look, we need to talk," Charlie said with a sense of urgency in his voice. Then the Captain paused and looked at the girl sitting in the chair. "Who the hell is she? Can we go somewhere where we can talk in private?"

"Oh, she's my latest honey, Samantha. Hey sweetie, this is my partner, Captain Jenkins. But you can call him Charlie."

"Thanks!" the Captain said.

Samantha sat still in her chair and winked at the Captain and then reached in her purse, retrieved a fingernail file, crossed her legs and started sanding her nails.

"Real lively one there," Charlie whispered to Jake out of earshot of Samantha.

"Yeah, but she's a hot date, if you know what I mean."

"Look, we've got a little problem you should be aware of. You know about those sailboat brats who found Ramos floating in the river? Two of my officers handled the investigation initially and now they won't drop the case. They keep digging. So far, they suspect the *Sun Ray* is involved in smuggling immigrants into Wilmingtown. They're persistent, but I am keeping their investigation at a low key. Hopefully, they'll drop the case soon. Fortunately, they haven't discovered anything about the car operations."

"Well, there's another issue that concerns me and that is Tampico," Jake said. "I heard today that the Mexican police are onto our business and are lying in wait to arrest our crew and confiscate our ship as soon as it arrives. However, I have arranged for a high-ranking gang official from Colombia, South America to meet with Captain Franco in Coakley Town and advise him to avoid Tampico at all costs and sail directly to Santa Marta. Her name is Francesca. She met with him yesterday. Do you know anything about that?" Jake asked.

"No," Charlie said.

"I was going to tell you tonight," Jake said.

"Never heard of this Francesca. Can we trust her?" Charlie asked.

"I guess so. Captain Franco likes her and is willing to head to South America now instead of Tampico. He's convinced there is a bigger market for our cars in Colombia," Jake looked at his watch. "As a matter of fact, the *Coral Sun Ray* should already be underway for Santa Marta as we speak."

"Sounds like a good decision. Who tipped the Tampico authorities?" the Captain asked.

"Don't know, but someone put a bug in their ears," Jake said.

"Well, maybe it's only a hunch. They don't have enough information on us to justify even a search warrant," Charlie said.

"You don't know the Mexican government. If they want to bad enough, they can bulldoze right in and tear our operation apart. After that and a few arrests, they conduct an investigation. But relax. We'll be fine," Jake assured Charlie. "Besides, we know you are the boss. We're not gonna let you down. You went through a lot to set up this international business. And the ingenious idea of smuggling Hispanics is a gold mine in itself."

"We can't make any more missteps. Shooting one of our immigrants and allowing him to fall into the Cape Fear River without fishing him out was a stupid mistake . . . and it's not over yet. I don't want any more screw-ups. Tell Captain Franco, he'd better make sure this Francesca is on our side and not an undercover agent for the police," Charlie warned.

"I've already checked her out," Jake said. "She's okay. She works for the most feared car gang in Colombia. She does have good contacts with the black market, and she has a waiting list of people to board the ship to come to the USA. So, I feel confident we're on the right track. That glitch in Tampico will go away once they learn the ship is not going to show up."

"Okay. By the way, I wouldn't trust that new girl friend of yours. What's her name again?"

"Samantha," Jake reminded him.

"Yes, Samantha. That's it."

Samantha looked up at Charlie and smiled.

The *Coral Sun Ray* continued to make its way westward across the Caribbean Sea, while Rafael, Carlos, Jon and Ming met with Captain Franco in his cabin for an important meeting. The Captain began, "Gentlemen, as you know our unwanted guests have discovered who we are and what we are doing, and as a result, they are a threat to our mission. We have to get rid of them. I brought them on board because I didn't want to risk leaving them with Jack Ringo and Sanchez in Coakley Town for fear of their escape. Now we have to decide the best way to dispose of them. One idea is to dump them overboard. Any other suggestions?"

There was silence as the four stared with blank expressions at the Captain and then looked at each other to see who was going to speak first. Finally, Rafael spoke up.

"Captain, I don't think dumping them at sea is a good idea. We're in international waters and if the Coast Guard found them dead or alive, they could link back to us for kidnapping, car thefts, murder, and who knows what else. We don't need the Feds breathing down our neck. I suggest we keep them peacefully on board until we reach Colombian waters where the U.S. can't touch us."

"Perhaps I did not make myself clear," the Captain said. "I meant we could dump them overboard with anchors tied to their feet. No one would ever find them."

"What would we do with them in Colombia?" Carlos asked the Captain.

"Santa Marta is a rough town. Lots of gangs, drug dealers, criminals walking the streets. They'll dispose of them . . . for a small fee. How about letting Francesca deal with this? She seems to be in charge down there," Jon insisted.

"Ah, I just thought of an idea," the Captain said as he broke out into a big smile. "We'll hold them for ransom and when we get the money we'll turn them over to the gangs in Colombia instead. They'll take care of them properly. Francesca can deal with them at that point."

They all hollered in agreement. "Okay, we'll keep them until we get to Santa Marta," the Captain said.

"Aye Sir. Is that all, Captain?" Rafael asked.

"Yes. You're dismissed. Thanks."

When the crew left his cabin, the Captain climbed up the ladders to the bridge to check on the ship's progress. He stood on the starboard side of the bridge and stared across the endless ocean while Juan manned the helm in the pilothouse. The tropical trade winds blew steadily out of the southeast creating an occasional blast of salt spray that reached the bridge level and showered the Captain's face. He retreated to the sheltered side of the bridge and reached in his pocket, pulled out his pipe and lit it. He took a couple of puffs then walked into the pilothouse to look over the charts. Juan saw this as his opportunity to talk to the Captain in private.

"Captain, have a question for you, Sir."

"Of course, what is it?"

"Well, Sir, who are those passengers we took on board at Coakley?" Juan asked.

"Oh, they are just some kids who wanted to see the world. We invited them to go on a little cruise with us. Ain't that nice of us?" the Captain grinned showing his tobacco stained front teeth. "They're our guests."

"Really? Then why were they locked in a stateroom when they came aboard and then set free? Did they do something bad?" Juan asked.

"Oh, no. It's just a precautionary procedure. Every guest who comes aboard has to go into quarantine for a while. Standard procedure," the Captain chuckled. "You know how it is. We have to play it safe. You see, we can't trust passengers until they have been on board awhile. Don't want strangers sabotaging our mission and ship."

"I . . . I don't believe . . . I mean, uh . . . so they were forced to come on board as prisoners, right, Sir?"

"I didn't say that!" the Captain growled getting irritated at Juan's interrogations.

"Uh . . . yes, you're right, Sir. Well then, what are you going to do with them when we reach port?" Juan asked.

"Now that's none of your business, is it? We're done talking about our distinguished guests. Anything else rumbling around in your thick coconut?" the Captain snarled.

"Well, yes there is, Sir," Juan said pushing his luck. "Where is our next port of call? As a crew member of this ship, I have a right to know, Sir."

"You'll find out soon enough. It's not important now," he grumbled.

In no mood to discuss the ship's business with Juan any longer, the Captain abruptly stuffed his pipe into his coat pocket, walked out of the pilothouse and headed below to his cabin. Juan stood alone, kept his hands on the helm, and steered the ship steady on a course of 260 degrees. He let out a deep breath of frustration.

Thirty minutes later Ming came up to the pilothouse to verify the ship's position and make a minor course change. "Juan, turn left to 250 degrees."

"Yes, Sir. Steady on 250." After a long pause, Juan tried to dig out information from Ming. "So, where are we headin?"

"Why are you askin' me? Don't you know?" Ming questioned.

"Uh, sure, I know. I was just testin' you to see how good a navigator you were."

"What? You're weird . . . asking the navigator if he knows where we are going. Weird!" Ming repeated.

"Yeah, that was kind of funny, wasn't it?" Juan laughed. "Of course you know where we are going. So, what are you going to do when we reach our port?"

"Hit the bars. What else is there to do? Wanna find me a woman. This sea life gets to ya after a while," Ming said.

"Oh yeah? What's your favorite bar there?" Juan asked.

"Don't know, never been there."

"Been where?" Juan asked.

"You know, our next port, of course."

"Uh, yes, that's what I meant," Juan said feeling frustrated more than ever.

"Maintain this course for the next two hours. I'm headin' back to my bunk," Ming ordered as he left the pilothouse and climbed down the ladder to the crew's quarters.

"Crap!" Juan muttered to himself and continued his focus on the compass heading.

The following morning, Juan decided to pay a visit to the mystery guests, knowing that his real motive was to see Maisy. As he skipped along the passageway toward their cabin while whistling a sea chantey, he casually combed his hair, straightened up his shirt collar and tucked in his shirttail. By the time he arrived at their door, he put on a big smile and knocked.

"Hello Juan," Jason greeted.

"Good morning, Sir, hope you all are doing okay," Juan said shyly.

"Yes. Looking for Maisy?"

"Well, yes . . . I mean is she available?" Juan asked.

"Of course. Just a moment." Jason left the cabin door open and called Maisy. She met Juan in the passageway and he reached out to shake her hand. Maisy responded.

"Hey, Maisy. Say, I was wondering if you'd like to go for a walk. I mean wander around the ship a bit. It ain't Central Park, but I can show you some things about how the ship works. Okay?" Juan asked hopefully.

"Sure. Is it okay if I call you Juan?"

"Oh yes, please do."

As Maisy and Juan walked down the passageway, she looked back and gave a thumbs-up to Jason behind Juan's back. The two strolled toward the stern, climbed down the ladders to the main deck and walked to the afterdeck of the ship. Juan then stopped at the railing and began a conversation of small talk with Maisy.

They watched the ship's propeller stir up the sea and leave a frothy wake as far as they could see, and twenty minutes later Juan invited Maisy to go with him below and see the engine room. Juan led the way down the steep ladders until they reach the lower deck of the control room near the keel. It was hot and noisy in the heart of the ship, and seeing sweat bead up on Maisy's forehead, he reached in his pocket, pulled out a handkerchief and gently wiped her face.

"Thanks. How can you guys stand it in this inferno?" Maisy shouted above the shaft noise.

"The engineer is used to it. He takes salt tablets sometimes to replace the electrolytes he loses, but it's still a tough job. Not for me, however," Juan said.

Maisy reached for Juan's hand for a second as a gesture of appreciation, which brought a smile on his face. After watching the turbines and shafts turn, they began their climb out of the depths of the ship into the cooler, salty air. Juan offered his hand to help her up the ladders and when they reached the main deck, Juan was still holding onto Maisy's hand.

"That was really interesting. Thanks for the tour," Maisy said.

"That's okay. I'm glad you liked it," Juan said. "Say, since you are from Andros, how did you get up with these other guys?" Juan asked.

"I met them in Coakley yesterday. We're just friends."

"So tell me, how did you manage to end up on the *Coral Sun Ray?*' Juan asked. "The Captain tells me you are our guests."

"Not exactly. We were too curious about what this operation was all about and were caught snooping around Ringo's and forced on board at gun point," Maisy said.

"Really?" Juan shouted. "But the Captain said you wanted to see the world."

"At gun point? Hardly not! But I'll tell you more later. I want to know more about you. How did you get interested in sea duty? You're obviously pretty smart," Maisy said.

"Thanks. Well, I signed up as a crewman in Wilmingtown, North Carolina, a few weeks ago, and this is my first cruise, but I am learning fast. When I started, I liked the job, but now I am not so sure. The crew is giving me a hard time."

"Oh yeah? Who?" Maisy asked.

"Well, one of them is Rafael. He makes me look dumb, and he won't tell me anything, like where we are going or what our mission is. Ming and even the Captain won't tell me anything either. And I thought at least Ming would let me in on a few things, but he's playing games with me, too. It's like I'm not wanted. I'm not one of them. They make me feel like an outcast," Juan confessed and he looked away from Maisy and out to sea searching for answers.

"You are not an outcast. Maybe this ship is not the right one for you. You can't even trust the Captain who lies to you." She paused for a few seconds and then said, "You know what, Juan. I like you very much. I think you can do much better on another ship." Maisy looked into his eyes and smiled. Then she leaned over and gave him a kiss on his cheek. Juan reached for her hand and they walked together toward mid-ship while he shared with Maisy his life story.

"I'm getting tired. I want to go back to my cabin. How about we meet again tomorrow at the same time, okay?" Maisy suggested.

"Sure, tomorrow. And thanks for your thoughts. I agree, maybe this is not the best place for me."

"Yes, I'm sure there are other ships around with a pleasant crew. We'll talk more tomorrow," Maisy offered.

"You're sweet."

When they reached Maisy's cabin, she gave Juan a quick squeeze on his hand. "Thanks, Juan. See ya tomorrow."

Juan waved goodbye and hustled down the passageway to the crew's quarters feeling as if he had just unloaded a huge bag of cooped up anxieties. He no longer cared about the harassment the crew was slinging at him. He no longer cared if the Captain lied. He was looking forward to getting off the ship.

"Well?" Jason asked with curiosity as Maisy walked in and closed the cabin door behind her. Maisy raised her hand in the air, rushed over to Jason, and met his hand with a smack.

"That was a high five. We're in, baby!" she exclaimed with excitement. "I can see our way out of this mess. I'm making progress with Juan. He is a rookie all right, and he feels betrayed by the crew in that they are keeping too many secrets from him about the ship's mission and where the ship is going. He's not a happy camper. In fact, he's ready to jump ship. So, I am developing a close relationship with him to get him to help us. It's a matter of trust between the two of us." Then she paused for a moment and looked at Jason. "Don't be jealous, silly goose," she said with a smile. "When I meet him tomorrow, I'm going to ask him to help all of us escape. I'm pretty sure he will be willing to do that," she said.

"I know. It just makes me feel uneasy," Jason admitted.

"We want to get out of here alive, don't we? Never mind, that was a dumb question," Maisy said.

Later, there was knock on their cabin door. Jeff opened it and a crewman from ship's galley stood in front of him holding a tray of food. Jeff invited him in but instead the man handed the tray to Jeff and then disappeared down the passageway. Jeff closed the door and sat the tray down on the table and then Maisy took the lead, picked some items off the tray, and began eating. "Come on guys. You'd better eat before I finish this up myself."

The following morning Jason was the first to wake up, and he climbed out of his bunk, stumbled over to the porthole, and looked out across the calm Caribbean Sea. From the position of the sunrise, he could tell they were heading south-southeast. He sat down, drew a crude map of the sea from Andros Island to the northern coast of South America, the east shore of Central American and the East Coast of Mexico. He sketched the island of Cuba in the center of his map. Based on some quick calculations of his estimate of the ship's speed, course changes, and the number of hours they had been underway, he drew a line from Andros southward, then west, then south. He placed an X on his chart about one hundred miles off the West Coast of Cuba. Beside the X, he wrote 'Tuesday 0620.' From this point, he drew a dotted line projecting where the ship might end up if it maintained the same course. The dotted line landed on the northern coast of Colombia.

"Well, that's interesting!" Jason squealed which woke up the entire crew.

Maisy stumbled out of bed first and came over to see what Jason was doing. He was staring at his work of art on the chart table.

"Good morning. You look like you're working on something serious. What's up?" she asked.

"Yeah, I just figured out where we might me going . . . Colombia, South America. Is that what Juan told you?" Jason asked.

"No. He claims no one tells him where the ship is going."

"Really? How could a crewman not know where the ship is going? He's gotta be lying," Jason said and shook his head.

A short while later, there was a knock on their cabin door. Maisy opened it and found Juan standing in the passageway with two trays in his hands.

"Juan, what a treat. You brought us breakfast. Come in, please," Maisy said. "We were just talking about you." Juan entered the cabin and sat the trays on a table. "We think we figured out where the Captain is taking this ship," Maisy said.

"Yeah? How did you find that out?" Juan asked.

"Jason did a little math exercise," Jeff said. "How does Colombia, South America, sound to you? Do you know anything about the ports in Colombia?"

"Well, I have a cousin who used to live in Santa Marta. His name is Raul Matinez, but I have not seen him for more than ten years. I don't even know if he still lives there. Do you think we are heading for Santa Marta?" Juan asked.

"I don't know. I can only guess somewhere along the coast of

Colombia," Jason said. "Have you been to Santa Marta?" Jason asked.

"No."

"Well, there is something else we need to tell you," Jeff interjected. "We know that the cars on board were stolen in the United States and are being taken to a foreign port for sale on the black market. Do you know anything about that?"

"I knew there was a car shop in the village of Coakley Town, but I figured it was just a normal repair shop. I never dreamed it might be a makeover shop for stolen cars. I must admit I was curious one afternoon and tried to go inside to see what was going on, but I was turned away by some tough looking thugs. I thought it was some sort of safety issue or insurance issue, like they didn't want visitors getting hurt," Juan said.

Jason added, "Well, we did sneak into the compound to check it out and got caught. That's how we ended up on board. Your fine Captain forced us on this cruise personally. Ringo Industries in Coakley is a makeover shop for stolen cars, and the mission of this ship is to sell stolen cars in foreign countries. So, I am guessing now that Colombia is our destination for the cars to be dumped onto the black market."

"Hasn't anyone on board talked to you about the car schemes or the ship's mission?" Jeff asked Juan.

"I saw them being loaded in Wilmingtown, always late at night. Sometimes only one car came aboard, sometimes two or three, but I never saw them arrive on a big car carrier like they do from a factory or dealership," Juan said. "A few days after I reported on board I asked the crew what was going on, but they kept quiet. I suspected the cars were stolen all along, but they told me to mind my own business . . . just do my job. I have been unhappy about working here shortly after I reported on board. I don't like working for a bunch of crooks! But I must tell you that there is another crime this ship is involved in and that is smuggling illegal immigrants into the U.S," Juan continued. "These poor souls pay huge amounts of money for their freedom. We lost one of them in the Cape Fear River. He was from Mexico . . . Ramos. He tried to escape but was shot. They left him floating in the river."

Jason's eyes suddenly opened wide, "That's it! That's the one Jeff and Lori found floating in the Cape Fear River alongside the *Southwind*."

"Well, I'll be . . . it's all coming together, isn't it," Lori added.

"Yep," Jason agreed.

"We've got these thugs figured out, except for what they are going to do with us," Maisy said.

"Yeah, and that scares the hell out of me," Lori said. "They are gonna dump us overboard, aren't they?" Her face turned white with fear as she shook her fist at Juan.

"I haven't heard anyone say that," Juan reassured Lori.

"I know. You haven't heard anything from anybody," Lori shouted.

Maisy jumped up, grabbed Juan's hand, and pulled him toward the door. "Juan, we need to go for a walk, get some fresh air," Maisy insisted. Before anyone could respond, she shoved Juan out of the doorway and pulled him down the passageway. They raced down the ladder to the main deck and headed aft. When they reached the afterdeck, Maisy looked at him and began talking.

"Juan, we are all stressed to the breaking point, particularly Lori. We need your help and you need our help. I don't think the Captain is going to dump us at sea. My hunch is that he *is* going to do something with us when we reach the next port; otherwise, he would have already gotten rid of us. We need to find a way to escape quickly as soon as we dock. Are you willing to join us and help with a plan to escape?"

"Well, uh, yes. I think I can," Juan pondered.

Maisy grabbed Juan's shoulders and held him firmly. "Look, Juan, this is a no brainer. You need our help and we need your help. We can work together and get out of this hellhole. All of our lives are at stake. Please join us," she begged.

"Okay," Juan agreed. "Since I know this ship is carrying stolen cars for our next port. I can volunteer to drive the cars off the ship to the storage warehouse in town . . . wherever that is, and maybe I can figure out a way to hide you all in the cars as I drive them off the ship."

"That sounds interesting. Yeah, I like that idea," Maisy said.

"Yes, I think it has possibilities. Do you have any other ideas?" Juan asked.

"Not at the moment," Maisy said. "If we plan this scheme out very carefully, I think it might work. Now, in return for our freedom, we'll swear to the authorities that you were an innocent victim and were not involved with the car thefts. When the rest of the crew goes to prison, you'll be regarded as a hero and get a big reward. I propose that once we get off this ship, we notify the FBI about what is going on. Let's go back to our cabin and talk my friends about your idea, okay?"

"Sure."

They walked quickly back to the cabin and shut the door behind them. Maisy and Juan discussed their plan and sought out other ideas from the group. But in the end, all were in favor of Juan's plan. After weighing the risks and working out some details, Juan left the cabin and return to the crew's quarters feeling confident that his plan had a good chance of success. Later that evening, Juan went to Rafael's office to talk about the ship's arrival in port.

"Rafael, got a few minutes?" Juan asked as he knocked on the opened door.

"Yes."

"I would like to volunteer to drive the cars to the warehouse when we arrive at out next port," Juan said. "I've always been interested in driving one of those high end cars."

"Well, that's interesting! My crew hates that job. When we were in Tampico, street gangs mugged our drivers while trying to deliver the cars. The cars were hot potatoes. Those street jerks will do anything to get their hands on them. I am sure it is the same situation in Santa Marta. It's dangerous. Still want the job?"

"Yes, Sir. I'm not afraid of thugs in Santa Marta," Juan said delighted to learn the name of their next port of arrival.

"Okay. Go tell Carlos you are going to deliver the cars. He always bitches when I order him to do this. I'm sure he'll be pleased. I'll let you know the details when we get to Santa Marta in three days."

"Thanks," Juan said and he turned his back and left Rafael's office to seek out Carlos.

Juan found Carlos asleep in his bunk in the crew's quarters. He leaned over to poke him then quickly changed his mind about waking him up. He stood beside Carlos in silence and watched him for a moment. With his thoughts whirling, Juan quickly left the crew's quarters and headed for the cargo hold to map out his strategy. When he reached the large, dimly lit cargo deck where the cars were parked, he began a methodical evaluation of the best prospects for smuggling Maisy, Jason, Lori, and Jeff off the ship. He looked carefully in the back seats to see which ones had the most room. He checked the trunk spaces. He found empty cardboard boxes and canvas in a pile along the bulkhead of the ship, and putting his hand to his chin, he made a mental note of how he could hide his friends in the back seats and the trunks. Excited with the prospects, he left the cargo deck and returned to the afterdeck to try to think of any possible flaws he might have overlooked. Leaning over the railing and watching the foam being generated by the ship's propellers, Maisy walked up behind him without warning and tapped him on the shoulder. He jumped with fear causing Maisy to grab his arm to keep him from falling overboard.

"You scared me," Juan exclaimed. "I might have been lost at sea."

"Not a chance," Maisy laughed. "You are an experienced seaman, remember? They don't fall overboard."

From a short distance away, Jason, Jeff, and Lori watched while Maisy talked to Juan for a minute and then motioned for them to join her.

"I was about to come to your cabin and talk to you," Juan said. "But we need to talk in private. I don't want the crew to get suspicious seeing us together. How about I meet you guys there in ten minutes, okay?"

"Sounds good. See you there," Jason said and they left Juan standing alone on the stern deck. Juan turned around and looked out to sea again and with a broad smile on his face, he felt a sigh of relief now that the taste of freedom was near. He could hardly wait to share the news with Maisy and the others.

Chapter 10

Plan B

Rafael knocked on Captain Franco's cabin door. "Excuse me, Sir; there is an urgent message for you from Tampico in the radio room."

"Thank you, tell them I'll be there in a little while," the Captain said.

"But the caller wanted you to contact them immediately, Captain."

"All right then, I'll be right there," the Captain muttered.

The Captain climbed out of his bunk and headed down the passageway to the radio room. He sat down in front of the control consul and tuned in the international frequency to make the return call to Tampico.

"Tampico Port Ops, this is *Coral Sun Ray* calling. Are you on frequency, Chico?" Franco radioed. A minute passed before he had to repeat his call. Finally, Chico answered.

"Captain, this is Chico. How do you read me, over," Chico inquired.

"Read you loud and clear. What's up?"

"Are you alone?" Chico asked.

"Yes," the Captain said.

"Well, Sir, I have very bad news. The Mexican authorities raided our offices this morning and confiscated important documents. They suspected we're involved with international car theft activities and decided to step up their investigation. In addition, they found records detailing our smuggling business, so we have shut down our Mexican operations completely and everyone has fled the area. I am slipping out of the country tonight myself. Tampico is finished!" Chico announced.

"Roger. Thanks for the warning. Keep in touch if you can . . . and good luck," Captain Franco said. The Captain turned off the radio, stood up from his chair, left the radio room and walked forward of the ship. He passed his cabin and continued walking toward the bow. Just a few feet from the anchor chain, he stopped, grabbed the railing, and reached for his pipe in his pocket. With the wind to his back, he lit his pipe on the first attempt, took several strong puffs before he took it out of his mouth, and held the pipe in hand. He had a stoic look on his face. Determined to keep his operation afloat no matter what, he smiled at his initial reluctance to accept Francesca's suggestion to sail to Santa Marta instead of Tampico. Watching the sea swells roll past the bow, he tried to unscramble his thoughts about how he was going to set up operations in a new port. After taking a few more puffs from his pipe, he turned around, headed to his cabin, and immediately picked up the ship's telephone.

"Rafael, round up Carlos, Jon and Ming and meet me in my cabin right away. I need to talk to you," the Captain ordered.

"Aye, Sir, right away." A few moments later, the three stood at the cabin door.

"Come in, gentlemen. Have a seat," the Captain said. "I wish to inform you that we have shut down our Tampico operations. That is why we have chosen Santa Marta as our new port operations to off load the cars and pick up passengers for the States. Our contact in Santa Marta is Francesca, so if you hear her name she is our new boss in South America. Treat her with respect. Any questions?" the Captain asked. The crew looked stunned and sat in silence for a moment until Rafael spoke.

"Sir, what happened in Tampico?"

"Some issue with the local authorities. They were getting too suspicious of what we were doing, so Chico closed the office and left."

"That's sounds serious, Sir. Did they find anything about us?" Jon asked.

"I don't know the details and am not going to worry about it. Tampico is history and that's all we need to know."

"Now, Ming tells me we should arrive in Santa Marta harbor in three days. I'll keep you posted if anything changes. You are dismissed," the Captain advised.

"Oh Captain, there is one thing I should tell you," Rafael spoke up. "Juan has volunteered to be our driver to take the cars off the ship when we arrive in Santa Marta. Have any objections to that, Sir?"

"That's fine. Just make sure he gets the job done right. He must understand the risks and the trouble he could encounter with the locals. No screw-ups. You are directly responsible for what he does," the Captain warned.

"Yes Sir," Rafael agreed.

The Captain closed his cabin door and lay down in his bunk to contemplate again the changes that were forth coming.

The following morning, Juan held a tray of food and knocked on Maisy's cabin door.

"Well, hello Captain Juan," Lori greeted him with a laugh. "What pleasures do you bring to us this morning?"

"Room service, Ma'am, just room service. Here's some hot breakfast," Juan said as he carried the tray of hot food into their cabin while Lori shut the door behind him. "Actually, I have some news for you. I stopped by the galley and picked up a tray of food as an excuse to talk to you."

"You are always welcome, my friend," Maisy said. "Sit down and talk to us."

"Rafael let it slip out that we are sailing to Santa Marta, Colombia, and Ming confirmed this morning that it is true. So, Jason, your guesses were right."

Jason walked over to Lori and patted her on the back. "See, Lori, I'm not so dumb after all."

Lori reached out and gave Jason a response slap on his shoulder. "Don't praise yourself too much. We're still prisoners and still could be dumped overboard. Besides, what if they do keep us until we arrive in Santa Marta and we escape into the town? What's gonna happen to us there? None of us speaks Spanish; we don't know anyone there. Maybe we'll be thrown in prison. It's bad news no matter what!" Lori became very emotional about the dreadful possibilities. Jeff immediately ran to her side and put his arms around her.

"Lori, I know it's tough. But like Maisy said, keep thinking positively. We are still alive, we met a crewman who is on our side, and I believe we are going to make it safely home . . . with Juan's help. It may take some time, maybe a few weeks but we'll find a way, right Maisy?"

"You bet," Maisy said and came over to give Lori a hug. Then she whispered in Lori's ear, "Look, I'm going to make it out of here . . . and you are coming with me. You have no choice. End of discussion, pal."

"Yes," Lori whispered back.

Juan sat down and explained his plan to his friends. "Rafael agreed to let me drive the cars off the ship to a warehouse somewhere in the city. So when the ship arrives in port and the rest of the crew is busy securing the ship to the pier, we'll high tail it to the car deck and hide in the cars. I plan to hide one person on the floor of the back seat and another person in the trunk of two cars. Along the bulkhead of the cargo deck, I found some canvas and sheets of cardboard that I'll use to cover the persons in the back seats. Then I'll drive one car to the warehouse, and come back and get the second car. When the coast is clear in the warehouse, we'll make a run for it in Santa Marta and blend in with the crowd. It's risky, but I think we have a good shot at it. This is our best chance to escape before the Captain comes to your cabin and takes you away."

"I love it. Sounds like a great idea, Juan," Maisy said. "But there is one thing that worries me. Won't we stand out in the Santa Marta crowd? We are not natives. We look different, we don't speak Spanish, and we don't act like we are from Colombia. I mean, we'll be spotted a mile away as being foreigners in Santa Marta."

"Not really," Juan assured them. "I have heard Santa Marta is an international seaport. The locals are used to seeing foreigners there. You could be tourists or students for all they know."

"Sounds too easy," Lori questioned. "There must be a flaw in this scheme somewhere."

"All right, where do you think it is?" Juan asked.

"Well, for one thing," Lori continued, "What if one of the crew spots us getting in the cars to make our escape. Or what if someone stopped you when you drove off the ship and decided to check out that lump under the canvas or cardboard . . . or even wanted to check to see what was in the trunk."

"I will make certain no one is on the car deck when you hide," Juan said. "That's why I chose the time when everyone is busy docking the ship. As far as someone stopping me while driving, that's a risk I'll have to take. I'll figure out something if that happens."

"Good plan, Juan. Next question. Where can we find help in Santa Marta?" Maisy asked.

"I don't know. We'll find out when we get there," Juan said.

"Wait, you said you had a cousin in Colombia? Can that person help us?" Jeff asked.

"I have not heard from him for a long time. I don't know where Raul is. I can try to find him, but we'll have to blend in with the city crowd in the meantime, find a temporary place to hide."

"How about the police?" Jeff asked.

"No. Raul told me once that they couldn't be trusted. They're tough on foreigners. Investigations can take a month, I hear. Meanwhile, they can hold you in custody until they decide what to do with you. That's not what you want. Sometimes they are in cahoots with organized gangs."

"Wow! Forget that route," Jason said. "Thanks, Juan. We can do this, right guys?"

"Yes," came the unanimous roar from the group. Juan looked at his watch and told them he had to get back to work before the crew started looking for him, and he left their cabin carrying the empty tray back to the galley.

At the Tiki Bar on the south side of Atlanta, the bartender wiped the counter with a damp rag and placed two beer mugs in the washer. It was almost midnight. Gina sat alone nursing her usual gin and tonic in a booth in the back of the bar unnoticed by two patrons sitting at the counter. A moment later, her partner, Gunner, strolled in the front door. He squinted in the darkness in an attempt to see the back booth, but he could not see Gina. The bartender recognized Gunner and pointed quietly in the direction of the booth while continuing his chores. Gunner looked toward the booth again but his eyes still had not adjusted to the darkness. As he got closer, he spotted Gina.

"There you are. I could not see you with that black outfit in the darkness."

"That's because you're blind, dumb head," she remarked.

Gunner ignored her sarcasm and ordered a beer from the bartender.

"So, how many cars have you grabbed this week?" Gunner asked.

"Two. And you?" she asked.

"One. I almost got busted, so I decided to lay low for a few days. I assume the *Coral Sun Ray* is due back in Wilmingtown soon. Have you heard when they left Tampico?" Gunner asked.

"No and that bothers me. Captain Franco usually calls me when they off load their cargo in Tampico and head back to North Carolina, but I have not heard from him," Gina explained.

"Why don't we call his boss, Captain Jenkins, in Wilmingtown? He knows what's going on."

Gina looked at her watch. "Yeah, why don't you just do that. It's midnight. I am sure he is sitting at his desk right now waiting for your call," Gina sneered.

"Ow. You are a nasty one tonight," Gunner responded.

"Just taking after you," Gina smiled.

"Peace. Let's call a truce, okay," Gunner pleaded.

"Okay. Call the Tampico port office. There's a security guard there all of the time. He'll know when the ship left," Gina ordered.

Gunner reached for his cellular phone in his pocket and scrolled down the list of phone numbers until he came to the one for Tampico. After a couple of rings, he heard a strange voice answer in Spanish.

"Uh . . . is this the *Coral Sun Ray's* office in Tampico?" Gunner asked.

"Maybe. Who's calling?" the voice switched to English.

"Has the *Coral Sun Ray* left port for Wilmingtown?" Gunner asked.

"The operations here are under the control of the police now and are under investigation. What is your name and where are you calling from?" the officer requested.

Gunner, taken aback, paused and then said, "Well, I have a friend on board who is coming to visit me. Don't know anything about the ship. Just wanted to know when I could see my friend."

"What's your friend's name?" the officer asked.

"Well, thank you for the information," Gunner said intentionally avoiding the question and hung up.

He looked at Gina with a fearful stare and then said, "The ship's in trouble. The police have raided the Tampico office and the ship never arrived. I suppose someone tipped off Captain Franco before he arrived in port. Sounds bad." Gina looked at Gunner with a blank face and sat in silence for a few moments. She then stood up and said, "I don't know what to think. I guess we'd better call Charlie Jenkins tomorrow. Meet me here at 9:00 o'clock in the morning, okay?"

"Yep, 9:00 o'clock."

Gina left the bar and Gunner ordered another beer from the bartender. Suddenly an idea popped into his head and he pulled out his portable telephone again and called the international marine operator. When the operator answered, he asked her to call the Vessel *Coral Sun Ray* on the short wave marine telephone circuit. Based on his time estimates, he thought the vessel was near the Bahamian Islands. The operator agreed to try it and told Gunner to stand by.

Moments later Gunner received a call back from the marine operator. "Mr. Gunner, I have a Mr. Rafael on the line from the *Coral Sun Ray*. Go ahead please."

"Rafael! This is Gunner calling from Atlanta. What happened in Tampico?

"Things got too hot," Rafael said. The local authorities raided the place, and we were advised to stay away from Tampico. Now we are heading for Santa Marta, Colombia, to set up operations there."

"Oh? Colombia huh. When will you be back in Wilmingtown? I have cars waiting for you," Gunner said.

"In about three weeks."

"All right, smooth sailing, Rafael. I'll let Gina, Merinda in Tampa and Dingo in Miami know the latest news," Gunner said.

The following morning Gunner met Gina at the Tiki Bar and began telling her the news from Rafael, but before she had time to take her coat off and sit down, she threw the newspaper in front of his face.

"Shut up and look at this," she said nervously and pointed to the headlines on page four.

Gunner read the article carefully. "Oh my God! This is incredible. I must call Captain Franco now. Rafael said nothing about Coakley or Wilmingtown operations," Gunner said.

"You got that right," Gina repeated.

Gunner leaped up, grabbed Gina by the arm, and pushed her to the front entrance of the bar and out the door. They ran down the street to his parked car and jumped inside where they could be alone and quiet. He reached for his cell phone again and dialed the marine operator. Soon he heard the operator call the *Coral Sun Ray*. But after several attempts, the marine operator explained that there was no one available to take the call on the ship.

"This is terrible! I need to talk to someone!" Gunner cried.

"Call Charlie Jenkins in Wilmingtown," Gina urged. Gunner picked up his phone again and dialed Charlie's number.

"Wilmingtown Police . . . Captain Jenkins here," the voice said.

"Charlie! This is Gunner. Have you read the paper yet?"

"What? What are you talking about?" Charlie asked.

"I am talking about a news article from Tampico, Mexico. It's about the *Coral Sun Ray* . . . and you. It's not good—"

"Wait! What article? I read the paper today, and I didn't see anything like that in our paper," Charlie said with some concern.

"Well, the article says that the Tampico Police raided the *Coral Sun Ray* Offices in Tampico, Mexico and confiscated incriminating documents. They said they found evidence that the *Coral Sun Ray* was involved in a major international car theft ring and smuggling immigrants into the port of Wilmingtown, North Carolina," Gunner said. "And they mentioned the car shop in Coakley on Andros Island. The Mexican Police found everything!"

"I gotta see that article," Charlie said.

"But the worst part is that the article mentioned your name as the person in charge of the whole international crime operation. The words

'Captain Charles Jenkins of the Wilmingtown Police Department' were clearly spelled out in print," Gunner explained.

"Crap. This is unbelievable! I've got to contact Captain Franco immediately," Charlie hollered over the phone.

"I already tried a few minutes ago but could not reach him. Good luck. Keep me posted," Gunner requested.

"Yeah. I've got to get a copy of that article. Where did you find that story?"

"In the *Atlanta Journal*, this morning's edition. I bet you could find it on the Internet, or I could FAX a copy to you if I can find a FAX machine," Gunner offered.

"No, I'll find a copy," Charlie assured him.

"What are you gonna do now, assuming this is true?" Gunner asked.

"I don't know. I just don't know." Charlie murmured and abruptly hung up the phone.

Gunner then turned and looked at Gina. "This is the beginning of the end of our empire, Gina. I'm quitting. I'm heading to the West Coast to find a real job. It is going to be hell around here. Atlanta, Wilmingtown, Coakley, Tampico, Santa Marta, Tampa, Miami . . . everywhere our operations have touched hands is going up in smoke. I'm outta here," Gunner yelled. He leaned over, gave Gina a kiss, and ordered her out of his car. She stared at him in complete disbelief, total confusion and then in desperation. She opened the door, stepped out, walked slowly down the street, and disappeared in the Atlanta crowd. He started his car, pulled out of the parking lot, drove down the street, and headed west to California, leaving Gina behind.

Later that morning, a bulletin lay on the Chief of Police's desk when his secretary walked into his office. Since the Chief was down the hall having coffee with his fellow officers, she could not help but glance at the note. It was marked urgent. Finding this irresistible, she sat down in his chair and read the bulletin:

> *From:* *Port Authority – Tampico, Mexico*
> *To:* *Chief of Police – Wilmingtown, NC, USA*
> *Ref:* *Criminal Activity – Vessel Coral Sun Ray*

Please be advised that we have suspicions that the vessel, Coral Sun Ray, is involved with international criminal activities, namely the importation of stolen cars from Wilmingtown, North Carolina and the smuggling of immigrants from Mexico to the United States through the port of Wilmingtown. On Thursday, we raided their operations office at the port in Tampico and seized important evidence that supports our suspicion. Specifically, we found records of a criminal nature that document that the ship has loaded stolen cars at a pier along the Cape Fear River and received payments from illegal immigrants for their freedom in the U.S. These immigrants came from Mexico and Central America. The records named a Captain Charlie Jenkins in Wilmingtown as the head of the international crime operations and Captain John Franco as the captain of the Coral Sun Ray.

We have also found that the operations have an auto rebuilding shop in Coakley Town, Andros, Bahamas called Ringo Industries. Apparently, the Coral Sun Ray transports the stolen vehicles to Coakley, remakes them, and ships them to Tampico for sale on the black market. We are in the process of notifying the Bahamian authorities to investigate these activities on their soil. Meanwhile, we have learned that the Coral Sun Ray has departed Coakley Town and presumably was heading for Tampico. We expected the ship to arrive several days ago but it has not entered our port at this time. Since the ship's Captain may have been alerted to our investigation, he may have diverted the ship to another port. We intend to keep you posted of any new events and findings as we continue to investigate. Please keep us posted of any new activity related to this case.

Thank you for your cooperation,
Simon Juarez – Director Port Operations, Tampico

Shocked when she read the part about Captain Jenkins, she grabbed the bulletin and stuffed it in her pocket. When she walked out of the Chief's office, however, she thought that perhaps the chief had already read it and would be looking for it when he returned. Frightened, she hurried back into his office and placed the paper back on his desk just as she found it. Uncertain as to what to say to the Chief or the Captain, she walked down the hallway to the break room where she found the Chief and Officer Black laughing together over a joke the Chief had just told. She stood frozen in the doorway and stared at them until the Chief caught a glimpse of her.

"Looking for me?" the Chief asked.

"Uh, no Sir," she said. With her mind scrambled with anger,

disbelief, sympathy, and fear, she quickly turned around and hurried back to her desk at the other end of the building. Before she sat down, however, she felt compelled to walk by Captain Jenkins's office to see if he were there. His office was empty. Realizing now the seriousness of the situation, she returned to her desk, sat down and placed her face in her hands. Then she walked down the stairs to the personnel office and informed the officer on duty that she did not feel well and was going home. After scribbling a few words on a note pad and leaving it on the Chief's desk, she headed out the door. Five minutes later, the Chief returned to his office and read the bulletin for the first time. He read it with intense interest . . . then his eyes suddenly stopped when he came to the words 'Charlie Jenkins'. He read his name again in disbelief.

"No! It cannot be true. There must be another Charlie Jenkins in town," he said aloud. He read the bulletin again to make sure he was not dreaming. Captain Charlie Jenkins's name kept flashing before his eyes. He set the paper down on his desk, paced the floor and mumbled, "Surely, Charlie is not involved with this," repeatedly. Very dismayed, he walked downstairs to Charlie's office to confront him only to find it empty. Now feeling betrayed he searched the headquarters, but Charlie was nowhere to be found. He called his home, but there was no answer. His emotions then turned to anger as he stood before his window and stared at the Cape Fear River flowing lazily southward. "How could he do this? Damn!" he hollered at the blank walls in his office and then slammed his fist on his desk.

On Coakley Town, a Bahamian police officer pounded on Jack Ringo's office door. After several knocks, Jack opened the door, smiled, and invited the officer in.

"Hey, how have you been, Carl?" Jack greeted him.

"My boss in Nassau just received a message from the police in Tampico, Mexico. It seems they raided the *Coral Sun Ray*'s offices there and shut down the local operations. The message said they found records that mentioned a stolen car remake shop here in Coakley, and so my boss sent me here to check it out," Carl said.

"I see. Did the Mexicans seize the ship?" Jack asked.

"Well, my boss said the ship never showed up in Tampico. It seems the police wanted to interrogate the Captain but got tired of waiting and decided to invade their port offices instead. The trail is getting hot. What should I tell my boss in Nassau?" Carl asked.

"Well, you just tell him that you checked it out and there is nothing going on here illegally. There's only a poor, local auto repair shop that's barely able to survive on local business. Tell him that this shop is not involved with illegal auto thefts or whatever is going on with the *Coral Sun Ray*," Jack insisted. "Tell him the ship stopped here for repairs . . . shaft bearing repairs."

"I know, but the bulletin from Tampico said that the Mexican authorities found evidence that you are directly involved with the international car theft ring," Carl argued. "What are you gonna do about that?"

"You heard what I said. Tell them the message is all a big lie. It's a Mexican scam." Jack then reached in his safe behind his desk and pulled out a wad of Bahamian bills. "Here, take this and buy your honey a nice present."

Carl reached out, took the cash, and stuffed it into his pocket. "Thanks. I'll see what I can do to cool the authorities down in Nassau," Carl said.

"Good. I knew you would find a way. Oh, by the way, you will let me know ahead of time if your boss or his cronies decide to pay us a visit won't you?" Jack said with a slight concern in his voice.

"Yes Sir," Carl affirmed.

Jack walked to the door and waved his hand for Carl to follow. Carl took the hint and left Jack's office smiling over the reward he just received from his friend.

Chapter 11

Grand Escape

That same morning Office Black rushed into Officer Paulo's office at the Wilmingtown Police Department and shut the door behind him. Holding a copy of the local paper, the Wilmingtown News, in his hands, Jerry quickly grabbed a chair next to the wall, pulled it up to Paulo's desk and sat down.

"Look at this!" Jerry said as he thrust the paper on Paulo's desk. Office Paulo glanced down the page until his eyes fixed on the headlines:

Local Police Captain Involved with International Auto Theft and Smuggling Rings

"Are you kidding me? Is this for real?" Paulo shouted.

"Shhhh, not so loud," Jerry cautioned. "I don't know, but the article originated in Tampico, Mexico where the vessel *Coral Sun Ray*'s offices were raided. Doesn't the *Coral Sun Ray* sound familiar?"

"It sure does," Paulo said. "But what about old Charlie Jenkins? He's our boss!"

"Yeah, what about Charlie? Sounds like he was our boss . . . if this is true," Jerry said.

"I can't imagine someone making up a story like this and then a newspaper publishing it without checking facts," Paulo said. "It's gonna hit the fan now! We'd better lay low. Not say a thing to anybody. Just keep our mouths shut and our ears to the wall to see what happens next. This is really bad stuff."

"Right. Good advice. I'll see you later, pal," Jerry said as he abruptly shoved his chair back against the wall and left his office. Jerry walked quickly past Charlie's office and found his door shut and the light out. Then he discovered that Charlie's secretary had called in sick earlier that morning.

Twenty miles north of the Florida/Georgia State line on Interstate 95, Jake and Captain Jenkins drove furiously toward Miami in a black

BMW. At regular intervals, Jake looked at the speedometer in front of Charlie and watched the needle wavering around 90 miles per hour.

"Slow down, man! That's all we need is to get picked up for a stupid speeding ticket. You know when the police stop you they check to see what else they can dig up in your record."

"I know, I know. I don't need a lecture. I just want to get to Miami before the police issue an all-States bulletin on us. There's a flight to Colombia that leaves Miami in twelve hours. I think we can just make it," Charlie said.

"You came by the office and grabbed me in such a panic, that I have not had time to think of anything. What are we going to do in Santa Marta?" Jake asked.

"Santa Marta is the end of the line for us. That is going to be our new home," Charlie said.

"You are joking, aren't you?" Jake questioned.

"No way. We are wanted criminals now. They'll hunt us down like hound dogs. We'll be safe in Colombia. Besides, Francesca will find us a place there and get us a job. Santa Marta is a big city, like New York. We'll blend right in with the locals," Charlie reassured Jake.

"Aren't you forgetting something? We don't speak Spanish, we don't look Spanish, we don't act Spanish, we don't eat Spanish food, and we don't have Spanish money. We'll stand out like a hen in the fox house, as the saying goes," Jake warned.

"That's not how the saying goes, but never mind. Santa Marta is an international city, like Rio, like San Francisco, any large seaport. They speak all languages there. They're used to seeing people from all cultures. We'll fit right in. Francesca will see to that."

"You're putting a lot of faith in Francesca. Have you met her?" Jake asked.

"Well, uh, no, not yet. But Captain Franco told me about her," Charlie hedged.

"That's what I thought. You don't know a damn thing. We are just running from the law for the sake of running. We may be jumping into a boiling pot of tar. We don't know what's going to happen to us!" Jake argued.

"All right. What's your solution, since you think you're so damn smart? Do you want me to stop the car on the highway and just sit here and see what happens next?"

"Man, you really are stupid! Maybe you should just get out and disappear in the woods while I drive on by myself and find a place in

Miami to hide instead of Colombia!" Jake threatened.

"Not me, pal! If that happens, you're the one that gets dumped along the side of the road. It's my car, remember? I invited you, remember? I'm your boss, remember? It's not the other way around," Charlie threatened.

"Okay. We're more likely to escape using the brainpower of the two of us than just one. Drive on," Jake said in a huff.

The *Coral Sun Ray* made its way toward the harbor of Santa Marta when Juan spotted the snow-covered peaks of the Sierra de Nevada Mountains on the horizon just south of Santa Marta. He grinned knowing that his ordeal on this ship was nearing the end. Letting go of the ship's helm for a moment, he turned around and asked Ming to come to the pilothouse to see the mountain peaks ahead. He handed Ming the binoculars.

"That's the northern tip of the Andes all right. In a few hours you should see the coastline of Colombia," Ming remarked. "I'll check our position on the chart with the GPS to see how far away that is." Ming left the pilothouse and walked back to the chartroom.

When the *Coral Sun Ray* was fifteen miles off shore, Ming picked up the ship's telephone and called the Captain to advise him that they were three hours from the Santa Marta harbor buoy. Shortly afterwards, the ship-to-shore telephone rang in the pilothouse.

"*Coral Sun Ray,*" Juan answered.

"This is the international marine operator. I have a call for Captain Franco. Is he onboard?"

"Yes, Ma'am. Hold on for a minute while I transfer this call to his cabin."

"This is Captain Franco, go ahead please," he informed the operator.

"Roger, standby for your party," the operator said and there was a brief pause.

"Hello, John, this is Francesca. Are you near Santa Marta?"

"About three hours out," the Captain informed her.

"Excellent. How are you fairing today?"

"Doing well at the moment, considering all that has happened in Tampico."

"What's the latest there?" she asked.

"The police raided our offices and shut down the operations," he growled.

"Yeah. You heard right. And Chico has left the country. Don't know where he went, but he got out of there just a few hours before the raid," Francesca informed John.

"Yes, I heard that too," John said.

"Well, there's more bad news," Francesca continued. "The Tampico Police have notified the authorities in Nassau about your activity in Coakley Town. They confiscated some of your records at the Tampico office that described what was going on at the car shop in the village."

"Really! Well blow me down! I didn't know about that. Man, Jack had better chase them away from Coakley Town or else. Come to think of it, Jack has friends on the local police force. He'll take care of those cranks," John replied, a bit concerned.

Hope you're right," Francesca said. Everything is all set for your arrival here. We have a secluded warehouse in town to conceal your cargo, and I have a list of eleven people who want to go to the States. They have already paid some upfront money."

"Good. Have you made docking arrangements?" the Captain asked.

"Yes, when you enter the harbor you will see on the starboard side a concrete dock with a large blue warehouse behind it. Keep going past it until you come to a small brown building with a wooden pier in front. The building has a circle F painted on the front. That will be your dock."

"I suppose the circle F is you, right?" John joked.

"Yes, but that is a long story . . . later," Francesca said.

"Will you will need a tug, Captain?" Francesca asked.

"Yes, any suggestions?" the Captain asked.

"Of course, we have our own tug. He is a member of our organization. When you reach three miles from the harbor entrance, call Sierra Marine on 122.9. His name is Captain Juarez. He runs a small blue and white tug. He's expecting you." Francesca continued. "When you arrive in the harbor give me a call, too, and I'll come to the dock to meet you."

"Good deal. Thanks."

"No problem. Oh, don't let anyone off the ship until I arrive. I need to talk to you about our set up here. And don't worry about Customs. They don't work on Sundays, so you can off load the vehicles without their interference as soon as I come aboard. They'll show up first thing Monday asking questions, but I'll tell you how to handle them when I see you in a few hours. Smooth sailing, John," Francesca said.

Lori, Jeff, Jason, and Maisy stood near the bow looking at the snow capped peaks in the far distance. Maisy, in particular, felt relieved now that land was in sight and their nightmare would be over soon. But Lori remained fearful. Her face was drawn with uncertainty as she contemplated the possibility of being shot on the streets in a strange country or put in prison if their plan failed. Jason and Jeff, on the other hand, were optimistic and anxious to get moving on their escape plan.

As the ship passed the outer harbor buoy, Juan knocked on his friends' cabin door to go over the latest details of their escape. Realizing no one was there and time was of the essence, he quickly searched the decks until he found them standing along the rail amidships looking at the harbor landmarks.

As he approached them, he whispered, "Hey, meet me in your cabin in five minutes. It's urgent," and continued his way towards the bow. They chatted among themselves until Juan was out of sight and then rushed back to their cabin. When Juan knocked once on their door, Maisy grabbed his arm and jerked him inside.

"Okay, here's the deal," Juan began panting for breath. "We should be docking in Santa Marta harbor in about half an hour. Rafael and the Captain are meeting someone by the name of Francesca as soon as we tie up. I've heard that she is in charge of the Colombian operations in terms of stolen car sales and smuggling immigrants out of the country.

"Fantastic. When do you want us to meet you on the cargo deck?" Maisy asked.

"Just wait here until it is safe. I'll come get you. I have to make sure no one is in the cargo area before we go down there. I'm going there now to pick out the cars we are going to use. I may have to jockey some around to make sure the ones I want are in front to drive off the ship first. And I want to get the canvas and cardboard covers ready. As I said before, the best time to make our move to hide in the cars is when the ship is actually docking. I know from experience, all hands will be outside manning the lines, ramps, and so forth."

"How come you are certain your boss is not going to call you for help in the docking process? After all, you are the rookie on board. Doesn't he think you need to learn the ropes of docking, too?"

"Normally, that would be the case, but Rafael has specifically ordered me to stay clear of the entire docking operations. He thinks I'll just be in the way, a hindrance," Juan said. "That makes a perfect setup for us, right?"

"Right, but what a vote of confidence! No wonder you're unhappy. We'll stick together. We're gonna help you, pal, get a real shipboard job," Maisy said as she walked up to him and gave him a hug.

"Okay, guys, keep a low profile and be careful. Get whatever you think you will need that can be carried in your pockets and perhaps a light bag. No suitcases and heavy stuff," Juan reminded everyone.

"We didn't bring anything on board except the clothes on our backs, remember?" Lori said to Juan. "We were taken as prisoners."

"Yeah, that's right. See you guys shortly," Juan said and left their cabin.

The four stood in silence anxious for their escape. Then Jeff was the first to speak.

"There is one thing no one has brought up yet. The Captain obviously has plans for us. What if he comes to our cabin before we arrive at the dock and pushes us overboard? That way he would not have to deal with us in port."

"We went through this already," Maisy insisted. "If he wanted to throw us off the ship, he would have dumped us at sea long ago, not in a busy harbor. There would have been far less chance of finding our. . . our . . . well, this is a ridiculous conversation. Forget it. We are going to get of this ship very soon. Period."

"Okay. You have been right so far," Jeff admitted.

From the pilothouse, Carlos steered the ship toward the harbor entrance two miles ahead. Somewhat bored, he left the helm and walked to a counter top behind him, emptied stale grounds from the coffee urn, added a fresh coffee mix from Costa Rico, refilled the water reservoir and turned the unit on. Just as he was focusing on his coffee preparations, Captain Franco appeared in the pilothouse.

"Good afternoon, Carlos. Have the ship on autopilot, do you?" the Captain tested Carlos. "In a busy harbor, no less!"

"Uh, no sir. I just left for a minute to make some coffee. There's no ship traffic coming toward us, so I thought it would safe if I left the wheel for a few minutes," Carlos attempted to convince the Captain.

"That's against all rules of the sea . . . that was stupid judgment. You never know when a ship or boat will cross our path. Get back on the wheel and pay attention to where we are going. I'll talk to you later," the Captain scowled as he scanned the harbor with his binoculars. Then he turned to Carlos again and added, "Make sure there is enough coffee for me."

"Yes, Sir, there're ten cups in the urn, Sir."

"That's fine."

The Captain then went into the chart house to talk to Ming who was stooped over the table plotting the course through the harbor with a set of dividers and parallel rulers.

"All set to navigate into the harbor?" the Captain asked.

"You bet, Captain. As soon as you announced where we were going to tie up, I immediately came in here and got the charts ready. The entrance channel and the harbor have good water. No shallows, sandbars, or obstructions in the channel to worry about."

The Captain told Ming about the tug, "Once the tug has tied up to our bow, stay on the bridge in case we need your help."

"Yes, Sir Captain," Ming acknowledged.

"When the lines are secured to the pier, get some rest, but stay on board until I send out the word for liberty for the crew," the Captain advised. Ming walked out to the port side of the bridge with his binoculars to take bearings on landmarks ahead and then returned to his charts and plotted the ship's position. When he walked by Carlos standing at the helm with a fresh cup of coffee in his hand, the aroma caught his attention.

"Like some?" Carlos offered.

"Yeah, where did you get that?"

"Over there." Carlos pointed behind him toward the table. "Made it myself, thank you."

"No way! You make coffee that tastes like black bilge water," Ming said as he grabbed his own throat and pretended he was gagging.

"Yep. So you don't want to drink my rotgut. Actually, that would leave more for me if you didn't," Carlos said with a toothless grin.

Ming left the pilothouse without the coffee while Captain Franco stood on the port side of the bridge and continued to gaze at the harbor entrance ahead. He then asked Carlos to call Rafael and Jon to the bridge for docking instructions. In less than five minutes, the two appeared before the Captain.

"Let's go in the pilothouse so Carlos can hear this, too," John ordered.

The Captain explained the arrival procedures for Santa Marta and ended with comments on his meeting with Francesca as soon as the gangway was put ashore. He also informed everyone that no one was to go ashore until after he had his meeting with Francesca. Finally, he ordered Rafael to go below and padlock his distinguished guests in their cabin right away until further instructions. The Captain then dismissed all but Carlos and Ming from the bridge.

When the ship reached the inner harbor, the Captain radioed the tug, Sierra Marine, for assistance. Immediately, Captain Juarez responded.

"Good afternoon, Captain Franco. This is Captain Juarez at your service, Sir. I have you in sight just entering the harbor. Correct?"

"Yes, good day, Captain. We're just passing the last channel buoy in the inner harbor," Captain Franco announced.

"Roger on that. You'll see a small blue tug waiting for you just ahead in the middle of the harbor. I'll pick you up on your port bow. Have your crew toss a line down to me when I come along side. Do you need a pilot to assist you in docking?" Juarez asked.

"No Sir. We can manage ourselves," the Captain informed Juarez.

"Aye, Captain. See you shortly, out."

Rafael returned to his office on the cargo deck below and searched for a padlock.

"Ah, there it is . . . and the key is in the lock. Perfect," he mumbled to himself. He left his office, climbed to the next level and headed straight to the passengers' cabin. Opening the compartment door quickly without knocking, he found the four sitting on their bunks. Expecting to see Juan, the four jumped up in surprise.

"You scared us. What do you want?" Lori shouted.

"Just a security check. We're arriving in port. The Captain has ordered you confined to your quarters. Enjoy your detention," Rafael laughed. Without further ado, Rafael slammed the door shut and snapped the padlock closed on the outside of the door. The four heard the lock click and waited a few minutes to assure Rafael had left the area. Then Jason rushed to the door and attempted to open it. The latch would not budge.

"Well, what's plan B?" Jason asked his friends. We didn't expect this to happen."

"We're still not in trouble. Juan will get us out," Maisy said.

"Oh yeah? You are assuming Juan has the key, Miss Maisy. You're forgetting Rafael has the key, not Juan," Lori said. "Your plan has failed!" Tears began to flood her eyes and she became hysterical.

"Calm down. You're giving up, Miss Lori. I'm not. Juan is smart. I am sure Juan will find the key or will cut off the lock. He's determined to get us off this ship and gain his freedom, too. He's not going to let a simple padlock stop us. Our plan has not failed," Maisy was getting increasingly irritated at Lori's pessimism.

The Captain announced on the ship's intercom, "Attention all hands. Man your stations for port arrival." Rafael rushed back to his office, hurriedly tossed the key on his desk, and ran up to the main deck to prepare for the tug to come along side. Captain Juarez maneuvered his tug to the port bow of the *Coral Sun Ray* as planned and shouted to Rafael through a bullhorn to toss down a line. Rafael complied and Juarez secured it to the tug. Then Captain Franco radioed Juarez from the bridge to push the bow toward the pier. Juarez tooted the tug's whistle acknowledging Franco's command, and the bow of the ship slowly turned to starboard.

Meanwhile, Juan ran to the passenger cabin where he discovered the padlock. He shouted through the door, "Hey, you guys still in there?"

"Yes, can you unlock the door?" Maisy asked.

"I don't have the key. Have to find the key," Juan shouted anxiously.

"Rafael locked it. He has the key. Maybe you can con him into giving it to you." Maisy urged.

"I'll try. We don't have much time, maybe ten minutes at the most. We are docking now. I'll do what I can."

"Bring a hacksaw if you cannot find the key," Jason yelled to Juan.

"Will do. I'll be right back," Juan said and rushed away.

While precious minutes ticked away, he vaulted down the ladders to the cargo deck and ran as fast as he could to Rafael's office. With incredible luck, he spotted a key lying on his desk. Hoping it was the right one, he rushed back to their cabin, inserted it into the lock and turned. The lock snapped open.

"I got it, guys," Juan shouted excitedly.

He abruptly opened the cabin door and pushed them into the passageway. Then he slammed the door shut, re-locked the padlock, and escorted them to the cargo deck. Quickly they found their way among the cars on the dimly lighted deck to the two he had set up for their escape. He placed Maisy on the floor of the back seat and Jason in the trunk of the first car. Then he helped Lori and Jeff into the car directly behind it. Continuing to move rapidly, Juan placed a piece of canvas on top of Maisy and Lori to hide them.

"Listen, this may take a while, so lie still, and be quiet. I'm doing the best I can. So far so good," Juan reminded all of them.

"Good luck, Juan," Maisy said in response.

Juan placed the keys to the two cars in his pocket and headed to the main deck to check on the progress of the docking. When no one was watching him, Juan tossed the key to the padlocked cabin door into the harbor.

As the ship reached twenty feet from the pier, Captain Franco ordered Carlos to reverse engines to stop the ship's forward motion. Ming stood by in the pilothouse and shouted depth soundings to the Captain every fifteen seconds. Then Franco radioed the tug to push the bow closer to the pier. Juarez tooted again in acknowledgment and slowly the bow eased up to the dock until Franco heard the wooden pilings and dock creak under pressure from the ship. Rafael tossed a large line over to a dockworker standing on the pier and then ran back to the stern and tossed another line onto the pier.

When the Captain ordered Carlos again to back the engines and turn the rudder to starboard, the bow pulled hard on the line and forced the stern of the ship to ease against the pier with another loud crack and groan from the wooden structure. Once all lines were secured and the Captain released the tug of its services, Juarez tooted a long blast from tug's whistle and steered his tug across the harbor to his home base.

While the ramp was being set in place, Franco spotted Francesca standing on the dock waiting to come aboard, but behind Francesca stood three others. The Captain took a double take because he thought one or two of them looked familiar but from his distance, he was not certain. He picked up a pair of binoculars, focused in on their faces, and jolted when he recognized them . . . Charlie Jenkins, Jake, and Chico. "What the crap! What are they doing here?" he yelled loud enough to cause Carlos to come out of the pilothouse.

"Did you call, Sir," Carlos asked.

"Uh, no, no. I was just looking at someone on the pier," the Captain said. "Never mind."

Once the ship's cargo ramp was secured in place on the dock with the aid of a crane, Captain Franco motioned to Francesca and the three others to come aboard.

Immediately, Juan sought after Rafael for instructions on where to deliver the cars. During his frantic search, however, the Captain announced over the ship's intercom for Rafael, Jon, Carlos, and Ming to report to his cabin at once. Fearing a serious delay in getting his friends off the ship, Juan rushed to the Captain's cabin in an attempt to intercept Rafael before the meeting.

Arriving in the passageway near the Captain's quarters, Juan waited impatiently for Rafael to show up. First Carlos arrived, and then Ming showed up followed by Jon. Rafael was still missing. Juan paced up and down the passageway and even peeked inside the Captain's cabin just in case he might have missed him.

Shortly afterwards Francesca walked by Juan without speaking and entered the cabin followed by the three others from Wilmingtown. Juan continued to pace in the passageway until he spotted Rafael climbing the ladder to his deck level. Rafael rushed along the passageway toward the Captain's cabin, but Juan blocked his path a few feet before the cabin door.

"Can I have a quick word with you before your meeting, Sir," Juan pleaded.

"I'm already late. I'll see you after the meeting," Rafael said breathing heavily.

"But Sir, I am ready to take the cars off the ship. I need the delivery address." Juan asked urgently.

"I don't know yet. That's what the meeting is about, I believe. Just standby and I'll give you instructions as soon as I get the word myself. Wait for me in my office," Rafael directed, pushed Juan aside and slipped into the Captain's cabin.

"Aye, Sir," Juan responded just as the door was slammed shut in his face.

Juan returned to the cargo deck and met his friends waiting in the cars. "Okay, at the moment guys, I'm waiting to get the warehouse address from Rafael on where to take the cars. He's meeting with the Captain now, so we'll just have to sit tight for a bit. Rafael asked me to meet him in his office when he is done." The four mumbled they understood and continued to lie quietly.

In the Captain's cabin, John addressed his passenger situation with Francesca.

"I had to bring four prowlers with me from Coakley. They broke into our car shop and discovered what we were doing. At first, I thought they would be a liability to our success, yet I did not want to leave them on Andros or dump them at sea for fear the authorities would find them and hunt us down. But now I think we could hold them for ransom. So, I brought them here. Can you hide them somewhere in the Colombian jungle?" Franco asked Francesca.

"Why the hell did you do that? You're already in hot water, and now you have thrown a wrench in the works. What a pain!" she exclaimed. Where are they now?" Francesca asked.

"They're locked up in our guest cabin," Captain Franco said. "Back to my question, can you help with the ransom demand?"

"Okay. I'll see what I can do. I've never had to deal with prisoners

before, but I know others in this country have done this and have made a lot of money. Keep them locked up. I'll get back to you tomorrow on a plan for them. Now we have another problem." She looked at Charlie, Jake, and Chico. "What are we gonna do with these three? You can't work here because you are not citizens of Colombia. The authorities will come looking for you when your passport restrictions expire. We'll have to find some work for you in the underground. I have a friend who has a small apartment you can hide in temporarily." Francesca turned to Franco and continued, "And that leaves me with your problem, what to do with you and the *Coral Sun Ray*." Already, your Tampico and Wilmingtown operations have been shut down as Charlie and Chico have confirmed. Now the Tampico Police have sent a bulletin to the Bahamian Police to be on the lookout for you and your ship in Coakley. You are now a ship and Captain without a country. You've reached the end of the line."

"That's right, Francesca," Charlie piped in. "Not only that but these brats that Franco forced onboard are responsible for our failure in Wilmingtown. This all started when they found Ramos' body floating in the Cape Fear River and reported it to our police dispatcher." He then looked directly at John and said, "That was really dumb on your crew's part to shoot him and leave him floating in the river. As the result, our officers were able to link the body with the *Coral Sun Ray*. I tried to downplay the investigation, but my coworkers were so persistent. As Captain of the police force, I had one hand tied behind my back. I couldn't stop them. You know the rest of the story."

"But, as Francesca said, we'll make money on these prisoners now. Sounds to me like we did a good thing. People will pay a lot to get their friends and coworkers back," the Captain insisted.

The meeting lasted half an hour before Rafael returned to his office. When Juan spotted Rafael coming through the door onto the cargo deck, Juan greeted him in a loud voice so that his friends could hear that Rafael was on deck. Rafael reached into his pocket and handed Juan a note.

"Here's the address where you are to take the cars." Also, here's a key to unlock the door to the warehouse. No one will be there. Just park the cars inside and lock up the place before you leave. The building is only ten blocks away, so you can walk back to the ship to get the rest of the cars. Glad you volunteered. Jon and Carlos are tired of doing this. It's risky. Be on the lookout for possible hijackers along the way. Don't stop for anyone or for any reason." He reached in his other pocket and handed Juan another piece of paper. "Here's a street map of Santa Marta. The route to the warehouse is marked. Any questions?"

Juan glanced at the map for a moment, and satisfied that he could find his way without difficulty, he bade Rafael goodbye. Stalling, Juan casually walked among the cars and waited for the opportunity to make his move. Out of the corner of his eye, he watched Rafael shuffle papers on his desk, place some documents in a file drawer, wash out his coffee cup, walk to the door, turn out his office light, and leave the cargo deck. Then Juan hurried to the two front cars and whispered that the coast was clear and he was ready to move out. A faint 'okay,' came from the two back seats. He climbed into the first BMW and turned the ignition key.

As soon as the engine started, he buckled his seat belt, pressed down on the accelerator, drove out the doorway onto the ramp to the dock. Trying to attract as little attention as possible, he kept a moderate pace as he drove out of the shipyard onto the streets of Santa Marta. He turned left on Carrera 1, drove four blocks, and turned right onto Calle 22. At one point, he looked at the map again to double check the address. Number 518 Calle 22 was circled on the map. Arriving in the 500 block, he soon spotted a rundown wooden building on the right badly in need of a paint job. Posted over the large, wooden, front door was a faded sign that read '518.' He pulled over to the curb in front of the warehouse and whispered to Maisy to be still while he unlocked the door.

Quickly unsnapping the padlock and opening the door, he returned to the car and drove inside. It was dark and he had to use the headlights to see his way to the back wall. As soon as he parked the car, Juan announced to Maisy and Jason that they were here and could get out. Maisy rolled out of the back seat while Juan opened the trunk for Jason to escape. They promised Juan that they would stay hidden in the warehouse until he returned. Juan then hurried out the door and walked quickly back to the ship.

Twenty minutes later, Juan ran up the ramp of the *Coral Sun Ray* into the cargo hold and jumped into the next BMW in line.

"Are you guys okay?" he whispered to be sure they were still there.

"Yes." Lori whispered. "We're fine."

"Good. The others are safe inside the warehouse. We're on our way to freedom. Hang on," Juan exclaimed in a soft voice.

When Juan started the engine and pulled forward, he spotted Rafael coming toward him straight in front of his path.

"Shhhhhh. Here comes Rafael," Juan warned Lori. "Lie still and quiet."

Juan put his hand over his forehead in disbelief, stopped and waited for Rafael to approach the car.

"Just a moment. I can't find the key to the passenger cabin? Have you seen it?" he asked.

"No, Sir."

"That's weird. I threw it on my desk before my meeting with the Captain, and you were the last one in my office after I left. Now the key is not there. You must have seen it on my desk. You had to take it."

"No, Sir," Juan lied.

"It was in plain sight. Keys just don't vanish. You must have taken it! Are you lying to me?" Rafael said suspiciously.

"No, Sir. I haven't seen the key," Juan repeated nervously. Then Rafael looked in the back seat.

"What's that piece of canvas doing in the back seat?" Rafael asked.

"Uh, well, I thought I would take it over to the warehouse and cover the cars to keep the dust and dirt off them. It's a dingy place. This'll keep them clean," Juan said. "Clean cars sell for a higher price you know."

"Oh yeah? We never did that before. The cars are inside. They don't get dirty inside," Rafael insisted. Suddenly Rafael noticed a small movement underneath the canvas. "Ah ha!" he yelled and without warning, he reached back, grabbed the back door handle and opened the door.

Immediately Juan jammed the accelerator to the floor, causing the door to slam shut and knocking Rafael onto the deck. The BMW squealed out of the cargo deck onto the ramp leaving a trail of black smoke and the smell of burnt rubber. He heard Rafael scream behind him to stop, but by the time Juan reached the bottom of the ramp, his excessive speed caused the car to hit the bottom of its frame so hard that Jeff yelled in pain in the trunk. Juan raced to the intersection of Carrere 1 and the harbor road when he saw Rafael drive down the ramp in a white Lexus, skid around the dock and roar toward him. Juan turned left onto Carrera 1 and sped into town only to discover a traffic gridlock three blocks ahead. He swerved right onto Calle 23 hoping to lose Rafael in the congested, narrow streets of the inner city, but Juan looked in his rearview mirror again and saw the white Lexus two blocks away turning the corner and heading toward him.

Instantly Juan pressed hard on the accelerator and screamed up the road another three blocks. He saw Rafael screech to a stop to avoid hitting pedestrians crossing the street behind him, and this gave Juan a few precious seconds to duck into a narrow, deserted alleyway unnoticed. Juan rushed to the end of the alley and turned right into another lane to escape out of sight. Shortly afterwards, he heard the roar of the Lexus speed by on the main road. Juan jumped out of the car, opened the back door and trunk lid and helped Lori and Jeff escape.

"We have to get away from here and hide somewhere. Follow me. Let's duck into one of these shops," Juan suggested. They agreed and fled out of sight leaving the car behind.

"Where is the warehouse where Maisy and Jason are hiding?" Lori asked.

"A few blocks from here. I locked the door, so they should be safe for the moment. But we have to get there as soon as possible before someone goes inside and finds them first," Juan insisted.

After running for a block in the back alley, they found a back door open to a shop and ran inside. It was a small clothing store and immediately Lori started looking though the racks as if she were interested in buying a dress. Jeff looked in the men's wear for shirts. The shopkeeper approached Lori and spoke to her in Spanish. Juan intervened and told the clerk in Spanish that they were just visiting Santa Marta, did not speak Spanish, and were just looking. The clerk nodded her understanding and left them alone.

Juan peeked outside the front door to check on the whereabouts of Rafael. Relieved that the white Lexus was nowhere in sight, he returned inside the shop and suggested that they make their way now to the warehouse and rescue Maisy and Jason. They left the shop cautiously and slipped toward 518 Calle 22.

A block away, Juan suddenly noticed the Lexus parked in front of the building. Rafael was frustratingly fiddling with the padlock on the front door. They could hear him cursing from a distance. To play it safe, the three hustled inside a small café half a block away and sat at a table where they could watch Rafael out the front window.

The café waiter approached them and began conversing in Spanish. Juan nodded his head, said something in Spanish and the waiter left them alone. A few minutes later they saw Rafael return to his car and drive away.

"Okay, I think the coast is clear now. Rafael probably went to get a key to the building. We have to move fast," Juan said.

Juan said a few words to the waiter, and then hurried out the café door and ran to the front of the warehouse. Unlocking the padlock on the front door, the three went inside and closed the door behind them.

"Jason! Maisy! Where are you?" Juan muttered in a loud whisper. A closet door opened near the front entrance and Jason and Maisy rushed out to greet them.

"We thought you would never show up. We were afraid something happened. Did everything go all right?" Maisy asked.

"No. Rafael caught us in the act just as I was about to drive off the ship. While I was sitting in the car talking to him, he saw Lori move under the canvas in the back seat and decided to open the back door to check it out. I jammed down on the accelerator and squealed out of there before Rafael had a chance to lift up the canvas to find her. I tore through town with Rafael chasing me in a white Lexus, but I managed to shake him by escaping in a back alley. We saw him here a minute ago, trying to open the front door, but he did not have the key to the padlock. I'm sure he'll be back here shortly. We've got to get out of here," Juan said as he grabbed Maisy's arm and led her to the door.

Juan shut and locked the front door while his friends ran across the street and hid in the doorway of another shop. Seconds later Juan joined them and ordered, "Follow me, we found a clothing shop a few blocks away. We can hide there for awhile and maybe buy some clothes to blend in with the locals before the gang spots us on the streets."

"Wait! Stop! This is all wrong! We need to go to the police, not a clothing shop!" Lori demanded as she began to run down the street. "We need their help, their protection from these savages."

"No, no, no . . . not in Santa Marta," Juan shouted and ran after Lori, grabbed her by the arm and brought her back. "The police won't know whom to believe. There'll be a big investigation and they'll hold us in custody . . . that's jail in plain English. They will keep us there until they gather information that could take weeks, maybe months. And the police may be on the take from these criminals. It's too risky! We could be here for months in confinement. We don't want to stay in Colombia for months. Remember the *Coral Sun Ray* is involved in an international criminal operation, not just Colombian. We have to get back on American soil before we report them to the authorities. We must find a way to get out of this country fast."

"How are we gonna do that? We can't escape. We don't have passports, money, don't know anyone here. We're trapped," Lori said. She began crying hysterically.

Jeff ran to Lori's side and said, "Look, Juan knows the people in

Colombia, in fact, he has a cousin here, right Juan?"

"I think he's still here. We're going to find out as soon as I can find a phone and directory," Juan said.

"I believe you, Juan," Jason said. "We will be safer in American hands, not Colombian hands. Let's work on getting away from these crooks and finding Juan's friend first."

"Stop arguing, you guys! If we stand in front of this warehouse any longer, we will be caught for sure. We have to get out of here. We can talk about this later," Maisy said near panic. With that warning, they high tailed it down the street to the clothing shop.

Lori, Maisy, Jason, and Jeff dashed inside and headed immediately for the clothing racks again. Greeting the shopkeeper at the door, Juan told her they liked what they saw and brought some friends along to buy some things. Meanwhile, Lori walked up and down the aisles and rummaged through the colorful dresses on the racks. She pulled a few off the hangars and placed them in front of her to check for size. Then she called Jeff for his approval.

Fearing a possible financial embarrassment, he looked in his wallet to see how much money he had, and then he asked Juan if the shopkeeper would accept American dollars. After conferring with the clerk, Juan assured him that she would. Maisy and Lori chose two dresses, and at the same time Jeff and Jason picked a couple of tropical shirts.

Meanwhile, Juan asked the clerk for permission to use the telephone directory to find Raul Martinez. There were several listings under his name. Scratching his head, he chose one at random and called. When the person answered, it was obvious Juan had reached the wrong number, so he tried another listing. Suddenly Juan shouted with excitement in Spanish.

"I suspect Juan found Raul," Jason said to Maisy.

"Yeah, I wish I could understand what he was saying," she said.

Juan remained on the phone for five minutes and then hung up.

"Good news, I. . . ."

"Yeah, we figured it out," Maisy interrupted. "You found him. So what's next?"

"Here's our plan. Raul lives in a small mountain village about three miles away in the Sierra de Nevadas. He grows fruit and vegetables on his ranch and brings them down to the farmers market each day to sell to the town people. He wants us to meet him at the market right away. From the map I got from Rafael, it looks like he is about fifteen blocks from here on the southern edge of town."

"So what good is that going to do, going to a fruit stand?" Lori questioned.

"Wait, let me finish. He offered to take us to his little ranch in the mountains to hide until we can arrange our escape out of the country. With the ship's crew, the local gangs, and perhaps the Santa Marta police hot on our trail, he believes we should get out of town and hide for a day or two until things cool down. And he added that kidnapping of Americans for ransom is common in this country."

"That sounds like a great idea. Thanks Juan," Maisy said as she patted him on the shoulder.

"So, you guys find what you wanted?" Juan asked.

"Yes," they said in unison.

"Good. Let's pay for the clothes, change and hit the road. I'm anxious to see Raul," Juan urged.

A short while later, they walked out of the shop dressed somewhat like the natives and headed toward their rendezvous with Raul. A block away, they came to an intersection where the traffic light was red, and while waiting impatiently for the light to turn green and for the traffic to clear, Juan suddenly spotted a waste can nearby and tossed the warehouse key in the trash. As they proceeded cautiously toward the farmers market, Juan spotted Rafael in the Lexus at the next intersection waiting for the light to turn green.

"Quick, separate into two groups, turn your back to the street, and look interested at something in the store windows. Rafael is coming our way again," Juan said.

Just as Juan feared, Rafael turned the corner and headed straight for them. Maisy and Jason stood in front of a store window pointing to something inside while two shops away, Juan, Jeff and Lori did the same thing. Fortunately, Rafael flew by without recognizing them. They remained separated in front of shop windows until the coast was clear several blocks down the street and then regrouped.

"Whew! That was close," Jason said.

"You're right. They are determined to find us. Luckily we only have a few more blocks to go," Juan assured them.

Turning the corner onto a small road near the south edge of town, they arrived at the beginning of the farmers market. As far as their eyes could see, there were stands full of fresh fruit, vegetables, bread, dairy products, meats, flowers and drinks. Longing for a good meal, the sight stimulated their hunger pangs as they strolled down the center of the road in search of Juan's cousin. Mid-way down the second block, Juan saw a sign:

RAUL
LAS FRUTAS Y LAS VERDURAS

That's it! We found it," Juan shouted. Behind one of the tables, a man stood with his back turned and was sorting out some of the fruit. Juan approached him.

"*Disculpeme, senor. Estoy buscando . . .*" Juan greeted him.

Raul turned around, set down the fruit he had in his hand, and rushed over to greet him.

"Juan, *usted sinverguenza. Gran verlo. Ha sido un largo tiempo,*" Raul responded.

They embraced each other for what seemed like eternity, and then came over to meet Jeff, Maisy, Lori, and Jason who were waiting in the center of the road.

"Juan told me a little bit about you and that you needed help. He didn't have time to give me details, but welcome . . . welcome. You are safe here," Raul said in English. He reached for Maisy and Lori's hands and shook them vigorously.

"You are beautiful ladies. It is an honor to meet you." Maisy blushed and thanked him for his help.

Then Juan said, "Excuse me guys, I want to bring Raul up to date on our situation, and I can do this faster in Spanish for Raul's sake." While Juan and Raul conversed, the four walked around the tables and admired the items in the baskets for sale. Watching them, Raul interrupted Juan at one point and said to the four, "Please, take whatever you want. You must be hungry." Thankful for the offer, Maisy and Lori smiled and said, "Gracias," and sorted through the fruit.

"Have you eaten fresh papaya?" Maisy asked Lori.

"No, these look like big pears," Lori stated as she picked one up and felt it.

"Well, they're not at all like pears. I can't really describe their taste. They're very sweet and juicy. Want to try one? I'm going to eat one," Maisy said.

Lori agreed and Maisy cut the papaya in quarters and peeled it before handing slices to her friends.

"Wow! This is good. I'll have to remember to buy these when we get home," Lori said.

"Do you realize what you just said?" Jeff exclaimed. "See, you do believe that we are going to make it home safely."

"Okay, I'll admit I feel better about this now. I feel we have a chance now that we are off the ship and have met Raul," Lori said.

"Of course," Jeff agreed.

They sat down on the curb and stuffed themselves with papaya as if they hadn't eaten in days. Juan continued with his story for twenty minutes and then turned to his friends, "Okay, Raul knows about our situation and is anxious to help, but he told me he has a surprise waiting for us behind the shed next to his stand. Come, let's go check it out."

Chapter 12

The Llamas

Jason, Maisy, Lori, Juan, and Jeff followed Raul around the shed to the back lot. To their delight, they discovered four llamas standing fifty feet away grazing peacefully under the shade of a mango tree. The first sight of them caused Maisy and Lori's eyes to light up like a child coming down the stairs on Christmas morning.

Lori raised her hands to her face and screamed, "Wow! Real llamas." As the result of the excitement, the llamas stopped grazing, looked up at the strangers, and pointed their long ears in their direction.

"Llamas are very curious and alert animals. Anytime something new pops up near them, they want to check it out," Raul said. "Just stand still and they will come to see what you are all about."

"Can I pet them?" Maisy asked as the llamas moved cautiously toward them.

"Sure, but pet them on their neck or back. They prefer not to be petted on their heads or faces. Let them sniff you first, then you can pet them," Raul informed everyone. "And talk to them in a soft voice. That helps them gain trust in you," Raul added.

"This is absolutely so cool," Lori said as the first llama came up to her and sniffed Lori's face. She reached out slowly and petted the animal on the neck.

"They're so soft," she exclaimed.

"Yes, we not only use them as pack animals to bring our fruit and vegetables into town from our mountain village, but we also us their fiber to make coats, scarves, blankets, socks, and many other things," Raul said. He pointed to a blanket on a rack in the rear of his shop that his wife made. "My wife, Roselle, does the spinning and weaving and we sell some of her things in the cooler months."

Lori and Maisy continued to pet the llamas for another fifteen minutes while they grazed.

"Do they have names?" Maisy asked.

"Yes. That half brown, half white one is Cookie, the dark brown one with a white chest is Matador, the one in back that is spotted brown and white is Wacissa, and the other one with light brown fiber and a little white is Jorge. A couple of them were born on our ranch and they all have very good dispositions. They make excellent pack animals. It takes about an hour and a half to reach our ranch in the highlands," Raul continued. "Are you up for a mountain hike?"

They all agreed. Raul turned to Juan and spoke to him in Spanish for a minute and then spoke to the group," We are going to head up the mountain around 4:00 o'clock. It is very peaceful in the mountains. There's no fear of gangs chasing you or the police harassing you. I'll let each of you lead a llama up the trail to our place."

Maisy jumped for joy and as promised when four o'clock rolled around, Raul placed the fruit and vegetables into sacks and laid them on the ground next to the llamas. Maisy and Lori watched intently as Raul showed them how to put the pack harness on Cookie.

"Always fasten the front belly cinch first and pull it tight before doing the back one," Raul instructed. "And you do the opposite when taking the harness off."

Cookie stood patiently while Raul made adjustments and tightened the harness.

"Okay. See how it's done?" Raul asked. Lori and Maisy nodded their heads. He then removed the pack harness and handed it to Maisy. "Here, put this back on Cookie," he said. With nervous excitement and uncertainty, Maisy took the harness, held it over her head, and walked quickly up to Cookie. Immediately Cookie moved away. Maisy approached her again and again Cookie stepped away always keeping about five feet distance between them before stopping. Raul laughed and then they all laughed together. Maisy looked back at them in frustration.

"What am I doing wrong?" she asked. "Cookie let you do this without moving at all."

"You were not paying attention to the details as I put the harness on Cookie," Raul said. "Approach her slowly and hold the harness at waist level. Give her a moment to gain a sense of trust in you. Cookie doesn't know you. She doesn't know if you are going to harm her or what. When you held the harness high in the air and rushed up to her, she saw you as a threat to her. In response she backed away."

Maisy felt a little stupid but regained her confidence and moved slowly toward Cookie on the second attempt. Cookie stood still.

"Keep talking to her. Tell her what a good girl she is," Raul said.

Cookie perked her ears up, watched Maisy cautiously, and gently set the harness on her back. Then she reached under her, pulled the front cinch around to her side, and snapped the buckle.

"Pull the straps tight," Raul reminder her. Maisy tugged on the two cinch straps and attempted to pull them tighter. Raul followed her and tugged on the cinches to test it.

"Ah, you have to get them tighter. Pull hard. It won't hurt her."

Wrinkling up her face in sympathetic pain, Maisy gave the cinches another hard pull. "Ow, that must hurt. Sorry Cookie," Maisy said while giving her a pat on the neck.

"No, she's not complaining," Raul pointed out. "The path is steep in places. We have to make sure the pack stays on and does not slip around on her back. I remember years ago someone put a pack on a llama, did not tightened it enough and while wading through a shallow rocky river, the llama slipped and the pack slid all the round upside down under its belly. You can imagine the reaction of the llama with its pack and load between his legs. That's when the real fun began. The llama panicked, of course, and scattered stuff from his pack all over the river. It was a hard lesson, so pull tight."

Then Raul placed chest and butt straps around Cookie and snapped them to the harness saddle to keep it from moving forward and aft during their climb up the steep slopes. When they were satisfied Cookie was ready, Raul handed the pack harnesses to Lori, Jeff and Jason for their turn to saddle them up. He assigned Cookie to Maisy, Jason took Matador, Jeff was given Jorge, and Lori was left with Wacissa.

"These llamas are trained to follow you on the trail. They know what to do. Just hold onto the lead and give them some slack. We call it a 'j' lead. They don't like to be dragged along. If for whatever reason they want to walk in front of you, just hold up your arm high in front of their faces and they'll step back behind you. If you have to stop for some reason, say *parada*, which means halt in Spanish. They know commands. Also, they are very gentle animals. They will not kick, bite, or spit at you," Raul assured them.

On a table under the shed, Raul reached for five sombreros and gave one to each of them to keep the sun off their faces and to disguise them from the gang members still prowling the streets. After the packs were loaded with the fruit and vegetables that did not sell during the day, they began their long trek to Raul's villa in the mountains.

In the beginning, the wide, straight path slopped gently uphill toward the snow capped peaks in the distance. With each step, the llamas kicked up a swirl of dust, and as Raul promised, Cookie, Jorge, Wacissa and Matador followed each handler in a single file several feet behind with a loose lead. The llamas knew the routine. They had done these treks hundreds of times before.

While Raul and Juan led the pack, Raul whispered to Juan, "Actually, these llamas don't really need leads. They know the trail and they'll follow us up the mountain regardless, but I'm not going to tell them that. I want them to think they are actually leading the llamas."

"Good psychology," Juan said. "They need this relief. They have been through hell this past week."

"Yeah. That's my point exactly," Raul said.

The path became narrower and steeper. When they reached the edge of the dense rain forest, the dirt path began to rise, twist, and turn under the thick jungle canopy. Raul suddenly stopped and everyone halted behind him like dominos.

"Okay team, from here on the trail will be steep and winding for about a mile. Then the trail will go downhill briefly to a river. We are going to cross the river by walking on the rocks but the llamas will wade through the water. Then the path goes up a steep, windy grade for another half a mile. At the top of that grade is our little villa. Anyone want to back out now?" Raul teased. No one spoke. "Okay. Onwards and upwards. Let's move out."

The trek moved forward again like a row of dominos in reverse. The pace slowed as everyone except the llamas began to show strain under the climb up the mountain.

"That's not fair," Maisy said breathing heavily. "The llamas are strutting along carrying weight as if there were nothing to this, and I am huffing and puffing carrying no weight and am about to crash."

"Are you surprised?" Raul asked.

"Well, yeah . . . I mean . . . no, I guess not. Just jealous," she said.

"If you had four legs, weighed three hundred pounds, and did this every day, you would think nothing of this little stroll in the park," Raul laughed. "These llamas love to do this. It's their job. They are work animals. They would rather do this than sit around under the shade of a tree and watch the world go by."

"Okay, trudge on," Maisy said trying to catch her breath.

In half an hour, they reached the top of the first peak. Maisy, Lori, Jeff, and Jason took a deep breath of relief and led the llamas down the hill toward the river. By now, they could hear the roar of the rapids and falls below.

"Wow! That sounds impressive," Jeff said when he stopped for a moment to listen to the sounds in the forest and the water roaring down the mountain.

"We have to cross that roaring rapids?" Jeff asked not able to see the river at this point.

"We're not crossing the rapids. There is a place where the water flows slowly before it reaches the high falls. That's our fording point," Raul assured him. "This is one of the many rivers coming down from the ice covered peaks of the Andes not far away. Trust me; the water is cold, even in the summer months. There are a lot of falls and rapids here. There are plenty of rocks to walk on to keep dry, but let the llamas wade across in the water. The water does not bother them and they know exactly where to step without getting hurt. I'm telling you, they are smart animals."

"I believe you," Jeff said. "They are even smarter than Lori."

Lori turned around and hissed at Jeff. "Good thing I have a llama with me. I'd come back and give you a punch in the side," she said half jokingly.

Soon they arrived on the bank of the river where Raul stopped everyone for further instructions.

"Now listen up. This is how we cross rivers. We must go in single file and follow the exact path of the person in front of you. Obviously, I'll go first. Do not crowd up. Stay at least fifty feet behind the person in front of you. Keep the llamas behind you with a loose lead. Giving the llamas distance between each other allows them to pick their way carefully through the river current. If they get too close to each other they cannot see very well where they are stepping and things could happen."

"Like what?" Jeff asked.

Lori stood next to Jeff and immediately poked him. "Will you shut up!" she hollered. "I don't want to know what will happen, thank you. Don't pay any attention to him." Lori said.

Juan and Raul snickered. "I guess you will find out if you don't pay attention," Raul said. They all laughed.

Raul led the way and Juan elected to bring up the rear in case of trouble. Jason followed behind Raul with Matador. Then Maisy and Cookie entered the river. Jeff and Lori decided to wait until everyone was half way across before making their move.

Finally, it was Lori's turn to go across. She was exceedingly nervous and took each step rock by rock with extraordinary caution. Jeff could

hear her holler with every step, "Oh my God!" Wacissa, completely relaxed on the other hand, trudged ahead at a steady pace and soon passed Lori standing on a rock in mid-stream. Wacissa's lead became taught as Lori held firmly on the line for balance, yet Wacissa continued toward the opposite bank.

With the threat of Lori being pulled into the river, Raul yelled to her, "Drop the lead! Drop the lead!" Lori dropped Wacissa's lead into the moving water, watched her llama slosh across the river alone and climb up on the bank on the other side.

Lori screamed, "Help. Someone help!" Juan jumped off the bank onto the rocks and started toward Lori until Raul shouted, "Hold up Juan, she can manage." Then he said to Lori, "You're okay. Don't worry about Wacissa. She'll stay right here with us and wait for you. Just stand still for a moment and try to relax, take a deep breath, regain you composure and balance, and then walk slowly toward us. Take your time. You can do it. Walk slowly." Lori thought for a few seconds and took another step, then another, then another, each time regaining her confidence in herself. Finally, she reached the bank and ran up to Raul's waiting arms.

"See, I knew you had it in you to do this. And you did it all by yourself. What a great accomplishment! Good job." Raul gave her a hug. "Wacissa is waiting for you over there. She wasn't going to leave you." He paused for a second then whispered to Lori, "I think Wacissa likes you." Lori ran over to her and gave her a hug, which prompted Wacissa to give her a sniff on her nose. "We call that a llama kiss."

Jeff and Juan crossed the river without incident and regrouped for the final steep, rigorous leg of their trek. The air was a little cooler at the higher elevation, and that made the amateur climbers feel better when they reached the top. Raul opened the small wooden gate to his compound, and they filed into a beautiful courtyard full of tropical shrubs, fruit trees, and flowers. There was a small pond and fountain in front of the house with a circular pathway around to the front door. When they reached the covered porch of the villa, their dog greeted them with enthusiasm and alerted Roselle inside of their arrival. She came to door to meet the new guests.

"Roselle, I want you to meet my new friends . . . and Juan. You remember my cousin Juan whom I have not seen in centuries it seems. He came to town on a ship today and brought some friends with him."

Roselle shook hands and hugged everyone. "But I must tell you, my sweets," Raul continued, "that Juan's friends are victims of a kidnapping in the Bahamas and smuggled to Santa Marta on Juan's ship. Miraculously with Juan's ingenious escape scheme, they managed to escape. Now they need our help to get them back to the Bahamas or perhaps the States without harm done to them. I offered to bring them here out of sight of the crooks in Santa Marta until we can arrange to get them out of the country. I hope you approve." Raul looked in his wife's eyes and immediately saw approval before she spoke.

"You know that's okay. We're glad to help. Please, welcome to our little home in the mountains. It's not much but it's our home. I am sure we have room for you. Come on in. Can I get you something to drink, perhaps some fruit punch and cookies?" she asked.

"Thank would be wonderful," Jason eagerly responded.

"Good, have a seat and I'll fix us all something," Roselle said.

Raul, meantime, excused himself briefly while he took the llamas to the shelter behind the villa. A few minutes later, he returned and met Roselle in the kitchen and brought her up to date as to how all of this happened. A short while later Roselle brought a large tray with glasses of punch and cookies to everyone in the great room.

"You poor souls. It's amazing you are still alive," she said.

"Yes. We are lucky thanks to Juan who really saved our lives. Who knows what would have happened to us on board on even here in Santa Marta, but Juan is our hero," Jeff said.

Raul walked over to Juan and put his arm around his shoulder. "Yes, Juan is a good kid . . . sometimes. If only he would keep in contact with us. It's been years since we last saw or talked to each other," Raul teased.

"Well, I could say the same about you. When was the last time you wrote me a letter?" Juan asked.

"Never mind," Raul said. He reached for the tray, passed it around, and insisted everyone take some food.

"You both speak English so well, where did you learn it?" Maisy asked Roselle.

"When you have a business that deals with the general public, you have to learn several languages to be successful. Santa Marta is an international city. We have some visitors and customers who speak English. We decided long ago that we had to learn the language to compete. We learned it at English classes at the University of Santa Marta," Roselle said.

"You folks must be extremely tired. Let me show you where you are sleeping and the bathroom," Raul offered. Jason, Maisy, Jeff, and

Lori followed him down a short hallway and into a bedroom. "This is one of our guest rooms. It only has one double bed. Would that work for you?" He looked at the group for a response.

Maisy stared at Jason for a second, and then turned to Raul. "Yes, this will be fine for us. Where will Jeff and Lori sleep?" she asked.

"Ah, follow me, please," Raul said. They walked down the hall to a den, where there was a pull out bed that slept two. "That's all we have, but perhaps under the circumstances this will work for you, too," Raul hoped.

"Yes," Jeff said and Lori nodded in the affirmative as well.

"Good. That leaves you, Juan. Come with me. I have a place for you down the hall. That takes care of our honored guest. We'll have dinner in an hour. You are certainly welcome to join us if you are not too tired. Meanwhile, I'll leave you all alone and let you freshen up, okay?"

"Perfect," Maisy said and gave Jason a big hug and immediately fell into the bed.

Later that evening all sat around the dinner table and talked about the events on the *Coral Sun Ray,* and how much they appreciated a real home-cooked meal.

"Okay, let's talk about how we can get you home," Raul said looking at his guests. There is no American Embassy in Santa Marta, but there is an American Consulate office in Barranquilla about 90 miles from here by road or 50 miles by sea. I suggest we call the Consulate's office tomorrow morning and explain your situation. I'm sure they will take you in under their protection and arrange to fly you out of the country to the States or the Bahamas."

"We want to return to Andros to get my boat. We left the *Southwind* at the dock in Coakley. I sure hope it's still there," Jason said with a hint of concern in his voice.

"Yes and I want to see my friends in Moxey Settlement. I'm sure they have been looking for me by now," Maisy added.

"And I'll probably stay in Miami or Ft. Lauderdale or wherever we fly to first in the States and look for a job," Juan said.

"Then that's what we'll do first thing tomorrow morning," Raul said.

"What about the market? Don't you have to be back in Santa Marta to set up your stand at the farmer's market?" Lori asked.

"Yes, but we can be a little late if necessary. The important thing is to start the ball rolling in getting you five back home," Roselle said.

"Thank you all so very much for your help and caring for our safety, and thank you for allowing us to stay in your nice home and the meals," Maisy said. At that point, Maisy stood up from the table and gave Roselle a hug.

"No problem. You are nice kids. We always like to help those in need," she said.

When they finished dinner, Lori was so tired she could hardly hold her head up and asked to be excused to go to bed. Maisy offered to help clear off the table and wash the dishes, but Roselle insisted that she would rather handle those chores herself.

"I'm sure you all are tired. Go get some rest. We get up early, so breakfast will be ready at 6:00 o'clock. We'll continue where we left off in the morning," she suggested. The others nodded in agreement and left the table for their rooms. When Maisy and Jason reached their room, Maisy shut the door and led Jason to the edge of the bed where they sat.

"Jason, I have been thinking. Without Juan, we would not be here, as you know, and maybe not even alive. He saved us. He's our hero. I like him and want to help him," Maisy began.

"Yesssss, what are you trying to tell me?" Jeff asked with some suspicion.

"No, no. Don't worry about you and me. I love you. But Juan is our friend and needs our help now."

"Go on," Jason urged.

"Well, Juan needs a job and we said we would help him find a new ship. He likes sea duty, and I was thinking of perhaps letting him take over the commercial fishing business my parents left in Moxey Settlement. He misses the sea, and yet he doesn't seem to fit as a crewman on a large ship. He certainly had difficulties on the wretched *Coral Sun Ray*. He may never admit it, but I sensed he would be happier doing commercial fishing on his own trawler. What do you think, honey?"

"Now where is he going to find a trawler?" Jason asked. "He probably doesn't have the money to buy a commercial fishing boat. And your parent's boat was destroyed in a storm, was it not . . . sorry, I didn't mean to bring that subject up." Jason put his arms around her.

"That's okay. We have to move on in life, don't we? The search party found my dad's trawler adrift at sea but not my mom, dad, and brother. The boat was damaged, yet they were able to tow it back to Moxey Settlement and haul it ashore and place it in a cradle for repairs. It is just sitting there with no work being done. Since I am the only survivor, I do not have the money to fix it. I thought I would give the boat to Juan and he could fix it up and run Dad's fishing operation."

"Wow. What an offer! That's a great idea. Yes, I like your suggestion. That means, of course, we . . . I mean you . . . would have to help him get a Bahamas citizenship or work permit. Can you do that?" Jason asked.

"I think so. I know the officials in Andros and Nassau. I have relatives in the right places. I am sure I can get it worked out," Maisy said.

"Let's talk to him about it tomorrow," Jason said as he let out a big yawn, leaned back and laid flat on the bed and closed his eyes.

"No, I want to make him the offer tonight and let him think about it overnight," she begged.

"Okay, I'll go with you to his room." He forced himself out of bed with a groan, stretched and together they walked down the hall and knocked on Juan's door.

"Come in," Juan said from inside.

Jason opened the door, "Juan, can we talk to you for a minute?"

Juan offered them a seat on the sofa while Juan grabbed a nearby chair. Maisy began explaining her offer to Juan, and when she finished she looked at Juan for a reaction.

"I . . . I . . . I don't know what to say. I can't believe you are being so kind about helping me start a new job. I don't deserve taking over your dad's business . . . and a trawler, too," Juan began.

"Yes you do. If it weren't for you, we'd probably be drifting at sea waiting for the sharks to have us for dinner. We have been telling you all along that we wanted to help you find a new shipboard job, but maybe working on large ships is really not your cup of tea, if you know what I mean," Maisy said.

"Yeah, you may be right," Juan said. "I like your idea. To be honest, I was even going to ask my cousin Raul tomorrow if I could stay with him in Santa Marta for a while and look for a seaman's job on a ship here in Colombia. Thank you for your offer."

"Sleep on it. We'll talk some more in the morning," Maisy suggested.

"Okay. You are such a sweetheart," Juan said.

"You'll have to decide by breakfast time," Jason reminded him. "We may be out of here tomorrow."

"I know. Thanks guys. See you in the morning," Juan said.

Maisy got up and gave Juan a kiss on the cheek. "Goodnight, Juan."

The following morning at 5:30, Raul was in the shed in the back of the villa feeding the llamas and filling water troughs. Maisy heard the clutter and looked out the window to see what was happening. Realizing the llamas were up and waiting to be fed, she jumped out of bed, dressed and ran out the back door to help.

"Good morning, Raul. Can I help, please?" Maisy asked hopefully.

"Sure. Grab a bucket, fill it with the feed mix from the barrels in the feed room, and follow me," he said. Maisy dipped the bucket into the feed barrel and headed for the corral. When she approached the corral, she saw Cookie standing first in line at the gate waiting with her ears perked up.

"I think Cookie likes you the best," Raul said as they came to the gate.

"Oh, you are just being nice. I think she likes the feed bucket," she said.

"You're right. Divide the feed in your bucket among all of them in their individual feed dishes," Raul said. When Maisy opened the gate, the llamas stepped back and let her through. Then all four llamas followed her to the feeding stations. One by one, Maisy portioned out the feed in the dishes and one by one, each llama waited in front of its own dish.

"Why are they not fighting over the feed in the dishes?" Maisy asked.

"That's because they have a pecking order," Raul answered. "Number one in their hierarchy goes first, then number two and so on. Pecking order is a very strong social instinct in llamas."

"That's interesting. Who decides who is number one?" Maisy asked.

"They do. Occasionally number two will challenge number one and may or may not win. But once they decide they respect the winner . . . for awhile."

"Who's number one now, Cookie?" Maisy asked.

"No, Matador. You noticed Matador came to the feed dish first while the others stood and waited for you to fill up the next dishes," Raul said.

"That's amazing. Llamas showing respect for each other. That's better than some humans do. Now that you mentioned it, I did notice Matador went for the first dish."

They finished the feeding chores in a few minutes and returned to the villa for breakfast. By then the rest of the crew were already up and getting ready for the day's adventures.

A little before 6:00 o'clock, Roselle called everyone to the breakfast table, and they sat down to homemade hot bread, fruit, cereal, juice and coffee.

"We have to pack up and head down the mountain by 7:00," Raul advised. "I figured we could call the American Consulate after we get to Santa Marta. Better take your stuff with you because you may go directly to Barranquilla from the market and not return here."

They acknowledged Raul's suggestion and continued eating. Getting impatient for Juan's decision, Maisy looked at Juan and asked, "Do you have any more thoughts about my offer last night?"

Lori suddenly choked on a mouth full of food, looked at Maisy suspiciously and immediately blurted out, "What offer? What's going on with you two? Have you two got a secret romance going on here?"

Maisy put down her fork and laughed at her silliness. Then Jason smiled, shook his head at Lori, and remarked, "What craziness, what craziness."

"Juan, tell Lori what Jason and I talked to you about last night," Maisy laughed.

"Okay, everyone. I have an important announcement," Juan said with fanfare by tapping his spoon on his drinking glass. Lori's face froze in anticipation of hearing some kind of hot, juicy gossip.

"Maisy offered me her dad's fishing boat and the opportunity to take over her dad's commercial fishing operations in Moxey Settlement when we return to the Bahamas. I gave this a lot of thought last night, and I think you are right, Maisy. Working on a large ship is not really what I do best. I accept your offer with huge thanks." He looked at Raul and Roselle and added, "I must admit I was going to ask if I could stay with you here in Santa Marta to look for a job on a ship, but Maisy and Jason came up with a better suggestion."

"Well, I'll be . . . " Lori said. "How long have you been pondering on this one, Miss Maisy? You didn't tell us about this deal."

"Actually, I have been thinking about it for several days, but I didn't really decide to go through with it until last night. You had already hit the sack when Jason and I made the offer to Juan last night. So now, Miss Lori, you know the whole story," Maisy said with a bit of arrogance in her voice.

"All right you two. Cool it," Jeff said.

"Actually, we owe him something special," Maisy added.

"Thanks, Maisy," Juan said. "It's strange because if you had not been taken captive, I would not have had this opportunity to help you and start a new career."

Following breakfast, everyone gathered their belongings, Roselle filled the sacks with fresh fruit and vegetables to sell at the market, and they gathered in the corral to pack up the llamas. Lori and Maisy were quick to grab the pack harnesses and put them on Cookie and Wacissa. Jason and Jeff followed suit with Matador and Jorge.

As before, Raul went around and double-checked the cinches. This time he was satisfied everyone did it correctly, and Roselle placed the sacks into the llama packs while Maisy, Lori, Jeff, and Jason hooked the leads to the animals.

"Looks like we are ready to head down the big hill," Raul said.

"Let's roll," Maisy said putting on her sombrero and feeling like a real cowgirl.

With sombreros over their heads and light blankets over their shoulders, they walked single file out of the corral with llamas in tow and headed down the trail to the river crossing.

"We're getting close to the river, I can hear the falls," Jason said half an hour into the trek.

"This time I'm not afraid. I'm gonna stay ahead of Wacissa," Lori said.

"Of course, the second time is always easier," Raul said.

The llamas and their handlers reached the river and crossed it like pros, and by eight-thirty, they arrived at the farmers market. Maisy and Lori led the llamas to the mango tree, tied them, and returned to help Roselle unload the packs. Jeff, Jason, Juan, and Raul placed the fruit and vegetables on the display rack in front of their stand when suddenly Jason saw the white Lexus moving slowly through the market crowd a block away. Immediately Jason grabbed Jeff and Juan and shoved them behind the shed.

"Sorry I had to do this. Rafael is coming down the road looking for us again, and I didn't have time to explain," Jason said. Watching the commotion, Lori and Maisy figured out what was happening and stayed put behind the stand next to the mango tree.

"You're safe there. He can't see you behind the shed," Raul hollered to everyone.

Raul and Roselle continued sorting fruits and vegetables on the tables while keeping a close eye on the Lexus. Slowly the crowd dispersed as the car moved closer to Raul's stand. Suddenly the car stopped directly in front of him, and Rafael got out and approached the merchant directly across from his stand. Raul held his breath for a moment hoping his friend across the street would not reveal any information about his guests. After a brief conversation, Rafael jumped into his car and drove slowly away searching both sides of the market. Curious about what was said, Raul strolled across the road and talked to his neighbor. With a smile on his face, he returned and spoke to his friends.

"Okay, I think the coast is clear. That was close. My friend refused to tell him anything that was going on over here. He sensed that this man was up to no good. Man, that crewman from the *Coral Sun Ray* is determined to find you," Raul warned.

The five came out of hiding and continued to help Roselle organize the stand, and by nine o'clock Raul decided to call the American Consulate in Barranquilla. When the receptionist answered, Raul requested to speak to the Consulate, and following a brief pause, Raul told the Consulate the story about his five friends. The Consulate agreed that they would be safer on the Consulate grounds and offered to take them in as soon as Raul could get them there. With the invitation in hand, Raul said he would call him back as soon as arrangements could be made to transport them to Barranquilla.

"Good news. The American Consulate has accepted my request to take you in and arrange to get you back to the Bahamas. Now we have to figure out how to get you to Barranquilla," Raul said.

An air of apprehension hung over the stand before Roselle spoke, "Maybe Santo could take them in his boat. It would take him about four hours to make the trip across the bay."

"Good idea. I'll call him and see if that's possible," Raul said.

After ten minutes on the telephone with Santo, Raul hung up and cheerfully announced, "Santo can do it. He asked if we could meet him at the dock in thirty minutes because he wants to be able to make the trip and return today."

Roselle looked at the five young faces and asked, "Well, what do you think?"

"Sounds perfect. I'm game," Jason said.

"Me, too," Jeff agreed.

"All right, we're ready," Maisy spoke for the rest of them.

"Great, I'll call Santo and tell him we'll be at the dock in thirty minutes," Raul said. "Then I'll call the Consulate and tell him he can expect you guys early this afternoon."

Maisy and Lori ran back to the mango tree and hugged Cookie and

Wacissa.

"Goodbye, love. You guys were a lifesaver. Take care of Raul and Roselle, Cookie," Maisy whispered in Cookie's ear. She gave Cookie another big hug. Lori did the same thing with Wacissa. When they returned to the shed, Maisy and Lori looked back and saw Cookie and Wacissa starring at them with their ears perked up. Sadly, Lori gathered her things, put on her sombrero, and joined her friends ready to begin their long journey home. They gave Roselle a hug and promised to stay in touch. Soon they left the market and headed down the road toward the waterfront with Raul in the lead.

Chapter 13

Homeward Bound

Jason and his friends remained huddled together as they cautiously walked along the back streets of Santa Marta toward the small marina where Santo was waiting for them on board his fishing trawler. During the thirty-minute journey, they kept a close eye out for the *Coral Sun Ray* crew. Luck was with them when they reached the marina without incident and spotted Santo standing on the bow of his boat. Raul waved to catch Santo's attention, and Santo responded, hopped off the boat, and walked toward them.

"Santo, how have you been, old buddy?" Raul greeted him.

"Hanging in there," Santo replied.

"I want you to meet my friends."

Santo shook hands with them and invited them to come aboard his thirty-eight foot fishing trawler.

"Listen, Santo, let me know what I owe you for fuel to take them to Barranquilla," Raul said.

"I'm not going to charge you for this trip. These kids need our help. Besides, I may throw out some nets on my way back and catch some fish. That will help with the cost," Santo suggested.

Raul bid them farewell with a promise to keep in touch, waved goodbye and stood by on the dock. Without delay, Santo started the twin engines, untied the lines and backed the boat out of the slip. He said the weather and sea conditions were good, but there was a three to five foot sea in the bay.

"I think we'll be fine. We're used to the rolling swells. For the past ten years, I have been ocean sailing off the coast of the United States, and if anyone gets seasick, I would be surprised." Jason said. His friends nodded in agreement.

While the rest of the crew remained in the main cabin out of sight, Jason sat in the pilothouse and studied the charts. Crossing the Santa Marta harbor they passed by the *Coral Sun Ray* tied to the pier. Juan,

Maisy, and Jeff looked out the portholes from inside the cabin and stared at the ship. Seeing the ship for the last time stirred up mixed emotions for Juan. Shattered dreams of a budding career as a seaman on the ship raced though his mind, yet he was thankful he escaped the disrespect and criminal activity that nearly destroyed him.

"Goodbye, *Coral Sun Ray*. "Hope you never sail again," Maisy shouted.

"Yeah, no tears from me," Jeff echoed. Lori could not bear to look.

The trawler left the harbor and turned left just outside of the jetty and headed across the bay. Santo set his course to 255 degrees and pushed the throttles full forward causing the bow to rise up. At the stern, the twin propellers created a white frothing wake as far back as they could see it. Impressed with the power surge, Jason looked at the knot log on the instrument panel and saw the number twenty pop up on the screen.

"That's amazing," Jason remarked. "Is that the fastest the boat can go?"

"This boat can go faster, but we'll have to slow down when we get into the big swells. We'll see how it goes," Santo said. "I've set the GPS for the Magdalena River entrance, the river that takes us to the port of Barranquilla. It looks like we'll arrive there around 2:00 o'clock."

"Perfect. We can't thank you enough for your help."

"That's okay. Glad to be available. Hope all goes well for you, and you get back to the Bahamas without any further troubles," Santo said.

"Me, too."

Jeff, Lori, Juan and Maisy lay down on the seats in the cabin and took short naps as the boat pitched and rolled toward the Magdalena River. Soon there were out of sight of land with fair weather and moderate sea swells coming from the north. By 1:30 in the afternoon, they entered the entrance to the Magdalena River and headed upstream for the ten-mile run to the port. As promised, they pulled alongside the dock at 2:00 o'clock in the town of Barranquilla. Without a prompt from Santo, Jason jumped off the trawler and tied the bow and stern lines to the cleats on the wooden walkway. With the boat moored, Santo shut down the engines and called the Consulate on his cellular phone.

After a brief conversation, Santo ended his call, turned to his crew, and said, "The Consulate is sending a van down to the dock to pick you up in about fifteen minutes. I'll wait to be sure you are safely in the van," Santo offered. They thanked Santo again for his help and remained on board until the van arrived.

Almost to the minute, a white van pulled up to the dock and a uniformed driver walked up to the group. After the formal greetings, Maisy, Jeff, Jason, Lori, and Juan turned to Santo, shook hands and wished him a smooth voyage back to Santa Marta. As soon as Santo started the engines, Jason untied the lines of the trawler and tossed them over the rail and then stood back and watched Santo steer the boat forward away from the dock and swing around to head down stream. After a final wave, the crew jumped in the van and headed up the hill to the Consulate's quarters.

The driver wound his way along the narrow streets toward Calle 72 and turned into a driveway that led to a locked, iron gate. When he pressed a remote button on the visor of his van, the gate slid open, and he drove into the compound. Arriving behind the facility, the driver stopped next to a door to the main building and let everyone out. The group went inside the building, climbed a flight of stairs, and walked down a long hallway to a large office where they met the Consulate sitting at his desk. He stood up and greeted them as they entered.

"Welcome to the American Consulate. You can relax now. You are safely on American soil. Raul told me some of your story, but I would like to hear the details, straight from the horse's mouth so to speak," the Consulate said.

Jason began his tale from Wilmingtown, to Andros, to Santa Marta, to Barranquilla. Occasionally, the others interjected details from their point of view. In less than half an hour, the Consulate understood the whole picture, and that prompted him to pick up the telephone and request two deputies to come to his office.

Addressing the deputies, the Consulate said, "These unfortunate people were kidnapped and brought to Santa Marta from the Bahamas on the vessel *Coral Sun Ray*, which I have been told is still in port at Santa Marta. As you can see, they miraculously found a means to escape, and they need our assistance in getting them back to the Bahamas. I want you to arrange for flights for them to Andros, Bahamas. I suspect they will have to go via Bogota, then to Miami then to Andros, but you can check that out. Put it on our Ambassador Services Account. See if you can get them on flights tomorrow morning." Then he turned to his guests. "Do you have passports or any ID cards?"

"We left them on my boat in Coakley Town, Andros before we were taken hostage. So, to answer your question, no, Sir."

"That's okay. As soon as we verify your identity with our office in

Washington, we will issue you temporary travel papers and ID cards to get you back to your boat. We have guestrooms for you to stay in tonight. There is a small dining room for our guests on site. Dinner is at six tonight and breakfast is at eight a. m. Now, my deputies will take you into their offices to get details from you about your identity so we can pass that information on to Washington. Plan to meet me in the dining room for breakfast at eight o'clock sharp tomorrow morning. Any questions?" the Consulate concluded.

"No Sir. Thanks you for coming to our rescue," Jason said.

"You are welcome," the Consulate said.

The following morning, Maisy woke up just as the sun began to rise over the foothills of the Andes. She looked out the window and wondered what Cookie was doing now. With the sudden splash of sunlight entering the room when Maisy opened the curtain, Jason woke up and saw her sitting by the window.

"Good morning, sweets," Jason said.

"Oh, good morning."

"See anything interesting?" Jason asked.

"Oh, just a view of the river and hills beyond. I was dreaming of Cookie. I'm going to miss her," she sighed.

"I am sure you are. She was a friendly llama," Jason said. He looked at his watch. "It's nearly seven-thirty; we need to get going to be at breakfast by eight. Since you are dressed, go make sure Jeff and Lori are awake, please."

Maisy slipped out the door, went down the hall to their room, and knocked on the door. "We're up, we're up," Jeff hollered.

"Okay, just checking. We have to meet the Consulate in half an hour."

By eight o'clock, the five stumbled into the dining room and sat down. The waiter gave them coffee and juice and took their orders for breakfast, and a few minutes later, the Consulate walked through the doorway and joined them. "Top of the morning to you, my friends," the Consulate greeted everyone.

"Good morning, Sir," they responded.

"I have your travel documents along with your airline vouchers. All five of you are booked on a local flight out of Barranquilla at ten-thirty to Bogota. Then you are booked on a flight from Bogota to Miami leaving Bogota at twelve-thirty, which gets you into Miami at four-thirty p. m. A special charter flight has been arranged to take you from Miami to Andros Town, Bahamas. When you get to the Miami airport, you will have to go to the General Aviation Terminal. An agent will meet your flight in Miami to escort you to the general aviation terminal. Your flight to the Bahamas leaves from there. We'll go over the details right after breakfast. So, did you all sleep well?"

"Yes, Sir," they said again in unison.

"Thanks again, Sir, for your help," Maisy said. "I can't imagine what would have happened to us without your rescue."

"I can . . . if we had . . ." Lori began.

"We don't want to hear it," Jeff interrupted.

"Change the subject," they all said in response.

After going over the details of the travel plans with the Consulate, the driver loaded them into the van and drove them to the local airport. When they arrived at the airline ticket counter, they handed over the documents to the agent who then riffled though them quickly and issued them the tickets and boarding passes for their entire trip.

A few minutes after ten, their flight was called and they proceeded to the gate and boarded the aircraft. The greeting by the flight attendant was mostly in Spanish with brief explanations in English. Juan laughed when he told his friends that the attendant did not explain her entire story in English as she did in Spanish.

"Oh well, we know the routine," Jason said. They sat in seats adjacent to and behind each other, fastened their seat belts, and were soon on their way. The flight transfer in Bogota was simple and by one o'clock, they were en route to Miami. Lori and Jeff finally realized they were free and felt a huge relief their ordeal was over. With that piece of mind, they slept most of the way to Florida. Juan, Maisy, and Jason, on the other hand, talked most of the flight about the possibilities of Juan's new job and their return sailing trip back to Wilmingtown. Time passed by quickly for them and by four, the Captain requested that everyone remain in their seats with seat belts fastened in preparation for landing at Miami International.

Jason led the group off the plane, went through U.S. Customs and Immigration without a hitch, and entered the main lobby of the international terminal when Maisy spotted a lady holding a sign that read: "JASON SHANNON."

"Jason, look over there, the lady with the sign," Maisy pointed out.

"That's me! The Consulate is a master at trip planning," Jason said. "We are really getting the royal treatment."

They followed the escort through the international terminal, took a shuttle bus to the general aviation terminal, and were led inside the lobby to the reception check-in desk. All five presented their ID's, tickets and documentation papers to the receptionist.

"Welcome folks to Miami," she said in a programmed manner. "How was your flight from Colombia?"

"Fine," Jason responded. "But we're glad to be home."

"On vacation in Colombia?" she asked in an I-really-don't-care tone.

"Yeah, I guess you might say that," Jason said not willing to go through what really happened to them.

"Okay, I'll tell the charter flight crew that you are here. Have a seat in the lobby. We'll call you when your flight is ready. Any questions?" she asked routinely and left before they could respond.

As they sat on the couch and waited to be called, Jason discovered a newspaper on the coffee table in front of them. Anxious to catch up on the latest news, he worked his way to page three when he suddenly leaped out of his chair and hollered, "Look at this." He quickly lured Maisy, Jeff, Lori, and Juan to his side and began to read the article.

International Auto Thief and Immigrant Smuggling Ring Busted

A large-scale international auto theft and immigrant smuggling ring was discovered operating out of the ports of Wilmingtown, NC; Coakley Town, Andros in the Bahamas; Tampico, Mexico and most recently Santa Marta, Colombia. Several ships have been involved but the largest freighter was the Coral Sun Ray now seized by the local police and under investigation at the port of Santa Marta, Colombia. Headquarters for the operations was located on the Cape Fear River in Wilmingtown, NC. And the most bizarre discovery was the leader of the crime organization Charlie Jenkins who was the Captain of the Wilmingtown Police Department. The collapse of the crime syndicate began when the Tampico Port Authorities became suspicious of the Coral Sun Ray's activities in Mexico. Impatient for the arrival of the vessel Coral Sun Ray, the Tampico authorities invaded the ship's port offices and confiscated a number of incriminating documents. Evidence indicated that the ship was indeed involved in selling stolen cars from the United States to the Mexican and Central American black markets and smuggling immigrants to the United States, namely through the port of Wilmingtown for large sums of money from the immigrants. Records were also found that linked the headquarters to Wilmingtown and an illegal auto alteration shop in Coakley Town on Andros Island.

Those currently held for questioning in Santa Marta are John Franco, the Captain of the Coral Sun Ray and his crew; and Francesca, head of the crime syndicate in Santa Marta. Others being held are Jack Ringo, operations manager in Coakley Town and his shop manager, Sanchez; and Gina, Merinda, and Dingo who were auto thieves in Atlanta, Tampa, and Miami. An all-points bulletin has been issued for the arrest of Charlie Jenkins; Jake, his operations manager in Wilmingtown; Chico, operations manager in Tampico, Mexico; and Gunner, an auto thief from Atlanta. It is thought that Charlie Jenkins, Jake, and Chico are in hiding in Santa Marta, Colombia based on preliminary checks with the airlines. The U.S. Immigration, Colombian, and airline authorities are continuing their investigations. Four people from a sailboat were kidnapped from Andros by the crew of the Coral Sun Ray and taken to Santa Marta for ransom but managed to escape with the help of one of the crew immediately upon arrival in Colombia. At press time, their names and whereabouts were unknown.

"Well, how about that?" Maisy shouted loud enough to cause everyone in the lobby to stare at her. "Justice is paying off! Whoopee!"

The general aviation receptionist approached them and announced, "Your flight is ready. Follow me to the ramp, please."

The five gathered their precious few possessions and headed out to the ramp to a small Cessna Citation Jet. Standing by the aircraft steps, the captain greeted them, helped them on board, and announced that their flight would take about twenty minutes. As the plane lifted off the runway and turned east toward Andros, Maisy began thinking about the events that started their bizarre adventure hardly a week ago in Coakley. Soon, Maisy spotted the island of Andros. Minutes later, she could see Coakley Town and Moxey Settlement in the distance toward the south. She became ecstatic and grabbed Jason's arm.

"Home at last," she said with excitement.

"Yes." Jason held her hand tightly and looked into her eyes with a smile.

The plane landed smoothly at Andros Town Airport and the pilot guided the jet to the ramp in front of a single, small cement block building. When the engines shut down, the captain lowered the steps to greet the Bahamian Customs and Immigration Official waiting for them on the ramp.

"Good afternoon, mon. Welcome back home," the local official said as the five climbed out of the plane.

"Jeffrey, what a surprise to see you here," Maisy said.

"Yes, I started this job last week. I heard all about you and your friends and I wanted to be sure I had this shift to meet you."

"Well, it's an honor," Maisy said and shook hands with her old friend from Moxey Settlement.

"Officially, I have to check your papers and look at your luggage, but not to worry. You all are welcomed to the Bahamas," Jeffrey said.

"Do what you have to do. Make it official. But we have no luggage," Jason added.

"I understand. I really didn't expect any under the circumstances."

The five walked with the official into the building and filled out the required arrival forms. After Jeffrey stamped the paperwork and gave them entry documents to the Bahamas, they were directed to the small airport lobby where they met their driver to take them to Coakley.

"Miss Maisy?" he asked the group while searching the faces for a response.

"Here I am," she said and raised her hand.

"Excellent. I am to drive you to Coakley Town. From there we have arranged for a boat to take you to Moxey. Come with me to the parking lot," he said.

"We can sail ourselves to Moxey Settlement on our boat the *Southwind*," Jason said.

"Oh, your boat is not there, Sir," the driver said. "Someone in Moxey came to Coakley and took your boat to Moxey Settlement. When they realized that you and Maisy were missing, we thought it best to guard your boat for you in Moxey harbor. We were afraid if the boat were left in Coakley, someone would think it was abandoned and maybe steal it. So you will have to take a charter boat to Moxey from Coakley. No roads go to Moxey."

"I see," Jason said. He leaned back in his seat and thought about the *Southwind.*

"Wow! What royal treatment! Are you the Queen of Andros, Miss Maisy?" Lori asked.

"No, of course not. I do have a lot of friends on the island, but I don't know anything about this," Maisy confessed.

They climbed into an old, rusty, faded station wagon, exited the parking lot and bumped along a dusty, pothole-filled road south toward Coakley Town. Along the way, Maisy could not hold back her curiosity.

"How did you know we were coming and who hired you to pick us up at the airport?"

"Ah, everyone in Moxey Settlement knows what happened to you. The word got out yesterday in the Nassau newspaper. I think the story came from Colombia, South America. A friend in Moxey contacted me this morning and asked me to pick you up at the airport.

"Ah, the Consulate in Barranquilla must have reported what happened to the news media," Maisy rationalized.

"Perhaps, but he also contacted people in the Bahamas about our arrival, so the news could have come by several different routes," Jason added.

"Yes, I know. Everyone has been so kind. I can't wait to introduce you and my friends in Moxey. It's gonna be a real treat," Maisy said to Jason.

"Yes ma'am, a real treat," the driver snickered and then burst out laughing.

"What's so funny?" Jason asked.

"Oh, you'll see soon," he said.

They continued down the road for another fifteen minutes when Maisy asked the driver, "Sir, can we stop by Ringo Industries for a moment when we get to Coakley before we board the boat? I want to see if that operation is still there."

"Okay. I can do that. But I must tell you that Ringo Industries is no more. The building is boarded up with warning signs from the Bahamian Police that say 'KEEP OUT—POLICE LINE.'"

"That's amazing how fast the word gets out. I wonder what they did with the expensive cars they were working on in the shop." Jeff asked.

"Don't know, Sir. The investigation has just begun and is being kept secret," the driver volunteered.

"Well, we'd still like to stop by the Ringo operation for a few minutes to look. That's where all of this horrible adventure began, where it all came together." Maisy stated.

"Okay, just for a few minutes," the driver said.

Soon they arrived in Coakley Town and the driver pulled up to the dock in the center of town along the harbor. The five got out and walked over to the spot where the *Southwind* was once moored. Then they looked across the harbor where the *Coral Sun Ray* was once moored. The harbor was empty except for a single boat tied to the dock a block away.

They all stood in silence reflecting the beginning of their plight more than a week ago as Jason reached for Maisy and put his arms

around her. Then they walked down the dirt road until they came to the offices of Ringo Industries. As the driver promised, the building was roped off with no trespassing signs. Maisy walked around to the side and stared at the long, chain-linked fence that led to the back of the property. She looked back at Jason, Jeff, Lori, and Juan.

"This is where our adventure began. Never again am I going to snoop around private property. I think we all learned our lesson," Maisy said.

"Amen," Lori, Jeff, and Jason answered.

Maisy and Jason told Juan the events that led them to be held captive on the *Coral Sun Ray,* and then they returned to the harbor and met the captain of the boat tied to the dock who was to take them to Moxey Settlement. Climbing on board, the Captain pulled in the lines, motored out the channel and turned south toward Maisy's home village. The Captain reached for his microphone and called on the radio to a friend in Moxey, "I've got 'em," and placed the microphone back in its holder.

"Roger that," came the response. "See you in an hour."

"What was that all about?" Maisy asked.

"Oh, nothing really. You'll see when we get to Moxey. I can't say any more," the Captain said.

That roused Maisy's suspicion that something was up. By early evening, the boat pulled into the small fishing village marina where the *Southwind* was tied. Jason was thrilled to see his boat again tied to the dock and could not wait to get off the boat and jump on board his own baby.

In a manner of a few minutes, the Captain eased alongside the dock just in front of the *Southwind* while Jason jumped off and secured the lines to the cleats on the dock. Without a moment to spare, all five scrambled off the boat and ran over to the *Southwind.* Jason quickly did an inventory and found everything as he left it. Jeff, Lori, and Maisy checked their personal belongings and found nothing missing. Jason and Maisy returned to the boat Captain and thanked him again for helping them return home.

While the five showered, changed into clean clothes, and freshened up on board the *Southwind,* Maisy heard a commotion in the parking lot nearby. She climbed up into the cockpit and saw a large crowd moving toward them.

"I can't believe this. Hey guys, come out here quickly. We have visitors, lots of visitors," she hollered into the cabin. All emerged from the cabin to an enthusiastic crowd who began waving banners, flags and shouting, "Welcome home." A small band consisting of a trumpet, clarinet and a drum set up on the dock and began to play.

Maisy put her head in her hands and started crying prompting Jason to rush to her side. Then they climbed over the railing together to greet the crowd. When all five of them stood on the dock stunned, the village mayor approached them and gave them a hug.

"You are national heroes. Everyone knows your plight and what you did," he announced to them and to the crowd. Then he reached for Juan's hand and said, "And ladies and gentlemen of Moxey, this fine young gentleman, Juan, was the key to saving their lives." He turned to Juan and added, "We hereby make you honorary mayor of Moxey Settlement," Then he draped a cape over Juan's shoulders and held Juan's arm up to the crowd. There were cheers from the crowd and music from the band that could be heard up and down the coast of Andros as people lined up to shake Juan's hand and the others as well.

"This is incredible! What a welcome! We'll have to do this again," Jason laughed.

"Will you shut up!" Lori yelled. "Never, never again!"

"Okay, never again," Jason laughed again.

The celebration continued into the night and by midnight, Jeff, Lori and Juan decided to crash into their bunks on board the *Southwind* leaving Jason and Maisy sitting in the cockpit alone. "How are you holding up?" Jason asked Maisy.

"A little tired, but okay," she said.

"Let's go for a walk on the beach. It's a perfect evening with a full moon. I want to walk with you in the soft sand, in the surf, around the dunes, the palm trees, just you and me and reflect what we have been through," Jason suggested.

"Okay, that would be nice."

When they reached the beach, Jason sat down in the sand next to a coconut palm and motioned Maisy to join him. Arm in arm, they listened to the sound of the rolling surf and watched the waves slide across the beach and retreat into the surf over and over again. Jason put his arms around her waist and kissed her for an eternity. "Maisy, perhaps I am crazy, but I love you," he whispered in her ear.

She looked into his eyes and responded, "I love you, too. I guess that makes us both crazy." They laughed. Jason stood up and pulled Maisy onto her feet, and silently they continued their walk slowly northward along the beach away from the village, away from civilization, just the two of them alone. Jason held Maisy's hand tightly and led her to the edge of the surf where the warm tropical saltwater swirled gently over their bare feet.

As they strolled hand in hand, Jason noticed something rolling in the tiny waves ahead and leaned over to pick it up. It was a small piece of a broken shell crudely shaped like a ring. The two looked at it for a moment and then at each other. Suddenly, Jason got on his knees and proposed, "Maisy, will you marry me?"

Maisy fell to her knees in front of Jason, put her arms around him, and squeezed him tightly. "Yes, yes, yes, yes," she kept repeating in his ear. Jason placed the ring on her finger as a surge of foaming salt water washed over their knees and feet. They remained locked to each other for a long time, and then Jason looked at Maisy and saw a wonderful sparkle in her eyes.

"Are you okay?" Jason asked.

"Of course. I am so happy it is hard to control my emotions," she said. "So many things have happened. So many wonderful things."

Jason looked at the shell ring on her finger. "It looks funny," he laughed. "It's one of a kind, that's for sure."

"I don't care what it looks like. I'll keep it forever. It will always remind me of this moment. One of the most important moments in my life."

They remained embraced in the shallow surf while the waves whirled around their feet. Finally, they stood up and began their walk back to the *Southwind*. When they climbed on board everyone was asleep, so quietly Maisy and Jason slipped into his cabin, shut the door and turned out the light.

The following morning, Maisy and Jason were the first to get up, and Maisy prepared breakfast in the galley. The smell of food on the stove woke Jeff, Lori, and Juan, and soon all were sitting in the cockpit eating together. Lori suddenly spotted the shell ring on Maisy's finger.

"Now that's interesting, where did you find that?" Lori asked innocently.

"Oh, Jason and I found it on the beach last night," Maisy said.

"What is it?" Jeff asked.

"It's a piece of a broken shell. Jason thought it looked interesting and gave it to me," Maisy said trying hard not to smile and give the real meaning away.

"Wait, guys, it's a ring, isn't it?" Juan suddenly blurted out.

"Yes," Maisy acknowledged with a slight twinkle in her eye.

"And it is on your left hand . . . your fourth finger, right?" Juan said as he caught on.

"Yes," Maisy repeated and grinned.

"Do you have something you want to tell us, Maisy?" Juan pushed on.

"Yes," Maisy said again.

"And? What?" Juan asked.

"Jason and I are getting married."

"That figures," Lori said and they all stood up and congratulated Maisy and Jason.

"Maisy wants us to stay a couple of days while she wraps up some personal things, then she wants to sail back to Wilmingtown with us. Is that okay with you two?" Jason asked looking directly at Lori and Jeff.

They both nodded in the affirmative.

"First thing I want to do this morning is to show Juan the trawler, give him the keys, and get him settled in the village. He can live on the trawler unless it is too damaged. If that is the case, he can stay in my apartment above the store. Is that okay with you, Juan?"

"Perfect."

"Good. As soon as I clean up, let's head over to the trawler and store. We have lots to tend to during the next couple of days. Another thing we have to do is help Juan fill out the application for a work permit until he can get his citizenship in order." Soon the five left the *Southwind* and walked over to the trawler.

On the morning of the second day, Jason, Maisy, Lori, and Jeff woke up as the sun peaked out of the sea. Jason listened to the weather forecast for sea and wind conditions and found it to be favorable to begin their voyage home. Meanwhile, Maisy prepared another breakfast while Jeff and Lori uncovered the sails and laid out the charts. Juan showed up at the dock following breakfast to help with the preparations and say goodbye.

"Good morning, guys," Juan greeted. "I have some good news. I called Raul in Colombia last night to tell him the latest in my adventures, and he said that he was given a position as Guide with the Santa Marta Ecologic Tour Service in appreciation for helping to prosecute the *Coral Sun Ray* crew and help with your rescue."

"Thank goodness for caring people. Raul is a jewel, that's for sure," Maisy said.

The galley and water tanks were stocked to last a month and the fuel tank was topped off. By nine o'clock, the *Southwind* was ready to set sail as Jason started the engines and Juan said goodbye to the crew. With all of the dockside chores done, Jason asked Juan to untie the lines and toss them onboard. In a matter of a minute, the *Southwind* was free from Bahamian soil. Jason backed the boat into the harbor, shifted into forward gear, and moved the boat slowly toward the entrance channel and open sea. They waved to Juan and shouted thank you again from the center of the harbor.

Jeff raised the jib and Lori and Maisy raised the main while Jason continued to steer the boat outbound. Then Lori secured the halyards and hauled in on the jib and main sheets to capture the trade winds coming out of the southeast. With the knotlog reading four knots, Jason shut down the engine and sat down on the bench for the long cruise ahead.

Soon they passed the last channel buoy, and Jason turned the *Southwind* to port to a new heading of 005 degrees. Maisy slacked the jib and main sheets to recapture the southeast winds and the *Southwind* surged ahead at greater than five knots. They looked back at the harbor entrance now half a mile away and they could barely see Juan standing on the beach waving. They waved back. Juan remained on the beach for a long time and watched them sail north along the Andros coastline until they were no more than a white speck on the horizon. He turned around, kicked up the sand in front of him with his bare feet and began walking slowly back to the village.

His harrying experiences on the *Coral Sun Ray* were now history. His escapades in Santa Marta, visiting his cousin Raul, and meeting the llamas were only memories. His daily conversations and adventures with Jason, Maisy, Jeff, and Lori had ended. Now a new life began not only for himself, but also for Jason and Maisy, and he wished them well. Then he stopped, turned around and looked northward along the coastline one more time. Nothing was there but the endless sea.

Jason continued to steer the *Southwind* northbound along the coast of Andros, and when they passed the channel buoy marking the entrance to Coakley Town harbor, Maisy cuddled up to him in the cockpit. Together they stared at the tiny harbor, the empty docks, Mangos and the village of Coakley as the *Southwind* proceeded on its journey home.

"This is truly an historic place for us," Jason pondered. "This is where we met the *Coral Sun Ray* again from Wilmingtown. This is where we discovered the stolen car shop. This is where we were kidnapped and taken aboard the *Coral Sun Ray*. This is where we had the good fortune of meeting Juan. This is where I met you, and this is where I fell in love."

Maisy pulled him closer, placed her arms around his shoulder, held him tightly, and gave him a long, passionate kiss.

"Yes, lucky me, huh?" she finally said.

They looked back again at Coakley Town Harbor.

"Coakley is the Andros Connection," she said to Jason.

"Yes, Maisy. It is indeed . . . the Andros Connection."

CPSIA information can be obtained at www.ICGtesting.com
Printed in the USA
BVOW052358181011

274002BV00005B/2/P